THE
MURDER
WALK

BOOKS BY ALICE CASTLE

THE
MURDER
WALK
ALICE CASTLE

bookouture

Published by Bookouture in 2022

An imprint of Storyfire Ltd.
Carmelite House
50 Victoria Embankment
London EC4Y 0DZ

www.bookouture.com

ISBN: 978-1-80314-492-4
eBook ISBN: 978-1-80314-491-7

To Ella and Connie, with love

ONE

'Magpie, you're a bad, bad cat,' said Beth crossly. Magpie, looking up from washing her paws after a delicious extra breakfast, gave Beth an affronted glance before continuing her ablutions. Feathers really did stick in the teeth.

'Listen, I'll stay and, er, clear up. You get off. You'll be late for work,' said York.

Beth knew when she was on to a good thing. Risking a quick look at the kill zone, and then wishing she hadn't, she scooped up her bag, phone and keys from the kitchen table. Jake had already left for school, walking himself the very short distance to the Village Primary in an experiment that had started, at his insistence, at the beginning of this new term. Beth had initially been fearful and resistant – sometimes she thought it was her default position since becoming a parent – but she had shelved her doubts and, with York's gentle encouragement, had allowed Jake this first taste of independence.

For the first week, obviously, she had tailed him at a discreet distance. But now, in week two, the new was becoming routine and today she'd barely given his perilous journey down the road a thought, thanks to Magpie's killing spree.

Closing the door after a lingering kiss on the doorstep – the least York deserved as a reward for his services as an impromptu undertaker – Beth mused at how quickly things could change. And she had a spring in her step as she passed the gingerbread brick buildings and neatly painted gates of the little Village Primary. The playground stood quiet and empty, the children already safely tucked inside. Even the straggle of sixth formers dawdling towards Wyatt's School had slowed to a trickle. But, instead of following the last of them up to the splendid wrought-iron gates of that august establishment, Beth veered off and headed down Court Lane instead.

She'd somehow neglected to mention it to York, but her first appointment of the day was not with her groaning in-tray in the archives department at Wyatt's, but with Katie, her great friend, who'd just acquired a puppy. Beth knew she'd been somewhat economical with the truth, but it really hadn't seemed quite the moment to correct his assumption that she was off to toil. As it was, she had a half-day's leave from her already extremely flexible job. There was a senior school open day today, which meant the place would be overrun with nervous parents, and children who'd either absorbed that stress or were deflecting it in any way they could. Definitely a good moment to give the place a wide berth.

As she walked, she enjoyed the few flickers of weak sunshine – a mild suggestion that better weather might be hiding somewhere around the corner after a miserably cold autumn, and a winter which had strewn Dulwich with drifts of snow.

Christmas was done and dusted for another year, thank goodness, and the decorations had been stowed as far out of sight as possible, much to Jake's chagrin. Beth didn't like to think of herself as Scrooge-like, but the season had not been designed with overstretched single mothers in mind. She just about had time to cover the bases in the normal run of events. Extra shopping, cooking and wrapping, all to be performed with a merry smile on her face, made her curse everyone from the Angel Gabriel downwards. The new spring term brought its own stresses, though, and that was why Beth was so keen to see Katie. They were going to have a serious debriefing session about the Wyatt's Year 7 interviews.

Beth had hardly dared to hope that her little Jake might get this far. The exam had not seemed promising at all. He'd already ploughed through the grammar school entrance tests by the time it came to sit the Wyatt's papers, missing out most of the maths and cheerfully admitting he hadn't a clue what non-verbal reasoning even was. Trooping along to the dauntingly huge hall at Wyatt's, sitting in serried ranks with what seemed like every smart kid in London and the Home Counties – not to mention a heavy contingent of boys who had been flown in specially for the occasion – Beth had been shaking in her boots, never mind Jake. He'd emerged a few hours later, a little pale and a lot more interested in finding out what was for his supper than in discussing the afternoon.

After that, Beth had done her best to consign her long-held hopes and dreams to the dustbin of history, and had started to research the other, really very good, alternative schools in the area. So what if her own brother had gone to Wyatt's in his day? And her grandfather, too? So what if there were Haldanes writ large on the school's honours boards, and even inscribed on the memorial to those who'd given their lives in the two great wars of the last century? Her father hadn't actually gone to the school, and he'd done fine – right up until the moment when he'd succumbed to a heart attack in his mid-fifties. Her late husband, James, hadn't set foot in the place either, and had been absolutely none the worse for it – until he, too, had died unexpectedly. Oh dear, was she seeing an unfortunate pattern here?

She hoped not. Because it looked as though Jake would not be going to Wyatt's.

For someone who made her living delving into and protecting the past, Beth had been doing her level best to put a brave face on this new leaf which seemed to have been forcibly turned. But when an envelope had swished onto the mat last week with the famous school's crest in the upper left-hand corner, the breath had nearly stopped in her body. At one level, she'd known it would just be the polite rejection she'd braced every cell of her body for... and yet, and yet...

Opening that letter, while Jake was safely out on a playdate, had been an out-of-body experience. She'd read the words on the flimsy slip of paper with the flourishing signature of the school's inspiring head, Dr Grover, at the bottom, but they hadn't made any sense. Indeed, they seemed to be swimming gently all over the page. She'd been expecting a terse, 'Not today, thank you', possibly softened by a kind word or two from lovely Dr G, as he now knew her so well. But to her astonishment, the first line seemed to read, 'I'm delighted to invite your son, Jake...'

He'd only gone and got an interview!

Beth had astonished herself by bursting into noisy tears. She rarely cried, and then only if something really bad had happened... like a friend getting murdered. Good news deserved a smile, not this storm of emotion. But a lot had happened in Dulwich over the past year. Maybe she was permitted a tiny wobble, she'd thought, as she blew her nose half an hour later and threw cold water on cheeks blotched with tears. Magpie had threaded anxiously through her legs as she'd sat hunched at the kitchen table, clutching an Earl Grey tea as though her life depended on it. This was only the interview stage. She had to hold it together, for Jake. What if he didn't get a place, after this? And what if he *did*? In a way, her worries would only just be beginning if he pulled off the seemingly impossible feat, as there was no way her meagre salary – grateful for it though she was – would actually stretch to cover school *and* food. Not to mention anything else, like lighting, heating, shoes...

'Oh, Magpie, you wouldn't be happy if your supply of extra-special Purina cat food dried up, would you?' Beth picked up the hefty cat and sniffled into her luxuriant black and white fur.

But that had all been a week ago. Beth had just about managed to get a grip since then. As usual, Jake had been her salvation. She'd needed to treat the interview with airy unconcern, in front of him, anyway, so that he wouldn't build it up in his head to be the massive, potentially life-changing ordeal that Beth, and all the rest of Dulwich, knew it was. Beth comforted herself that Katie, who'd got the self-same letter for her son, Charlie, who was Jake's best friend, had reacted in a much more extreme way. She'd promptly gone out and bought her boy a brand-new puppy.

Beth, whose musings had by now brought her to the door of Katie's huge Court Lane house, rang the bell and then jumped anxiously as a volley of yaps greeted her. The puppy was already making its presence felt. The creature must have been just behind the door. Either that, or it could run terrifyingly fast. Beth took another step backwards. Then there was the sound of a scuffle, with a lot of shouts of, 'No!' and 'Bad dog' and a frantic scrabbling as Katie finally got the door open. Her blonde hair was all over her face, and she was using both hands to restrain a tiny ball of silky black fluff on the end of a thick lead.

'Beth, meet Teddy,' Katie said breathlessly. She whipped round as Teddy scampered for the door and flung himself towards the oblong of daylight like a lifer attempting a jail break, winding his lead through her yoga-honed, enviably long limbs and Beth's own short stumps. Katie yanked him back at the last moment and he flopped onto the marble tiles, slobbering all over them as he panted like a marathon runner.

'Do you want me to shut this?' said Beth, hanging onto the front door as Teddy suddenly picked himself up, shook himself like a small black mop, and hurled himself towards freedom again.

'No, better out than in. He needs exercise, then he'll calm down. A bit. We'll have to get him in the car, though.' Katie was flushed.

'Why? What's wrong with the park?' Beth looked down the road towards the entrance, only a few metres away. This was one of the many reasons why Katie's house was so perfect – for once, an estate agent wouldn't be lying through their teeth by describing it as right on Dulwich Park's doorstep, round the corner from the village's coffee shops, and within easy walking distance of the best schools. As Beth watched, a mother with a pushchair was trundling in through the park gates, nodding good morning to a jogger in wall-to-wall Lycra, doing stretches so complicated they looked like origami. A professional dog walker, being towed by a brace of pugs, a cockapoo and a retriever, whisked past next. Was it Beth's imagination, or did he glance sharply in the direction of Katie's house?

'I can't take Teddy there again,' said her friend with a shudder. 'I'll explain when we've got him in.' She wrapped the puppy's lead round her wrist several times, picked up a roll of plastic bags, a tin of dog treats, a squeaky duck toy, a ball, a long plastic throwing stick and a spare lead, and tried to jam them all into her minimalist handbag. Beth wordlessly took the dog treats, duck and stick. Katie squared her shoulders, locked her front door and took a breath. 'Right. Let's go,' she said.

Her estate car was parked on the street right outside, but the trip from doorstep to boot seemed to take forever. Beth was forcibly reminded of their days with Jake and Charlie as toddlers. The amount of kit you needed to sustain these tiny lives was incredible. And the endless prevarication and circum-locutions a child was capable of!

She thought she'd seen it all, until Teddy stopped and attempted to pee on every single one of Katie's precious spring bulbs. The poor things had only just started to pierce the wintry earth, now they were greeted by enthusiastic streams of dog widdle. Luckily, Teddy ran out long before Katie's planting scheme did, but that didn't stop him from going laboriously through the motions as though still in full spate. When he wasn't weeing, he was snuffling in the shrubs and around the rose bushes as if dozens of sausages were hiding behind every leaf.

'Is he part-hound?' wondered Beth out loud.

Katie rolled her eyes and started to drag on the lead. Teddy, who'd found a promising smell under a rhododendron bush, refused to budge. She picked him up bodily, whereupon he squirmed like a furry black eel.

'Nope. I'm beginning to think he's at least half Tasmanian Devil. But I bought him as a cavapoo,' she said, passing her car keys to Beth as she fought to contain Teddy's struggles.

Beth clicked the boot of Katie's enormous estate open and they bundled the fluffy creature inside, just managing to get the door shut again without trapping any of Teddy's busy limbs or even his questing head. Both paused for a moment.

'Does he calm down at all?' Beth asked tentatively. She didn't want to sound too negative about her friend's new acqui-sition, but on a purely selfish note she could see that Teddy might seriously put a crimp into the quiet coffees with Katie that she so relied on.

'Thank goodness, he does. He crashes out like a light. I defi-nitely like him best when he's asleep.' Katie peered carefully through the window into the back of the car. 'Look at him now. Butter wouldn't melt,' she said, with the sort of gooey eyes a mother reserves for her child.

Teddy, chewing heartily on one of Charlie's trainers – not even a particularly old one, by the looks of it – put his head on one side and panted at Katie, and she put a hand to her heart. 'Bless him. He's settled now. We can get in,' she said confidently.

Beth cracked open her car door gingerly, in case Teddy went nuts again and tried to escape. Apart from the odd growl as he disembowelled the shoe, he was quite peaceful, and once they were driving down Court Lane, he started to snore. 'Aw, listen to that,' said Katie, smiling at Beth.

'Tell me though, why a dog? Why now? Was it just because of the interviews?' Beth knew it wasn't really her place to cross-question her friend, but she wanted to understand the thought process that had led to young Teddy's arrival. It was quite a major shift in thinking. Katie was extremely house-proud – on the outside at least; Beth knew her cupboards hid a multitude of sins – and she had suffered, rather than enjoyed, Charlie's brief enthusiasm for hamster ownership. Of all the people suddenly to acquire a dog, Beth would have put Katie reasonably far down the list, after even herself. And she was *never* getting one.

'Oh, well, Charlie did do so brilliantly, getting through the exam. They both did, didn't they?' she said, glancing over at Beth, who nodded enthusiastically, reliving her thrilling moment with the envelope again. 'And he's wanted a dog forever. You know that,' said Katie, negotiating the junction with Lordship Lane with a slight frown. 'Remember that PowerPoint they did ages ago?'

Beth couldn't help smiling. Three or so years ago, the boys had taken a brief break from the PlayStation – in itself quite a momentous occurrence – and concocted a presentation on why both mothers should cave in and immediately buy them puppies. Plucking the cutest possible images of cuddly dogs from the internet and interspersing them with slogans like, 'A boy's best friend', it had been hilarious and touching – but had ultimately failed. Or so Beth had thought.

A child couldn't possibly know how much time and responsibility went into dog ownership. As far as Beth was concerned, single stewardship of a small human life was tricky enough. Magpie, she could just about manage. The cat was pretty self-sufficient and could even, at a pinch, feed herself on unwary visitors to the garden, if today's grisly scenes were anything to go by. Not that Beth wanted to encourage that. But a puppy was about as much work as a baby, everyone said so. And Katie had always had her heart set on a yoga empire.

'What about all your classes?'

'The idea was that we'd get a nice quiet breed and the dog would just sit in the classes with me, keep me company. So many of my ladies love dogs. It really seemed like a puppy would be an asset,' Katie explained.

Beth closed her mouth. Even on such short exposure, it was hard to imagine Teddy sitting sedately in a basket and watching the Lycra-clad ladies of Dulwich stretching their stuff, without wanting to give them a very thorough sniffing – and probably wee on them into the bargain.

'I know what you're going to say. I must have been crazy picking Teddy. But you see, when we went over, he was so docile. He was just adorable, like a rag doll.'

'Did they drug him?' asked Beth, before she could stop herself.

Katie shot her a look. 'I think it's just a bit of youthful exuberance. He'll grow out of it soon. Well, that's what Michael says, anyway.'

Beth had been wondering how Katie's husband was adapting to the new addition. 'How does he feel about it all?'

'He absolutely adores him. But then, he only sees him for a couple of hours a week. By the time he gets back in the evening, Teddy is pretty relaxed – to the point of being comatose –

because he's run me ragged all day and then usually just eaten his weight in puppy food.'

'Where exactly are we off to now? I've got to be back at work after lunch,' said Beth, suddenly anxious. She peered out of the window. The car was already purring down Forest Hill Road.

'Don't worry, we're just going to the Rye. It's a bit more... anonymous,' said Katie evasively.

'The Rye?'

'Don't tell me you've never been before? To Peckham Rye?'

'I've been past it in a car, obviously. Not sure I've ever got out and wandered around,' Beth admitted. 'But we've got Dulwich Park right on our doorstep, so I suppose I've never felt the need to go anywhere else. And that reminds me, what actually happened with Teddy in Dulwich Park?'

'Oh, people can be so precious about things in Dulwich,' Katie said vaguely. 'The Rye is a bit more... real.'

'That's not an answer,' Beth said mildly.

Katie sighed and seemed to make up her mind to speak. 'Dog owners can be ridiculously oversensitive. You've no idea, Beth. Honestly, you'd think little Teddy was some kind of Lothario, the way people were dragging their mutts out of his way. He's only a baby. He did try and jump on a pug or two, but that's just his way of being friendly, saying hello. He doesn't mean anything by it, let alone, well, *you know*.'

Beth looked at her friend, but she was fully occupied swerving round a bus and avoiding an oncoming SUV. All she did know was that Katie had only had Teddy two minutes, but already she was as blind to his faults as any doting mama.

'I bet Charlie loves him to bits,' said Beth ruefully. She had no intention of changing her own mind on the subject, which meant Jake was going to be horribly jealous and bound to pile on the pressure.

'You should see them together when he gets home from

school. They're inseparable,' said Katie, peering down the road in search of a parking spot.

They'd come down the hill, and the green of the Rye now stretched out and opened up before them, a welcome slash of green in the relentless brick and tarmac swirl of south London. On the left-hand side, a row of beautiful Georgian houses stood, like enormous tea caddies, looking out over the swathe of grass. It was here that Katie was searching for a space.

With some difficulty, Katie edged her behemoth of a car into a gap, the parking sensors waking the sleeping Teddy and provoking a pitiful wailing.

'He's going to have to get used to that sound. No way I can park this bus without them.'

For the thousandth time, Beth wondered why Katie, with her one child, had a car big enough to transport the entire Brady Bunch, but she knew that the answer must lie with Michael. Not only did he want his wife and son to travel in the urban equivalent of an armoured vehicle, safe against the slings and arrows of outrageous fellow road users, but he'd never really accustomed himself to the idea of such a small family. He'd been born and bred to be a country squire with a quiverful of children, and it still seemed a bizarre accident that he'd ended up running a publishing empire and living in Dulwich with one lad. Having a dog was a step as natural to him as breathing, as long as he didn't have to concern himself with walking, feeding or training the creature.

It was a position Beth could heartily sympathise with as Katie began the extraction process, wrestling Teddy back into his lead while he was still confined in the back of the car, then straining to stop him from chucking himself under every moving vehicle that passed once he'd been liberated. At least they didn't have to wait long at the zebra crossing. Teddy launched himself across it, causing a taxi and a cross mummy in a Volvo to fracture their brake discs in unison.

Sensing freedom in the air, and with the springy grass of the Rye under his young pads, Teddy pulled like a tug-of-war team on the maximum dosage of steroids, until Katie was leaning backwards on her end of the lead like a water-skier. Neither of the women had the breath or the time to speak, as Katie was towed forwards and Beth trotted to keep up.

The wide-open spaces of the Rye were dotted at irregular intervals with other dog walkers. In the distance, Beth could see an enviably tall woman walking a red setter, then way ahead was a meaty, thickset man, head down, bundled into a nondescript coat, keeping up a spanking pace with a small dog that looked as though it would like to tone down the speed a little. Was he familiar? Before she had time to think, her eye was caught by a group of women straggling across the path, wandering and chatting with a retriever and a couple of spaniels.

Beth wondered what it would all look like from above – the seemingly random routes taken, their intersections and divergences. She'd once been up in the London Eye and had marvelled as the chaotic, crowded thoroughfares of the metropolis had become a chiselled, three-dimensional carpet of exceptional beauty, seeming to make a perfect sense which was entirely lacking at street level. Would all these meanderings be dignified with a purpose if seen from afar? The stout lady ahead of them with a frisky spaniel? The youngish man, head down, coat collar up, powering past them with a large black poodle on a red lead? What did they call those big poodles, anyway, Beth wondered idly. Standard, was it, like the lamps? Yes, she thought it was that, and the weeny ones were called miniature, which made sense. All these thoughts swirled through her head as they chugged along – partly to take her mind off the unwarranted amount of exercise she was getting. Beth started to pant.

Eventually, Katie turned to her friend. 'I'm letting him off the lead,' she said breathlessly.

Though she was already getting a stitch in her side, Beth was instantly worried. 'Are you sure that's such a good idea? Will he come back?' she asked, eyebrows steepling.

'Well, he's got to learn. And my arm's total agony,' said Katie, reaching forward and slipping the lead off. Teddy, unchained, was a silky black bullet out of a gun, racing across the Rye, his ears and tail surging in the wind like pennants. It was a truly beautiful sight. He zigzagged across the green for a while, pausing briefly to sexually assault what looked like a small spaniel – then he disappeared completely into a clump of trees in the far distance.

Katie started to run, and Beth, reluctantly, followed suit. If she'd known she'd be jogging, she'd have worn different shoes. Her little pixie boots were not built for speed – a bit like their owner. By the time she reached Katie, the stitch in her side was burning ferociously, her fringe was plastered to her sweaty fore-head, and she was not feeling at all well disposed towards small, furry creatures. It was just as well, perhaps, that Teddy was nowhere to be seen.

'Teddy! Teeeedddddy!' Katie was calling in a sing-song voice.

Beth looked around. Even on this short acquaintance, she was willing to bet that Teddy would be in motion, wherever he was. Surely they'd see the undergrowth moving, leaves rustling, a tree being thoroughly Teddied? But all was still and quiet in the little grove of trees. A bit too quiet for Beth's liking.

She'd had quite a lot of unfortunate experiences recently, and something about the atmosphere in this little glade got the hairs on the back of her neck standing up. She looked from one side of the path to the other. Nothing untoward. Nothing that could possibly give rise to this level of unease. But the feeling didn't go away.

Right ahead of her, veering off the tarmac, was a track through the undergrowth leading deeper into the thicket.

Should she follow it? For a moment, thoughts of Red Riding Hood flashed through her mind. She shook them off. This was silly. She was a grown-up. She wasn't carrying a basket of goodies for her grandmother, and she definitely wasn't wearing scarlet. Yet she did have the feeling that someone, or something, was watching her. Knowing south London, it was most likely a feral pigeon, or a hungry rat. Better than a big bad wolf, but still not the nicest thought. She decided to stay on the path.

But now she'd lost track of both Teddy and Katie too. Where was everybody?

Beth stepped forward, and suddenly everything was in motion again. A twig under her foot snapped, and she heard the snuffling of a very busy Teddy not far to the right of her. She walked on, the long tufts of unkempt grass brushing over her boots, still slightly damp from last night's drizzle. Where was that blasted dog? And where, for that matter, had Katie vanished to?

Teddy was whining now, as well as making unmistakable digging sounds. Beth picked up her pace, hurrying towards the noise and, round a tree, saw him at last. But he wasn't alone.

The first thing she saw, next to the puppy but apparently impervious to all his fervent attempts to scrape up a friendship, was an elderly-looking chocolate Labrador, which looked round solemnly as Beth approached then thumped its thick tail against the grass. The dog was sitting bolt upright in a curiously human way. If Beth had believed in anthropomorphism, she would have said it appeared both responsible and worried. Having studied her with sorrowful brown eyes, it turned immediately back to the cause of its concern – a form by its side, lying so still that Beth had somehow overlooked it before. Wait, was that someone lying on the grass?

Beth did a double-take, then wondered what on earth they could be doing there. Surely it was much too cold to be resting here, in this copse? And too wet? Her own boots were feeling distinctly soggy now. She would have hated to lie down, even for a second. Something was wrong. She stepped quickly forward, wondering suddenly if the person had been taken ill.

But one look told her that, as usual, things were much worse than that.

TWO

Part of Beth was wondering, for what seemed like the umpteenth time, why she was always getting mixed up in this stuff. But even as she was grappling with the shock, her mind whirling in denial, her vision going blurry and a ringing starting up in her ears, another part of her was taking in as much as it could of the horrifying tableau.

She took a deep breath and walked closer on steadier legs, trying not to disturb the Labrador. It was just as bad as she'd feared.

A man lay in the grass, arms stretched out, face mercifully turned to the side, as though he'd fallen in an ungainly way. But he'd never be getting up again. His pale beige windcheater coat was speckled and slashed with dark red, and there were rusty patches at his side in the grass which Teddy, horrifically, was dancing between, digging and licking at them as he bounced.

Beth darted forward and grabbed his collar just as Katie appeared in the clearing.

'There he is! Naughty Teddy,' she said, running straight over to Beth's side, then stopping dead as she suddenly took in the hideous sight before her. The look on her face might have

been funny, Beth thought – under entirely different circumstances. They stared mutely at one another, then looked down
at the body again.

'Oh no! I don't believe this,' said Katie, her face blanching.

Beth's first thought was that Michael was definitely going to
want to up sticks and move house now. Her second was that she
must ring Harry straight away, and her third was that she
needed to catch Katie before she fainted.

Looking back on the situation later, Beth realised that,
however bad you might think it could possibly be stumbling on
a murder victim, there was nothing like an exuberant, untrained
puppy to make everything much, much worse. If Teddy wasn't
barking at the elderly Labrador, who seemed so static that he
must be in shock, he was digging at the prone man's feet or
making ghastly lurches for the blood seeping away into the
earth of the Rye. Every time Beth slackened her grip on the
puppy, trying to take in the details of the murder scene, he got
overexcited again. And if she hadn't yanked him back very hard,
he would have pranced all over the victim and probably
attempted either to slobber him back to life or, more horribly, to
eat him whole.

It was almost as much as Beth could do to drag Teddy a bit
further off, so that she could ring Harry. The conversation was
short and to the point. Beth could feel him restraining himself
from saying a great deal more, and guessed he was in his office at
Camberwell Police Station, with interested subordinates
listening in. He and Beth would be able to talk more freely
when he arrived, but from the sounds of his clipped words and
terse instructions, that might not be very much fun. Honestly,
he was acting as though she *wanted* to stumble over dead bodies
and was doing it to annoy him. Nothing could be further from
the truth. She was heartily looking forward to turning this
whole matter over to him the second he arrived, and getting
Katie away for a much-needed coffee.

She felt terrible as she made her second call – to work – and explained that she wouldn't be able to make it in, even for the tiny sliver of time she'd allotted to her job that day. She spoke to her friend Janice's temporary replacement, Sam. She was lovely but didn't have such a sure grasp on the tiller, and was thrown into twittering panic by Beth's quick outline of her predicament. Janice, now married to the headmaster Dr Grover, was on maternity leave and spending every waking minute cooing over her new-born miracle. Beth sorely missed her comforting presence on the phone. Janice would have known what to say, and what to do.

Beth did her best to bring Sam back from the edge of hysterics, and promised she'd be in tomorrow morning – with all the details. Most schools ran on custard creams and gossip, and Wyatt's, though in many ways a sleek oceangoing liner in a sea of beaten-up fishing smacks, was not a jot different in this respect. Beth was willing to bet that once Sam got over the initial horror, she'd be bombing over to the staffroom to spread the tidings that a body had been found on the Rye.

Beth herself knew a fair bit more these days about the drill surrounding sudden death. Until Harry got here with the forensic bods, she really had to stay at the scene. The Rye was much larger than Dulwich Park, and the chances were that many dog walkers would be wending their way through the little grove this morning, which meant that potentially vital evidence could be worn away forever by paws and feet.

As Katie had more or less collapsed at the base of a tree, Beth had to do her best to keep people away single-handedly. At least the Labrador showed no signs of going anywhere. His gaze, now directed at what must be his late master, seemed full of dignified sorrow.

Soon the only sound that could be heard in the copse was Teddy's sporadic yapping, interspersed with frantic scratching and digging. A bird started to sing high in the trees. Despite the ghastliness of the situation, her acute awareness that Katie was suffering, and the knowledge that, just feet away, a man had lost his life, Beth couldn't help listening to the liquid pattern of the notes and appreciating its beauty.

It wasn't long until she heard the reassuring tramp of feet that sounded much too purposeful to be ordinary walkers, and soon DI Harry York was elbowing his way into the little stand of trees, accompanied by a troop of white-clad SOCOs. Beth could tell, even from this distance, that Harry was in a truly towering rage.

He was an impressive figure any day of the week, standing six foot four in his socks. Fully suited and booted, in his navy blue peacoat with a cream Shetland jersey underneath, with dark chinos and, she happened to know, boxers with a rather special red heart print that she'd bought him herself, he was drop-dead gorgeous. Normally, she would have melted into a puddle at his feet. Unfortunately, today's outfit was accessorised by a mean and narrow-eyed stare from flinty blue eyes, and it was directed right at her.

She supposed her discovery was a bit much, coming right on top of having to get rid of Magpie's kill this morning. But it was hardly *her* fault, was it? She rushed over to him, hoping a good dose of candour would win him round.

'I found him like this, with the dog sitting there. Obviously, I haven't touched anything...'

'No, you know the drill by now, don't you?' York ground out, his eyes reduced to slits.

'I don't know what you're so cross about,' Beth said, lowering her voice. She was conscious of the interested glances of the SOCOs, who were rustling about, assessing the scene and opening up their boxes of tricks, but perfectly able to eavesdrop at the same time.

'Honestly, Beth, is there some sort of unwritten rule of the universe that if someone gets murdered in south London, you have to find the body?'

'That's a bit unfair, Harry, it's not like I want to be constantly falling over corpses. And Katie was with me this time. We were walking her puppy, Teddy.' She pointed over to where Katie was now smiling rather greenly up at York. In fact, Katie hadn't been exactly with her, as they'd both been looking frantically for Teddy – but this wasn't the moment to go into that. The little dog, hearing his name, rushed towards Beth, inadvertently tripping up two of the SOCOs with his trailing lead. Harry tutted, and Beth made to start disentangling everyone.

'Look, it'll be best if you take Katie and, er, that dog, and just leave us in peace. You'll both need to be interviewed later, of course. And Beth...' York stepped closer to Beth and stooped to whisper in her ear. She felt the brush of his scratchy chin as he leant down, and the heat coming off his body. In other circumstances, it would have been quite urgent and sexy, but now all she sensed was his white-hot anger. 'I thought you were going straight to work?'

'Um, yes. Well, via Katie's. And the park. And then we couldn't go to the park, so we came to the Rye...'

'Spare me the details,' he snapped.

'You did ask,' said Beth, stung.

'Look, I don't think you realise quite how difficult this is for me. It's one thing you enjoying a bit of amateur detection in your spare time. But this? It's beginning to look like a habit. You've got a better hit rate than most cadaver dogs. And this stuff is dangerous, don't you understand? My job is hard enough without having to worry about you all the time.'

'Well, for your information, it was actually Teddy who found this one. Maybe he's got a career ahead of him in the Met dog squad, or whatever you call it. And however hard this is for you, I know someone it's much harder for,' snapped Beth.

'Who? Not you? Because I really don't think—' said York, folding his arms across his broad chest and staring down at her.

'No, not me. Him,' said Beth, pointing at the corpse. At that moment, the Labrador let out a piteous howl. One of the SOCOs had got very close to its master's head, taking a close-up of the injuries. Beth turned away quickly. She knew how the poor dog felt. It wasn't pretty.

'I tell you what, you could do something useful,' said York slowly, looking over at the corpse with a speculative glint in his eye.

'What?' Beth asked a little warily. Much though she wanted to get back into York's good books, she wasn't sure what role he could give her to play in a murder enquiry – officially, at least.

'You and Katie could take that dog away.'

'Teddy? Don't worry, I was only waiting for you. We'll finish our walk now.'

'No, not that mutt. I mean the big chap, sitting there. Poor old boy. We don't need him in our hair right now, and it sounds like he's going to make a real fuss when we have to shift the body.'

Beth felt mulish for a moment. The one thing worse than being out for a walk with the ridiculously bouncy Teddy must surely be having to take a recently bereaved, ponderous Lab along for the ride as well. But she could see the truth of York's remark. It was definitely going to be traumatic for the poor old dog when his master was zipped into a body bag. And, perhaps if she was helpful now, Harry'd be a mite less cross later. Though there was something about the stern side of him that she did find rather appealing. She surprised herself by giving him a coquettish little smile and, after a beat, the corners of his mouth tugged up by a millimetre or two in a slow response.

'Only if you give me a kiss,' she said, astonished at her own daring. Who would have thought, a year ago, that she'd be flirting with a big policeman in the middle of the day? If anyone had even suggested to her that it might be a possibility – and in the presence of a dead body – she would have said they were crazy.

That thought suddenly sobered her. There was an appropriate time for a bit of jousting with her paramour, and this surely wasn't it. A man had been killed here, and that was a serious and desperately sad business. Although she'd been at more than her fair share of crime scenes recently, she must never get used to it or treat it lightly. If she did, part of her own humanity would be leached away.

As if thinking the same thoughts, York tutted again, but bent down and brushed her cheek very quickly with his lips. Then he turned back to the SOCOs, daring them to have noticed the exchange. Unlike her, they didn't seem to enjoy any aspect of his grumpy side and they all bent to their tasks, brushing and bagging with redoubled concentration.

'And don't forget – get yourselves over to the police station today to give your statements about finding the body. Just the factual stuff. No embroidery or speculation,' York said brusquely to Beth, almost as though he wanted to undo the revealing tenderness of that little kiss.

Beth, not nearly as chastened as York clearly felt she should be, walked over to Katie with Teddy, and passed his collar over to her friend. 'Do you think you're well enough to go on? I think they're going to start to get busy quite soon, we might want to, erm, not be watching...'

As Beth had hoped, this grim prospect was enough to get Katie on her feet.

'There's just one bit of bad news...'

'*More* bad news?' asked Katie weakly.

'Maybe I didn't put that very well,' admitted Beth. 'The thing is, we've got to take the other dog with us. Harry thinks he might not react well when they have to, well... move the, er, body.'

'OK,' said Katie, closing her eyes briefly and taking a deep, calming breath, then exhaling through pursed lips. Beth rather envied her friend's instinctive ability to delve into her yoga training in moments of stress.

Looking a lot better already, Katie seemed to be taking things in her stride again. She clipped Teddy's lead on, as the dog pirouetted around her, licking anything that didn't move fast enough to evade him. One of the SOCOs trailed over, lugging the reluctant Labrador by the collar.

'Doesn't he have a lead?' asked Beth.

'Not that we've found so far. We'll keep you posted on that,' said the young technician.

'Great. But in the meantime, how are we supposed to take him away?'

'Oh, don't worry, Beth, I've got a spare. I always bring one in case Teddy manages to lose his,' said Katie, fishing in her bag. 'Prepared for everything, I am,' she said with a smile, unrolling a fabric leash and attaching it to the big Labrador's collar.

'There we are, boy. You can be Teddy's new chum,' she said kindly, patting the old dog's head. His tongue lolled pinkly, and he panted at her in a friendly and accepting way.

Something on the dog's collar winked in the weak sun, and Beth had a brainwave. 'Let's see what your name is,' she said, bending to look at the small metal disc that dangled there. 'Colin.' The Labrador barked once, in a tired sort of way. Beth smoothed his velvet head absently. 'Can that be right? Colin? Funny name for a dog. Or is that, could that be, your master's name?' Beth asked excitedly. 'Is your owner called Colin?' The Labrador barked again, listlessly.

Beth could see she wasn't going to get far with this game. 'Well, we might as well call you Colin anyway, until we know more,' she said, turning the disc round. There was a mobile phone number etched on the back. 'Have you got that?' she asked the technician, fired up again, but he only nodded and plodded away. Beth kicked herself. Yes, of course. She'd thought she was being so clever, but searching the murder victim's dog for clues was probably on page one of the SOCO Handbook.

Nevertheless, she couldn't resist getting out her phone and quickly dialling the number.

'Do you think you should be doing that?' asked Katie anxiously, guessing what her friend was up to.

Beth turned away slightly, hunching over her phone.

The SOCO team were bustling around now and York was rapping out orders, but they all heard the sudden warble of a ringtone. Unfortunately, it was the *Star Wars* theme tune, its triumphant notes rendered horribly tinny by the phone's speakers. It sounded sorely out of place at this most sombre of gatherings. Beth was tempted to cut the call immediately. After all, it would be little short of a Lazarus-style miracle if anyone picked up. But, despite herself, she wanted to hear the answering machine message.

After four agonising rings, while the SOCO team prodded and patted down the corpse to find the phone, a recording blessedly clicked in. 'Leave a message after the tone,' said a man's pleasant, light voice. It sounded educated, with a smile in the words that made Beth instinctively warm to the speaker – who had to be the crumpled body lying in front of them. Poor man.

Beth pressed cancel immediately, just as one of the SOCOs unearthed the handset, but not before York had looked over in their direction and, from Beth's guilty and surreptitious stance, put two and two together. He'd just started to stride across the clearing towards them when Beth shoved her phone back in her bag and yanked on Colin's lead.

'Come on,' she said urgently to Katie, leading the motley group out of the copse and back out onto the Rye. Luckily, Teddy was useful for once. As soon as he'd realised they were on the move, he started pulling like an express train and soon the group of trees was just a speck behind them. When Beth looked back, she was pretty sure she could still see York staring crossly after them, those blue eyes tracking her every move like lasers.

Ten minutes later, and Colin was panting heavily as Teddy led them a merry dance all over the open heathland. Katie, having learnt her lesson earlier, kept Teddy firmly on his lead this time. Although that horse had definitely bolted – Beth was pretty sure even she wouldn't be stumbling over another corpse on the Rye that morning – Katie decided she'd had enough experiments for one day. Teddy's lead was still long enough, though, for her to be dragged hither and thither, while Beth and the trailing Lab brought up the rear, plodding along in a companionable silence.

Beth had been expecting a bit more reluctance from Colin, perhaps even a Greyfriars Bobby-style refusal to shift from his owner's side, but it turned out that any walk was a good walk – even a walk away from everything he'd ever known. Every now and then, he turned his head to give Beth a mildly surprised glance, as if they were at a cocktail party together and he just couldn't quite remember her name. But he was so well brought up that he would no more have dug his paws in and refused to budge than he would have bitten the hand that might well soon end up feeding him. Beth hoped fervently that York, once he'd got over his sudden burst of ill-temper, would be making some urgent enquiries about where Colin lived – and who was going to look after him from now on.

She hadn't recognised the dead man at all. That wasn't altogether surprising, she supposed. She always felt that Dulwich was essentially a small community, a slice of white-picket-fenced heaven that had managed to carve out a charmed existence despite the rest of south-east London pressing in on every side. But that, she knew, was an illusion. People came and went in the city as relentlessly, regularly and anonymously as waves on the sea shore. With a population of ten million and counting, it simply wasn't possible to know everybody, even in her own street. The truth was that her own world was very small, and bounded by crucial factors like attendance at the schools Dulwich did so well. It gave her the illusion of continuity and cohesion. But there were plenty of other sides to the place that she really knew nothing about.

Now she cast her mind back, trying to edit out troublesome details like the damage to the side of the man's head, the clumps of rusty blood and, worse, his pallor and stillness. With that airbrushed away, could she get a sense of what he had been like, even if she hadn't actually known him?

Not old; in fact, probably not much older than her, she decided. Late thirties? That, in itself, was difficult to get her head around. Could life really be cut short so easily? But she knew it could.

And what had he been wearing? She squeezed her eyes closed for a second, nearly tripped over a tussock of grass, and realised this wasn't perhaps the moment for a reconstruction. But nevertheless, she'd managed to get some details fixed in her mind. He'd been wearing red jeans. The type that only posh boys bought.

In this area, that hardly narrowed the field much. But at least it meant she was pretty sure he wasn't just a wandering tramp. She'd heard there were a few who congregated on the Rye, camping out at nights, getting what shelter they could under the trees, and spending their days anaesthetised by Strongbow. None of them would be wearing red trousers, she was willing to bet.

What had he been wearing on his top half, though? A beige windcheater. Well, it had started out beige, at any rate. That was harder to identify. It didn't seem to belong to any sort of urban tribe that she recognised, though she'd be the first to admit that the nuances of outfits often passed her by. As a perennial jeans wearer who considered buying a new T-shirt quite a major event, she wasn't typical of women in general, or Dulwich in particular. Most of the mothers she knew were impeccably turned out, with a different, perfectly coordinated and accessorised outfit on every morning, even if their most pressing appointment of the day was with a changing mat and a toddler's bottom.

Men's clothes were always that bit more difficult to calibrate, anyway. Their colour palette was so restricted, compared to women's. Blue, black, brown, beige. If it hadn't been for the red chinos, for example, Beth wouldn't even have been sure that the chap was from SE21 at all. But when there was little to go on, every element that she could glean about his appearance, position, and even his dog, could be vital in identifying him. So far, Colin – an impeccably well-brought-up dog of a popular middle-class breed – and the man's trousers were telling their own story loud and clear.

She didn't need to do this; she knew that full well. It was York and the rest of the Metropolitan Police who were responsible for finding out who the man was and why he'd met his end here. But she also knew, by now, that she wouldn't be able to rest until she too had done as much as she could for him, in her own small way. Fate seemed to be pointing her at these mysteries, and the least she could do was use the talents she'd been given to help unravel them.

Had this poor man known his attacker? Beth couldn't remember whether his hands had been damaged. Defensive injuries, they called them, didn't they? Signs that he had fought back. The SOCOs would be looking for traces under his fingernails, preserving them with plastic bags on his fingers. Even the pattern of wounds would tell them whether he'd resisted or been taken unawares. Maybe the blow to his head had immobilised him, and then the killer had been able to do his worst.

There she went again, making assumptions. The killer might well have been a she. If recent experience had taught

Beth anything, it was that there was often a lot more to even the simplest scenario than met the eye. The frustrating thing was that she'd have no access to any of the nuts and bolts of the investigation, unless Harry was prepared to take her into his confidence. And judging from the look on his face as he'd watched her walk away, that wasn't going to happen any time soon.

Before Beth had time to get downcast, they'd crossed the side road at the edge of the common and reached the grey and orange painted café. For years, there had been a café on the Rye itself, close to the car park and the children's playground, but it had been closed for some time for refurbishment. While the work was going on, this little place was reaping the benefit.

Beth was more than ready to stop and get a calming coffee. It had been quite a morning already, and it wasn't even eleven o'clock. But the presence of Teddy and Colin was immediately problematic.

'We can't take the dogs in, can we?' said Katie, looking a little hopelessly at the façade of the café. The décor looked fresh and zingy in the weak sunshine, and a window display of intricately iced cupcakes, millionaire's shortbread and brownies was calling to Beth. The heavenly aroma of cappuccino wafting from the doorway made it all the more appealing. It was suddenly a Shangri-La that these two most determined coffee drinkers might be banished from.

'Do you think you can manage both dogs for a second? I'll go and get the coffees and we'll just have to sit outside,' said Beth. It wasn't exactly tropical weather but, thanks to Teddy's exuberant pace, and Beth and Colin's doughty efforts not to be left too far behind, the women had rosy cheeks and the dogs were now panting steadily like deflating airbeds.

A few minutes later, and Beth was back outside with a tray bearing a large slab of brownie each, as well as their drinks. They deserved something to keep their blood sugar up, after the shock they'd had. She also had a plastic cup of tap water, to top up the doggy bowl on the ground near the table Katie had chosen.

Katie was a little hunched into her brand-new dog-walking outfit – an expensive waxed jacket with as many pockets as Teddy had naughty tricks. Beth could tell this was soon going to take the place of the minimalist handbag that Katie still loved, but which was manifestly failing to fit in with her new lifestyle. She'd soon go bagless, as Beth had seen dog-owning women do in the playground, and just have paper twists of Bonios exploding from her coat. Beth felt a little sad. She'd loved Katie's look – part yoga guru, part lady of leisure. She supposed she'd just have to get used to this new phase.

Thank goodness cat owning didn't require any special sort of uniform. Beth sometimes wondered if Magpie would miss her at all, if she suddenly disappeared from her life. But maybe she was being unfair. Magpie did always seem to know when her owner was upset, and would generously arrange her bulk over Beth's lap in such cases, seeming to believe that a good layer of shed black and white fur could improve any crisis. Beth would be devastated if Magpie ever wandered off or... she didn't even want to finish the thought. Strange, that she'd looked with a degree of equanimity on the sudden death of a fellow human being today, yet could not contemplate the demise of her cat.

But many were the times when she'd shed a bitter tear into that fluffy coat, and whispered secret sorrows into those sensitive triangular ears when Jake was safely abed. In theory, she now had York to confide in when things went wrong, but years on her own had made Beth rusty at the whole trust business. She would have said Magpie never judged her, as York often did, but that was not the case. Anyone gazing into those emerald chip eyes could be in no doubt that Magpie was a highly judgemental cat. The soothing thing was that she never, ever shared her views.

Had Colin's owner confided in this big, safe lump of a dog, Beth wondered. She inadvertently caught the Labrador's eye and looked away again quickly. Maybe it was ridiculous, but she felt obscurely guilty, knowing so much more about his master's fate than this clearly devoted boy did. It was very sad.

'Poor old thing,' said Katie, smiling ruefully.

'Awful, isn't it?' agreed Beth. 'I just hope they find out quickly who he belongs to now. Do you think the man was married?'

'You were having a good look,' said Katie with a shudder. 'Did you see a ring?'

'I don't think I did,' Beth said, screwing up her eyes to picture the scene again, then wishing she hadn't. Suddenly, the brownie didn't look quite so tasty.

Katie's was untouched, too. 'I've never seen a dead body before,' she said glumly.

Beth could no longer say the same. She scrolled through some unpleasant pictures in her mind's eye and shook herself. 'Come on, let's think about other things,' she said bracingly. 'There's nothing we can do for that man now. And Colin doesn't want to be sad,' she said, smoothing a hand over the dog's ears. He thumped his tail on the ground politely.

'You're right. Yes. And we've got plenty to talk about.'

'I suppose we have. The new café in the village?' Beth had rather guiltily tried this out recently with her new friend, Nina, while Katie had been away skiing.

'Puccini's? No, not that. Though we do need to discuss it. But don't say you've forgotten? Only the interviews,' said Katie, with the ghost of her usual enthusiasm coming back.

'Yes! Getting the letter. That was such a moment,' said Beth. Remembering the keen mixture of joy and astonishment she'd felt at seeing the contents of that slender envelope helped enormously to shove away the sorrows of the morning's discovery. It wasn't that she wanted to downplay the awfulness of what they had seen, more that neither of them needed to wallow in it. After all, if Harry and his team did their thing efficiently, then neither Beth nor Katie need be involved in the situation for a moment longer, once they'd got their official statements out of the way.

'I sort of wish it all stopped at the letter,' said Beth whimsically.

'What do you mean? Don't you want Jake to get in?' Katie was suddenly bolt upright on her bench.

'Well, of course I do,' said Beth slowly. 'It's just that now, with the letter and the prospect of the interview ahead of us, all the hope is there. If we could stay in this moment, enjoy that feeling of possibility forever, it would just be lovely.'

'You mean you don't think he'll pass the interview,' said Katie sagely.

'Oh, I don't know.' Beth took a sip of her coffee. 'He's lovely and chatty, if that's what they want. I'm just worried they'll test him on stuff that's out of his comfort zone, like current affairs. I was trying to chat to him about Novichok the other day – I thought he'd love all that Russian spy stuff – and he just asked me if it was a new type of Nutella.'

Katie laughed. 'They're so young. I don't think they expect them to be fully fledged members of the debating team... yet.'

Beth gave Katie a rather dark look. She knew full well her friend had been subscribing to *The Week* for at least eighteen months in order to prepare Charlie's brain for the ordeal ahead. And not even the children's version, either. She was pretty sure she'd also seen a massive pile of newspapers in Katie's hall when they'd trailed Teddy out of the house earlier. Charlie probably knew more about policy hot potatoes than most members of the Cabinet by now, but Jake had had his chips. He couldn't possibly catch up.

It was Beth's own fault for half-expecting Jake to fail at the first hurdle. Now she had less than a week to cram the past thousand years of political and social history into her boy so that he could converse like a middle-aged banker at the drop of a hat. The thought made her wonder quite why this school was such a good idea. But it had been her dream for so long that she couldn't step back from it now. On second thoughts, maybe thinking about the murder would be more fun.

'Do you think he lived around here? Or closer to Dulwich?'

'Who? Oh Beth, for heaven's sake, not the, um, victim? Tell me you're not going to get wrapped up in that now.'

'*Wrapped up* might be overstating it. But don't you feel curious about who he was and what he was up to?'

'Not in the least little bit,' said Katie. 'Whoever he was, he obviously got up the wrong person's nose, and I don't want to know why he had it coming, but he clearly did.'

'But that's a terrible way to look at it, Katie,' said Beth, a bit shocked. 'You know it could have had nothing at all to do with him. It could have been a loose madman on the Rye...'

'Thanks for that thought, Beth,' said Katie, taking a hunted look around her. 'You don't think the killer is still somewhere around, do you? Maybe we should get home. The Rye was a mistake. I'll have to try Dulwich Park again.'

They were still the only ones sitting outside, but a slow stream of dog walkers passed the café and Beth realised Katie was now scrutinising them anxiously. They all seemed to be marching purposely across the expanse of green, collars up against the wind, and not exhibiting any overt signs of psychosis or brandishing blood-stained murder weapons.

'The killer will be long gone, Katie, don't worry. Anyway, the body wasn't even warm when we got to it.'

'Don't tell me you touched it?' said Katie in horror.

'Just inadvertently,' Beth mumbled. 'Anyway, I washed my hands inside when I was getting the coffee,' she added, mentally crossing her fingers. 'That's not the point. The thing is, the killer could be someone who wanted something he had, or killed him because he had a secret... nothing to do with the poor man at all.'

'Please don't start all this again, Beth! Haven't you had enough of being clonked on the head and terrified out of your wits?'

'Well, neither of those things is fun, granted. But don't you feel you owe the victim something? After all, we were the ones who found him. That must mean something. Isn't yoga all about karma and stuff?'

'That's a low blow, Beth. You know I only do the *namaste* out of the corner of my mouth,' said Katie.

'All the same. The universe made us find him, Katie. Out of all the people on the Rye, all the people in Dulwich, in south-east London... we were the ones.'

'*You* were the one, you mean,' said Katie mulishly.

'Me – and Teddy, who is yours,' Beth pointed out. They both turned to look at the puppy, who'd been silent for a while. He gazed innocently back, a well-chewed and almost unrecognisable tartan umbrella clamped in his jaws.

'Is that yours?' Beth asked.

'Never seen it before,' Katie admitted.

'We'll just chuck it in the bin as we leave,' said Beth. 'But you take my point? I feel a sense of responsibility now that we have found him, for whatever reason.'

'You've got much more pressing responsibilities. Your son, your job. Even your boyfriend, who is, by the way, the person who's supposed to be dealing with stuff like this.'

'Oh yes, but you know what Harry will say. "Huge percentage of unsolved crimes, motiveless attacks, statistics, blah blah..."'

'All of that is completely true,' Katie said.

'I'm not denying it. But where's the justice? That man is dead, and even if you want to pretend nothing's happened, there's at least one other person apart from me who definitely wants answers – and deserves them.'

'Who's that?' asked Katie pettishly.

'Colin, of course.'

Hearing his name, the old Lab peered round from where he'd been quietly surveying Teddy's devastating attack on the umbrella. He looked at Katie with kind, limpid eyes.

'You see? He's beseeching you,' said Beth, with a little triumph in her tone.

'Colin isn't a person,' said Katie tightly. But she also stopped protesting.

Beth smiled to herself. It looked like she had Katie's tacit approval for her quest. She wasn't expecting to get anything like such a favourable reaction from Harry. He'd be furious if he even so much as suspected she was going to make her own enquiries into the case. But then, he'd be happy giving up himself the moment things got hard. True, he had stuff like this stacking up yards-deep on his desk, and had no manpower or budget for more. It was just as well he was able to let these things go, or they'd drive him mad.

Beth, on the other hand, knew that she was a terrier when she was on the scent of a mystery. And she did have a powerful incentive to get things sorted out. If she didn't, where was Colin going to live? It might make one small boy very excited if he acquired a dog out of the blue. But Colin wasn't exactly the sprightly puppy Jake had ordered. He was an old gentleman, set in his ways, and would no doubt be missing his master very much indeed.

And there was someone else to consider, who'd be even less enthusiastic about the prospect of dog ownership than Beth. Magpie. Beth shuddered to think what her beloved black and white moggy would make of the day's developments.

THREE

Perhaps it was York's revenge on Beth for her trick with the victim's phone, or perhaps it was just the way his day panned out, but it was a subordinate who eventually took statements from both women down at the police station. The whole process seemed to take forever, and it felt as though several days had dragged past by the time they found themselves standing outside the school gates that afternoon, waiting patiently for the boys to be liberated.

'I can't believe I'm doing this,' said Beth, shaking her head.

'What? I know you've been doing that experiment, letting Jake walk back, but surely on a day like today, you know, *finding a body*, you'd like to pick him up yourself?' Katie was surprised.

'Not that. This,' said Beth, shaking the brown lead she still had clasped in her hand. Colin, feeling the shake, looked round patiently. 'And why do I feel this dog is just tolerating me?'

Katie, who was a lot more relaxed now as Teddy was slumped asleep at her feet, laughed. 'I must say, it's funny seeing you with a dog. I never saw you as a dog owner, really.'

'Whereas you're an expert, now, I suppose?' Beth said, a little tersely.

'Don't be like that. Come back with us and I'll give you one of Teddy's spare bowls and some dog food to keep you going, just to get you started off.'

'I'm still hoping Harry's going to ring me and tell me someone's rushing round to pick Colin up,' said Beth. 'But that would be wonderful, thank you. Sorry to be such a grump. It's just that I know this is going to cause... Oh, here they come.'

With that, the boys were upon them. Charlie made a beeline for Teddy, who was suddenly alert and yapping in sheer delight at seeing his chief accomplice again. Meanwhile, Jake ran over to Beth, looked incredulously at Colin, and astonished her by falling on his knees before the dog and gathering him into an enormous hug. Colin, meanwhile, was acting as though he'd been given a blood transfusion, wiggling his entire, solid body in pleasure, wagging his tail like an outboard motor on full speed, panting with joy and licking Jake's face.

Katie and Beth looked at each other in astonishment.

'Have they met before?' Katie asked.

'Not that I know of,' said Beth, her eyebrows disappearing into her fringe. She'd been braced for Jake to find babysitting Colin almost as much of a chore as she did, and was certainly expecting a lot of renewed pressure to get a puppy instead. What she hadn't anticipated was this apparent reunion of souls separated at birth. It was going to make things much easier tonight – but a whole lot trickier in the long run.

Beth, looking down at her beloved boy and seeing the smile on his face, couldn't begrudge him this happiness, and wondered if she'd been in the wrong all these years denying him the pleasure of a pet. Yes, they had Magpie, but as far as she chose to interact with humans at all, Beth was her point of reference. And the cat wasn't mad about Jake at all. She had spent the first six or so years of his life running off every time she'd seen him, and steadfastly spurning his love. Even now, if she deigned to sit on anyone, it was Beth, and frankly that was usually when she was cold and fancied a human hot water bottle.

Would a dog have helped Jake through those first years without his dad? But no, Beth was the one who'd really suffered James's absence. Jake had been too small to register the change in their lives, and had grown up knowing no different. And during those early years, Beth had not been in a state to take on a dog as well as the unwanted position of widow. She needed to give herself a break on this one.

'Have you noticed, Beth, Colin seems to be showing Teddy the ropes?' whispered Katie as they straggled home, the two dogs in front being proudly led by the boys. Beth looked and, as usual, thought that Katie was being wildly optimistic. Teddy was managing to take at least five paces for every measured plod of Colin's, and seemed to be dancing around the old boy's paws in a way which certainly would have led Beth to cuff him one over his silly fluffy ears, if she'd been a dog. But Colin was loping along patiently, pink tongue lolling from side to side, a little slow but apparently perfectly happy. Was he missing his owner at all? Beth wondered.

Once they were at Katie's, and Teddy and Colin had been turned out into the chilly garden, the boys were suddenly a little less keen to keep up the façade of responsible dog ownership and sneaked off to Charlie's PlayStation instead. Beth looked at Katie. 'So, how long do you think the novelty's going to last?'

Katie smiled. 'You've got a point, but the thing is, Teddy's here for keeps now, whereas Jake doesn't come over much midweek – he's the main attraction tonight. Sure, Teddy's a bit mad at the moment,' she admitted, as they watched the puppy attempting to clamber up the big copper beech after an anxious squirrel. 'But he'll get a lot steadier, and then he'll be a great companion for Charlie. You'll see.'

Beth noted that Katie was feeling a lot more positive about Teddy this afternoon than she had been this morning. That probably had a lot to do with the fact that Teddy was currently safely outside, wearing himself out, which ought to mean a long, long sleep was on the agenda quite soon. Nevertheless, she felt she ought to sound a note of caution.

'I think he's basically going to be your dog. Charlie and Michael might think they want one, but the day-to-day stuff is going to be down to you. But you're happy with that, so it's fine,' Beth added quickly, not wanting to be too much of a doom-monger.

'Well, don't look now, but I think you've got a new fan, too,' said Katie, nodding to the huge glass garden doors where Colin was now seated, nose against the window, gazing fixedly and expectantly at Beth. He'd had enough of the great outdoors, it seemed. In the background, Teddy was literally barking up the wrong tree, as the squirrel executed a heroic leap onto the fence and bounced away across the neighbours' gardens.

As they stacked the boys' plates in the dishwasher later, Beth realised she was moving at half her normal speed. She was trying to put off the evil hour when Magpie was going to have to make the acquaintance of their impromptu houseguest. But there was nothing else for it. Collecting an unwilling Jake and a patient Colin, and with a carrier bag full of must-have dog accessories that Teddy had already managed to tire of or find superfluous, Beth set off for home.

As soon as she got her key in the lock, Beth braced herself for the inevitable. Sure enough, Magpie was laid out in the hall like a fluffy monochrome rug, waiting for the special tummy tickles which she consented to endure when her humans got home. They were a bit late back today, but she was willing to let that pass. As soon as the door swung open, though, and she got a good sniff of her least favourite perfume – *eau de dog* – Magpie shot a good five feet up into the air.

Pausing only to direct a vicious green glare at Beth, who quailed, Magpie zoomed towards her cat flap in the kitchen like an Exocet missile. Beth wasn't even sure if she'd put a paw on the ground in her flight, which took seconds. Colin looked up at Beth, head on one side, pink tongue still lolling, as if to say, 'What *was* that?' And Jake bounded, oblivious, into the hall.

'Straight up to do your teeth now, it's a school night.' Beth was using her special firm voice and Jake, for once, did as he was told with minimum '*aw, Mum*' whining.

Beth and Colin were left in the tiny hallway. 'Don't look at me like that, Colin. I don't know what we're supposed to do next, do I?' she said, a little exasperated. To say the day hadn't panned out as she'd hoped was a massive understatement. She'd had the utter horror of discovering yet another body. If that wasn't catastrophe enough, she selfishly still rather resented Katie having purchased such a demanding pup. And now, just to add sprinkles on the top of all the awfulness, she seemed to be lumbered with a dog of her own. Things couldn't really get much worse. Could they?

Just then, she heard the sound of a key in the lock and York appeared, looking exhausted. He stopped short at the sight of Colin, who was taking up a large amount of hall. Colin immediately leapt up with a deep woof and wagged his tail madly, brushing the walls on both sides of the narrow hallway, at the first sights and sounds of a man approaching. Then he seemed to take a closer look and his tail stilled abruptly. He sat down, then sprawled out on the tiles, head on his paws, eyes facing the wall, and let out a tiny whine.

It was his first sign of distress in what must have been a confusing and terrifying day. Immediately, Beth felt dreadful. No matter how much things had sucked for her, it had been a thousand times worse for this poor old boy. He must have seen his master being murdered, and now he was with strangers, far from everything familiar. At least he couldn't possibly understand all that had gone on. She hoped.

Her eyes met York's. He shrugged a little, then squatted to

pet the Labrador just at the moment when Beth's hand smoothed over the velvety old head. Their fingers met – and entwined.

York sighed. 'I'm sorry I was cross earlier. I just hate it when you put yourself in danger.'

'I know. I'm sorry, too. But I wasn't doing anything reckless this morning. I was just out walking...'

'Only you could go for a stroll and fall over a body,' said York ruefully, straightening up.

'That's not even true,' said Beth, rising to her full height and tilting her chin to look up at him. 'Dog walkers are *always* tripping over corpses. I shouldn't have to tell you that.'

York made a noise that sounded like a harrumph, turned away for a moment, and said hopefully, 'Supper?'

Beth grimaced. It was a bad night to have to admit the cupboard was bare. Jake had eaten with Charlie, and Beth had assumed she'd make a meal of whatever was lurking at the back of the fridge. That wouldn't tickle Harry's palate, though. Sure enough, he peered optimistically into the bulging carrier she'd brought back from Katie's, only to find tins of dog food that Teddy had turned his wet black nose up at.

'I'll pop out for some fish and chips,' said Beth in a conciliatory tone, picking up her bag from its usual spot on the paint tin.

York looked at the can of emulsion and sighed. 'I'll go. Safer that way. Don't want you tripping over multiple stabbing victims in the chippy, do we?' He ruffled her hair and banged the door shut behind him.

Beth tore the scrunchy from her ponytail and ran her fingers through her mane. She hated it when he messed her hair up like that. She bundled it all back off her face again, and trailed into the kitchen, followed by Colin. As she bustled about getting the wine glasses out of the cupboard and finding cutlery, he sat, staring up at her expectantly.

'Is it your dinner time, too?' she asked, finally realising what he was telling her.

She got the bag and took the haul of dog food out. Teddy seemed to have rejected at least half of the contents of Waitrose's pet aisle already. She held out each tin to Colin in turn, waiting to see which one he liked the look of, but she got the same panting enthusiasm for them all.

There was even a bowl in the shape of a bone in the bag, so Beth put that on the floor and scraped a tin's worth of disgusting meaty mess into it, hoping Colin would eat fast so she didn't have to see or smell it for too long. He obliged her, showing a spurt of speed for the first time that day, and snuffling hopefully around inside the bowl long after it was licked clean. Beth wasn't sure if that meant she'd been a bit mean with his portion, but she had a dim memory that Labs were quite greedy – and Colin was already a solid chap. Still, she hoped she wasn't depriving him. But with any luck he'd soon be moving on to a new home where people knew a lot more about this whole dog ownership thing.

A clattering at the door meant York was back with the catch of the day, so she busied herself putting the plates on a tray with everything else and taking it to the sitting room. For some reason, a take-away always meant a TV dinner. She wasn't sure why, but maybe it was to do with standards slipping. If she was feeling lazy enough to buy instead of cook, then the full piggy experience of eating in front of a screen seemed only fitting. Tonight, having their eyes glued to the box meant York wouldn't be able to tell Beth off again for finding another body – something she was already heartily sick of.

The slight prickliness she was feeling had hardened into something more resentful as they sat in silence, tucking away cod and chips twice. He hadn't even gone to Olley's this time, but to the much closer shop on Half Moon Lane that she wasn't so keen on.

Maybe she'd been wrong giving York a key. At the time, it had seemed like a logical next step. He worked such antisocial hours that normal dating – whatever that was; Beth certainly didn't claim to know – was almost out of the question. If she hadn't given him the run of the place, she would never have seen him. And that, she admitted, would have been a shame. But now, several months into the relationship, she didn't quite know where they were or, perhaps more importantly, in what direction they were headed.

It all seemed to be on his terms. Ridiculous as it seemed, she'd never yet been to his flat, even though he was so much at home in her little house that he now had his feet up on Jake's schoolbag as he licked a heady cocktail of salt and ketchup off his fingers. Noisily. In fact, tonight, he was making the sedate Colin look like the ideal male companion.

The dog had curled up at her feet with his head just on the edge of her toes, keeping them lovely and warm. Every now and then, he'd gaze up at her with affectionate, if puzzled, eyes. The rest of the time he was content to stay peacefully silent, giving out the odd gusty sigh which, in Beth's head, meant that he was missing his master. She leant down to pat him, then tutted and picked York's used chip wrappers off the floor, stuffing them in the carrier bag.

York, glued to a re-run of *The Wire*, remained oblivious, then turned to her, jabbing at the screen with a chip in hand, saying through a thick mouthful of cod, 'See? That's where they get it so wrong. No way could they have done that, it's completely impossible.'

Beth murmured something that could have been assent, confident that York wasn't really listening. He was more inter-ested in putting his own point across than hearing hers. His legs were spread out wide, dominating the small room. He was taking up three-quarters of the sofa, and his whole attention was wrapped up in the goings-on in Baltimore. Well, better that than nagging her again about things that were outside her control.

She put her plate aside and got her phone out and flicked idly through her messages. She should be cross-questioning York about what he was doing to find out where Colin belonged now, but she supposed a night with the old boy wouldn't be the worst thing in the world. The dog was quite a comforting presence.

As though he knew she was thinking about him, Colin looked up at her again and thumped the floor with his tail gently. She didn't have any sort of bed for him – did dogs need them? She'd bought a few, over the years, for Magpie, but her cat had always taken great pleasure in ignoring such rash purchases, however cushy the fake fur or enticing the fleecy interior. She much preferred vital paperwork, school projects or, of course, any garment of Beth's left foolishly lying around; the more expensive the better.

'I suppose I'd better take Colin out for a final walk. That's what people do, right?' asked Beth, nudging York and hoping he'd get the message and jump up to do it himself. But he was deep in the murky world of America's war on drugs, and barely grunted.

Beth sighed, collected up their plates and wrappers, shoved the rest of the rubbish into the bag, and put it by the door to take out. Once the dishes were rinsed, she slipped on her shoes and picked up Colin's lead, looking round in surprise. Where was he?

Out in the hall, she found the old boy with his head stuffed in the chip bag. When he emerged, looking slightly guilty, Beth didn't have the heart to tell him off. After the day he'd had, he deserved a few extra carbs. And by the looks of his muzzle, he'd eaten her lemon quarter, too. Hmm, she thought. That was probably not such a great idea.

On the street, it was decidedly nippy, but Beth enjoyed the

quick saunter round the block more than she'd thought. It was a good way of clearing that greasy *après*-junk food feeling from her system, and she felt a sense of camaraderie with the other dog walkers who seemed to be the only people around at this time of night. No one seemed to be astonished to see her with a dog. Perhaps, contrary to her long-held belief that she and dogs didn't mix, she might be a natural, after all?

Colin seemed to be loving his airing, stopping to wee methodically every now and then, but showing no signs of wanting to do more. Which was just as well, as Beth hadn't brought any bags and she'd already jettisoned the chip wrappings in the wheelie bin outside the house. She definitely wasn't looking forward to that aspect of dog ownership. But hopefully, York would have found the boy his rightful home before his bowels had time to move.

FOUR

The next morning, she opened her eyes to find an admiring male gazing at her as though she was the most beautiful creature in the world. Unfortunately, he had the most ghastly case of dog breath ever.

'Colin! Get off,' she said, shoving at him ineffectually and looking wildly round at the other side of the bed. York had upped and left, it seemed, leaving the bedroom door wide open for marauding Labradors. She'd missed her chance to have a proper talk with him about what on earth was happening with this dog – and much else besides. Were there kennels, for instance, where dogs like Colin could be stored until relatives came to claim them? And was it time that she got her whole relationship with York onto a clearer footing?

These were just two questions that were going to have to wait. Top of the agenda was getting everyone up and ready for work, and all of a sudden that now included a grieving dog. Beth wished, yet again, that Janice was back from her maternity leave. Would Wyatt's allow her to bring the old boy in until something could be sorted out? Janice's replacement, Sam, wouldn't have the authority. Beth's great friend Nina was now working at the school as an admin assistant, after her old job had come to a very abrupt, somewhat messy end, but she didn't yet have her feet far enough under the desk to help Beth out.

But wait a minute, maybe there was a way of sneaking the old boy in by the back door, so to speak. As long as Colin didn't go on the rampage in school grounds, then Beth couldn't see that the poor chap would really pose any sort of a problem. He could stay in her room with her, help her with the archives. He'd be well out of the way. Her office in the old Geography block was off the main drag, far from the headmaster's office. She often felt she could do with an assistant – usually just so she could lumber someone else with the less enticing bits of her in-tray – but still.

She wasn't at all sure what the school policy with dogs was. She imagined it would go something along the lines of, guide dogs good, all others bad. But if she didn't ask, then she couldn't know, and if she didn't know, she wasn't infringing anything. It wasn't perhaps the most morally upright code, but Beth decided it would have to do for the moment. It was hardly as though it was a situation of her own making. She'd acquired Colin entirely accidentally, and was as keen as the next person to move him along.

Well, she told herself that. But actually, looking down into his dark eyes as they meandered along to school later, she knew it wasn't really true. Already, he'd encroached a little into a heart which she'd firmly felt was a dog-free zone. Even Magpie, whom she'd expected to have a lot to say about the matter, had just decided to evade the issue, making herself scarce yesterday evening and not showing so much as a whisker this morning either. Her little bowl of goodies was empty, though. Assuming Colin hadn't done the dirty on her and scoffed her food – and if he knew what was good for him, he wouldn't try that more than once – then she'd been back to have breakfast and ready herself for a day of hanging out with the neighbourhood cats, no doubt having quite a hissy-fit about the new addition to the family.

Beth had a moment of doubt as she passed George, the porter, in his little glass cabin, but he just smiled at her as though he saw her saunter in with a large dog every day of the week. Rather anxiously, she and Colin padded down the corridor to her office, and she then installed him in her little used conference corner, where there was a table he could sit under. From the doorway, you'd never even know there was a dog here at all, thought Beth, hoping all her visitors would keep out of range of Colin's pungent halitosis.

At some point during the day, she knew she was going to have to take him for a walk, and presumably the moment she dreaded would arrive. But she had remembered to shove a roll of Southwark Council's compost caddy-liners into her bag as she'd left home. It wasn't, by any means, the intended use of these little sachets, but in an emergency she hoped she'd be forgiven. Until then, there was plenty of work to be getting on with.

Two hours later, Beth realised she'd had her most productive morning for, well, she hesitated to say years, but... Decisions had been taken, documents corrected, emails returned, and all under the watchful eye of Colin, who seemed to be willing her endeavours on with his every measured breath. Suddenly, though, he got to his feet and whined.

This was so unusual that Beth stopped what she was doing immediately. 'What's up, boy?' she asked.

Colin put his head on one side and panted. Beth smiled at him vaguely, then returned to her screen. He whined again. She got up, went over to him, patted him a few times, then returned to her desk. The whine came again. And he wasn't sitting back down. This was serious. She thought for a moment, then realised he probably did finally need to use the facilities, as it were. And it was lunchtime. Both very good reasons to try and meet up with Katie in the park. She collected her bag and jacket with one hand and stabbed at her phone with the other.

Twenty minutes later, Beth was at the café in the park, waiting for Katie. Despite the chill, she was sitting at one of the monolithic picnic tables with a much more relaxed Colin keeping her feet toasty. The deed she had dreaded was done and dusted. She'd found it slightly less revolting than she'd thought. It was a long while since Jake had been in nappies, but the principle was much the same. Though her hands hadn't come into contact with anything, she'd still tethered the dog to a bench and had a thorough scrub in the café loos before she felt able to put the incident behind her.

She'd been more particular about this, in fact, than when she'd handled his dead master and then eaten a brownie, she realised with a faint wave of nausea. No doubt she'd get used to it. But she stopped herself there – no, she wouldn't have to. Because York was going to take Colin off her hands, as quickly as possible.

Beth was just fulminating on this point and wondering crossly whether York was dragging his heels to punish her in some obscure way for becoming the Dulwich mums' circuit equivalent of a vulture, with her unerring eye for a carcass, when she saw Katie striding towards her with her customary easy grace, only slightly hampered by Teddy doing a slalom through her legs. Unusually, Katie was wearing a hoody pulled up right over her sunny blonde hair and, if Beth was not mistaken, she was peering a little furtively from side to side as she bowled along. She slipped onto the bench opposite Beth and they air-kissed – the table was just too wide to permit the normal double Dulwich greeting.

'You OK?' Beth asked, wrinkling her brow beneath her fringe.

'Yep, yep,' said Katie, seeming to scan the horizon a little nervously, then hunkering down to whisper across the table. 'Would you mind getting me a coffee from inside? I can't risk taking Teddy in.'

The puppy, who was now busying himself bouncing up and down on Colin's paws, looked round briefly at the mention of his name then redoubled his efforts to get the older dog's attention by nibbling his ears. Colin, very sensibly, gave a deep sigh and rolled over onto his side, pretending to be asleep. Beth looked at his glossy brown coat, picking up dirt and leaves, and worried in advance about her floors. But she could see the old boy had a point.

'Flat white?' she asked, and Katie nodded.

The café had recently changed hands. Gone were the passive-aggressive notices about baby wipes in the sewers – but gone, too, was the soft-play area for the tinies. It didn't cause Beth too much of a pang, as her boy was so far beyond all that now, but she did wonder how the mothers with toddlers would cope. She and Katie had spent endless summers here when the boys were small. It was very chi-chi now, with Farrow & Ball's entire selection of relentlessly tasteful taupes on the walls and the sandwiches tucked into faux-artisanal stencilled wooden farm crates, which had never been within ten miles of a real farm for hygiene reasons. And the coffee, hand-ground on the premises and brewed in the latest machine that looked as though it could nip to Mars and back, had suffered a huge price hike. On the plus side, it was now delicious.

Beth left the café somewhat reluctantly. It was lovely and warm in there and the fug of steamy coffee and hot milk was very soothing. The cold bit as soon as she was out of the door, and she could almost feel her nose going red. She sat down at the bench again, seeing in surprise that Katie was hunched over her phone. That was very unlike her. She usually hardly bothered with it, in public at least.

'Everything all right?' she asked tentatively, pushing the coffee across the expanse of wood.

Katie looked up briefly. 'I'm sorry, Beth. Lot on my mind,' she said mysteriously, just as a woman walked over to their table and burst into speech.

'Excuse me, I thought I recognised...'

Katie immediately shrank into her hoody and turned away quite rudely. Beth stared in astonishment. Normally she was the chatty, friendly one and Beth was content to remain in the background. Not today, apparently.

Beth looked up at the woman with a questioning smile. 'Um, hello?'

'Yes, it *is*, it's Colin. How are you, lovely boy?' asked the woman, stooping to pet the dog, who looked up at her with his pink tongue lolling and his heavy tail banging the ground. He even staggered to his feet and pressed his nose into her crotch, like someone very politely remembering his manners.

'Oof, that's definitely you, old boy. Never forget a fanny, do you?' said the lady, petting his ears and stroking the velvety head.

'You know Colin? You aren't his owner, are you? Or one of them?' Beth asked, slightly desperately. Maybe this lady was going to take the dog off her hands. 'Do sit down.'

'But where's Mark?' the woman asked at exactly the same time. 'Oh, sorry, after you,' she said with a laugh.

Dressed in expensive jeans, with a silky top just showing beneath a snug rose-coloured cashmere cardigan, and feet in knee-high suede boots against the chill, the woman looked a typical well-heeled Dulwich lady of a certain age. Teddy was now nibbling at the ends of her sugar pink pashmina, which had come unwrapped as she leant forward to pet Colin.

Beth looked over at Katie, who'd angled herself away from them and couldn't see her protégé's latest transgression. The lady yanked the scarf good-naturedly away from the puppy, settling the soft folds back around her neck. With some difficulty, she inserted herself onto the wooden bench, at the other end from Beth and across from Katie, who was now pulling fruitlessly on Teddy's lead. Colin waddled over and collapsed at her feet, and Beth, to her surprise, felt a little bereft.

'Do you know Colin's owner, then? Is he... called Mark?' Beth said tentatively.

'He isn't here with you, then?' Confused, the woman looked from Beth to Katie and back again. When neither enlightened her, her expression changed. 'What's going on here? Why have you got Mark's dog?'

'Look, we haven't stolen him, if that's what you're thinking,' said Beth, as Katie got up and pulled Teddy away from the woman. He whined a little. He was always being yanked away from new friends. Katie trudged back to her seat with Teddy on a very short lead.

Peering at her watch, then shifting restlessly on the bench, the woman seemed on edge. 'What's all this about?'

'There isn't an easy way to say this, but Mark – or a man who was with Colin yesterday, on Peckham Rye – has been found, um, dead.' Beth's voice, not loud at the best of times, tailed off towards the end. She'd never had to break bad news before, and she really wasn't enjoying the responsibility.

'Dead?' The woman felt no such qualms about volume. She virtually shouted it, and everyone hardy enough to be sitting at the outside benches swivelled in their direction.

'I'm afraid so.'

'I don't understand,' said the woman. 'He was fine. It can't be true. He was in perfect health...'

'It wasn't his, um, health,' said Beth, while Katie, sitting across, shook her head silently at her friend. Beth realised she was right. There was no reason to go into all the circumstances. 'Look, I can give you a number you can ring, maybe they can explain more. If you're a friend of Mark's?'

'Yes, of course I am,' said the woman crossly, as though Beth should have been aware of that. 'I've known him since he was a boy. Mark is – *was* – my son's best friend... This is awful. How am I going to tell John?' She looked wildly at the two women, who had no answers for her.

'Did Mark often walk on the Rye? Was that his usual route with Colin?' Beth couldn't resist asking.

'Every morning, they'd be out there, rain or shine. They've been best friends since school. Both with their dogs. John with Bubbles. His poodle, you know?' The woman raised her eyebrows, as though expecting some sort of reaction. Beth and Katie exchanged blank glances.

'Mark loves the Rye,' said the woman absently. 'More than John, probably. They've gone their separate ways a bit over the years – well, that's inevitable, isn't it? School was ages ago now, after all. But they were so close. They had so much in common, with their art.'

'It's lovely when boys have hobbies they can share, isn't it?' Beth worried that this effort to keep the conversation going would seem too transparent. But what she'd said was true. Jake and Charlie's hobby, gaming, might be a lot less creative than art, but they certainly loved doing it in tandem.

'Yes, yes,' said the lady, seemingly lost in a reverie. 'But, of course, Mark went on with the painting... and John didn't. Such a shame. He was so talented; he had more of a gift, as a boy. I really thought so. And I wasn't biased.' She looked up at Beth, seemingly expecting to meet opposition. But she wasn't going to get any. Beth might have no clear idea what the lady was on about, but she knew it was vital to keep her talking. At this stage, they knew nothing about their victim, and every word that was being said expanded their knowledge exponentially. She nodded emphatically. It seemed to work, as the woman continued, almost as though she'd forgotten Beth and Katie were listening.

'Well, best friends do grow apart, don't they? I'm not denying it was difficult for John. Particularly in view of, well, everything... But there we go. Some people have all the luck, don't they?'

If the woman was still talking about Mark, this was rather odd. Beth certainly wouldn't have put him in her top ten of fortunate folk this week, put it that way. She shuddered slightly as a vision rose, unbidden, of the man lying there prone, liberally covered with those red slashes. It had not been a pretty sight.

'People have to take on other, well, responsibilities, don't they?' the lady continued, now twisting her pashmina nervously between long, mobile fingers. On them glittered several of what Beth thought of as Dulwich diamonds – gem-encrusted eternity bands of the type that her poor James used to refer to, laughingly, as 'maternity rings'. Lots of the yummy mummies had them; the mothers of earlier generations, too. She liked to think James would have got her one, eventually, to celebrate the birth of her beloved Jake. Particularly if she'd nagged him enough. But then, time and fate had got between them and all their plans. It happened. All too often. And James was just another man who had not been so lucky, she supposed.

But she brought herself back to the park and the bench with a bump. The lady was still trying to explain away something that made sense only to herself, and it was vital that Beth paid proper attention. So far, this was the only person they'd found with a connection to the victim. She could be an absolute gold mine of information. Thankfully, she didn't seem at all bothered by the inattention of her audience, with Katie apparently trying to merge into the bench in case any Teddy-haters spotted her, and with Beth wandering away on her usual flights of fancy. Beth kicked herself and resolved to concentrate. The woman was still talking, her beautifully modulated voice rippling on like silk, only snagging sometimes on emotion.

'But the one thing Mark and John still always agree on is their morning walkies. Despite everything. They both say it's so important to them. Bubbles and Colin absolutely love it. And so do the boys. *Did*. Oh. Oh, this is too much...' the woman tailed off, searching through her pockets for a tissue. Beth found her one from her handbag, mercifully clean and fluff-free. Katie was still sitting a little aloof, clutching at Teddy's collar, but Beth could tell she was in bits just hearing the woman's story.

'Then Mark always comes – came – here to Dulwich Park in the afternoon, but just for a quick saunter. Mark always says, *said*, that Colin needed his postprandial stroll... I'd often bump into them here; we'd have a catch-up. Not every day, of course, but I usually walk my poodles here, you know.' Again, there was a little pause here and, despite her grief, the lady seemed to be looking for a response from Beth and Katie which, unfortunately, they just couldn't provide.

Katie was keeping a profile so low that even the wooden bench itself seemed more animated. And the only thing Beth herself really knew about poodles was that, nowadays in Dulwich, they always seemed to be mixed with something else – labradoodles, cockapoos and so on. Even Teddy was part-poodle. The psycho part, thought Beth a little sourly, as the puppy made an unprovoked assault on her pixie boots. She whipped her feet back under her seat quickly. But the lady was still talking.

'Mark was such a good soul, such a thoughtful boy. Are you sure? *Really* sure that he's dead? How do you even know?'

Beth shifted uncomfortably on the bench, and Katie darted a glance at her under her hoody. Beth spoke a little reluctantly. 'We're pretty sure.'

That was a bit of a white lie. There was no doubt about it. Unless Mark was taking part in some sort of over-realistic *Crimewatch* reconstruction which involved being dead for real, or he was such an outstanding actor that he'd managed to subdue his pulse and all other bodily functions, and splatter himself with blood, then he was definitely dead. But Beth didn't want to keep rubbing it in. And it was outside her remit to give away too many details. Didn't the police always err on the side of vagueness, in case of copycat killings? She didn't think this lady was the sort to rush out and commit an equally horrific crime, but she might well tell the story to someone else... Dulwich being what it was, within a few hours everyone would know. And Harry York was bound to suspect that Beth had something to do with the dissemination of the information. Was it fair to keep this poor lady and her son, a friend of the victim, in the dark, though? Beth thought for a moment.

'Look, call that number I gave you if you want to know more about the, er, circumstances,' she said gently. 'But anything you can tell us about, er, Mark in the meantime would be really useful, though.'

'Why would it be useful? I don't understand. Why should I tell you anything? And what on earth could I tell you anyway?' The woman looked wildly from Beth to Katie and back, her voice rising again. Though there weren't many people having their coffee outside, those that were appeared glued to what the lady was saying.

Beth thought fast. She could see it was beginning to infuriate the woman that they knew so much more about the fate of her son's friend than she did. A little bit of information, though well shy of the full quota, wouldn't be wrong in these circumstances, would it? She instinctively leant her head in and spoke quietly, and the woman followed suit.

'Look, I know this is really difficult, but *we* are the ones who found Mark dead. And that means we have an interest in the whole business,' Beth said.

'Speak for yourself,' Katie muttered from the other side of the table, but although the woman looked across at her sharply, she then turned back to Beth.

'I just don't understand all this at all. Mark was young and fit. Well, I suppose he's in his mid-thirties, like John, but that's young these days, isn't it?'

Beth, also in her mid-thirties, nodded her head emphatically. As far as she was concerned, it was a fine age and very definitely much too young to die. Even Katie, aloof as she was trying to be, gave a quick assent from her side of the bench.

'Was it a heart attack or something? How odd. And how awful. His parents are dead, so that's a mercy, I suppose. There's nothing worse than having to bury a son. And he was an only child too. But I don't see how I can really help.'

'But you knew Mark. You might know... why this happened.'

'But that's the thing I don't know, and that you aren't telling me. I haven't got a clue; how could I have?'

Beth sighed inwardly. Without coming clean and revealing that Mark had been murdered, she wasn't going to get much further. She really wanted to ask whether he'd had any sworn enemies or received any threats recently – a dead giveaway, if that wasn't a too horribly apposite way of putting it. But she wasn't at all sure how this poor lady would react to the full, brutal truth about what had happened on the Rye. Should she be inflicting that kind of a blow on a stranger? And would she be compromising Harry's investigation if she did?

Usually, this wasn't a consideration. She knew that Harry, a pragmatist to his fingertips, was only too happy to let cases drop into the great unsolved folder that seemed to lurk at the centre of the Metropolitan Police like a huge swirling vortex. Even though she'd successfully sorted out quite a few unpleasant incidents now (and she inwardly marvelled at herself for passing off so much murder and mayhem as merely 'unpleasant'), she knew he'd still much prefer it if she didn't get involved. She wasn't entirely sure that was because he didn't like her to put herself in the way of danger, or whether he was worried about her treading on his size elevens.

She'd done pretty well, so far, in tidying these situations up. It wouldn't be ridiculous of her to worry that he saw her as something of a threat. He, of course, was convinced of his own chivalry, but that didn't mean he was right. Most people had more than one reason for thinking things, though often they weren't comfortable admitting it.

All this windmilled through Beth's mind. At the end of her thought processes, she mustered a sympathetic smile. 'I'm very sorry for your loss, and for your son's. If Colin is anything to go by, his master was a very nice man.'

It was too much. The woman's eyes filled with tears and, to Beth's horror, she began to cry in earnest. Beth looked mutely to Katie for support. Usually, when things got emotional, her sunny friend stepped in to comfort everyone and diffuse the situation. Today, for reasons of her own, Katie was being most unhelpful. She turned away a little further and seemed to be focusing on a tree at the other end of the park, as far away from Beth's current crisis as she could get.

Beth took a breath and rooted in her bag for another tissue and handed it to the lady, who clutched it gratefully and blew her nose. Restored, she looked up tremulously. 'I suppose I'd better take that number from you, and get on,' she said.

'Yes,' said Beth cannily. 'Give me yours and I'll ping it over to you by replying. What's your name?'

'Um, I'm Rebecca Grey. Spelt like the colour,' the woman said helpfully.

'Thanks, Mrs Grey. It is Mrs?' Beth asked, and got a nod of assent.

The woman seemed to hesitate, before saying, 'Look, I suppose I should give you my son's number, too, so you can send the contact to him as well. Just in case he needs it. John deals with a lot of stuff for me these days. He's always saying I forget things, you know.'

Beth suppressed a little smile of satisfaction. The more the merrier – everything was potentially useful in a murder investigation. It wasn't until she'd sent Harry's number over to Mrs Grey and her son that she realised: she'd made a decision. Whatever Harry – or Katie – thought, she'd have to look into this death. She felt a compulsion. Of all the people on the Rye that morning, it had been she who had stumbled across the corpse. She, who'd already sorted out several similar situations. It couldn't be coincidence. Not again. There had to be a reason why death and disaster kept finding her. Why she'd been able to help clear up so much.

And, this time, that was enough for her. She wouldn't do the usual, worrying forever over the rights and wrongs of getting involved. She wouldn't even be anxious about Harry's anger levels. She'd just get on and look into things, in her own way. And try not to get hit on the head this time.

Just one more question to ask, for now.

'I don't suppose you'd like to take Colin home with you, would you?'

Colin perked up at the sound of his name, but Mrs Grey shook her head sadly. 'I'd love to, Colin's such a dear. But I can't. We've got all the poodles, you see. And a cat.'

'I've got a cat, too,' Beth said glumly. But Colin already felt like a fait accompli, and she could see the other woman wasn't going to relent and take him off her hands. In fact, she was moving away pretty quickly now, as though concerned that Beth would run after her proffering an unwanted Labrador. Possession was nine-tenths of the law, and Colin had Beth firmly on the other end of his lead.

As soon as Rebecca Grey was out of earshot, Beth turned to Katie, who was still staring moodily into the far distance.

'What was all that about?'

'What do you mean?' asked Katie, not quite meeting her eyes.

'What's with you today? Is there something wrong?' Beth was perplexed. Katie was her fixed point, the perpetual sunshine that enlivened her sometimes gloomy world view, and convinced her that things would always turn out right in the end. If Katie went all weird, then what hope was there for Beth? 'Katie?' she asked again, really worried now.

'Oh, it's just Teddy,' said Katie, after a long and troubling pause. 'I think I might have bitten off more than I can chew this time.'

'Well, it definitely looks like Teddy has,' said Beth, looking down to where Teddy had his jaws clamped round something that looked suspiciously like the sorry remains of Katie's eye-wateringly expensive handbag.

'Christ,' said Katie, dragging it out of Teddy's clutches and trying to brush off a couple of layers of dog slobber. 'God, he's chewed right through it. That's it. I've just about had enough. *Bad dog.*' She gave Teddy a look which would have made Charlie wet himself, but which the puppy laughed up at, mouth wide open. She put her head in her hands. 'Michael's going to be furious. He bought me that bag for our anniversary two weeks ago.'

'You're not going to cry, too, are you?' Beth asked nervously. She knew she should be offering support, but two weeping women in one morning was pushing it, as far as she was concerned.

Katie laughed ruefully and shook her head, but Beth came round and sat on her side of the bench, tentatively putting her hand on Katie's shoulder just in case. 'Look, it's probably not too late to give him back to the breeder... stick him on eBay... auction him at the school gates,' said Beth tentatively.

'I can't do that. What would Charlie do? What would he think? No, I've committed to this dog and I'm stuck with him. A dog is for life, and all that nonsense. Little bleeder,' said Katie, jogging his lead. Teddy looked adoringly up at her out of eyes dark and sweet as molasses. 'Look at that. Pretending to be so innocent.'

'I thought you were really happy with him, even though he's a bit, erm... energetic,' said Beth tactfully. She didn't want to get caught in the trap of bad-mouthing Teddy if Katie was really keeping the mutt and they both had to endure another ten years of his continual presence. It was a bit like her teenage years, when a friend had broken up with a boy. Beth consoled her by confessing she'd always loathed him, then the couple promptly got back together, and Beth was on the outside from that day forth.

'Oh, I love him when he's behaving... but that's five minutes a day at the moment. And it's just made it so difficult coming here. I mean, this is *my* park. My house is a stone's throw away, we've always walked here, we love coming here for coffee. And now, well...'

Katie tailed off, darting a look left and right and readjusting her hoody. Beth peered around, too. She would have said Katie was being paranoid but, if she wasn't mistaken, the owner of a spaniel sitting at the bench closest to the playground was giving her friend a filthy look.

'What on earth did happen here? You never really explained,' Beth asked.

'Oh, do I have to? It was so awful,' said Katie.

'It can't have been that bad, surely? This is Dulwich Park, Katie. No one's going to be really *nasty*.'

'You haven't seen the owner of an ancient dachshund who's being enthusiastically buggered by a puppy,' wailed Katie.

Beth couldn't help it. She burst out laughing. 'Probably did it no end of good,' she said bracingly.

'I'm not sure about that. It could hardly walk afterwards. Teddy was madly in love.'

'I thought it was a pug he went for?'

'It turned out that was just the warm-up act. It's dachshunds he's really got the hots for. They can't run as fast as him,
and their bits... *you know*, are really close to the ground. On his
level.'

Beth shut her eyes to banish an unwelcome vision. 'Oh
Teddy, Teddy. You look such an innocent boy. No one would
think you're Dulwich's answer to Casanova,' she said, reaching
under the table and petting Teddy's black silky coat. He immediately rolled onto his back, paws in the air, oblivious to the
chill, and blind to everything except delicious sensation, accidentally revealing the surprisingly large cause of all the trouble.
'You're incorrigible, aren't you? So, you're telling me there's a bit
of a #MeToo movement building up in the park against young
Teddy here?'

Beth's shoulders shook as Katie nodded sadly. 'Look, I know
it probably seems ridiculous to you, Beth, but I'm not used to
this sort of treatment. I'm not saying you are,' she rushed to add.
'But I don't think you're that bothered if people don't like you.
You're so independent, you just shrug it off. But for me, well,
it's a bit of a shock. I'm not used to people whispering about me
and basically running off when they see me and Teddy
coming.'

Katie looked so miserable, Beth's heart really went out to
her. She could have said she didn't love it when people didn't
warm to her, either – frankly, who did? She'd just had to get
used to it over the years, whether she liked it or not, as she'd
never had Katie's happy knack of being popular, charming and
lovely. But perhaps now wasn't the moment. And she could see
that from Katie's previous position on a sort of golden pedestal
of niceness, her current status as delinquent dog-owning pariah
was pretty grim.

'I'm sorry you're having all this hassle, Katie. You – and
Teddy – don't deserve it.'

'Well, he definitely deserves it, no doubt about that,' said Katie crossly, jerking his lead again.

'I can see you've got your work cut out with him, the naughty boy. But I don't understand why you were acting so oddly when Rebecca Grey was here just now,' said Beth.

Katie looked at her bleakly. 'The trouble is, I think the dachshund's owner was a friend of Rebecca's. I knew I recognised her from somewhere, and then I realised it was during that whole, well, um, unfortunate... session. God, that woman was beside herself. And Rebecca Grey was just standing there, looking judgemental, with her bloody poodles. Needless to say, they were impeccably behaved.'

'I wondered why you were treating her like a plague carrier. You'd turned so far away from us I thought you were going to fall off the bench.'

'I didn't want her to recognise me. People are really precious about their pets, you know,' said Katie in righteous tones. Beth just nodded. Magpie might shred her soft furnishings with determined regularity, but she'd defend to the death her moggy's right to dump hairs on any visitors to the house. And she knew that, whatever Katie's current levels of disappointment in Teddy's morals, she'd still stick up for her dog against all-comers.

And that gave Beth pause for thought. Could this whole thing on the Rye be about the dog, not the owner? And if so, did that mean Beth already had the key to the puzzle on a long lead? She looked down at Colin and he placidly returned her gaze. If only he could speak, she thought. And if only he'd been a better guard dog. Then none of them would be here now.

That was another point, Beth realised. So much for a dog being man's best friend. Colin's human had been done to death, while he apparently looked on with his usual doggy half-smile on his face. What kind of chum did that make him? Hardly a bestie, Beth thought. Shouldn't he have protected his master?

Barked, at least? Well, he might have done that, she realised, as she had stumbled on the scene sometime after the murder. But he couldn't have barked loudly enough to have attracted much attention, or the frenzied knife attack would have been interrupted before his owner died. What was the point of having a dog, if it didn't see off would-be assassins?

All right, no one would buy a Labrador expecting an attack dog, unless it was sandwiches they wanted mauling. But you'd expect an 'Excuse me, would you mind not stabbing my human?' wouldn't you, in return for all that Pedigree Chum? Not to mention the endless walkies and poop-scooping over the years.

Wait a minute. Maybe Colin had a reason for holding off. Maybe his size, inertia and general good-natured approach to life concealed a secret loathing of his late master. Had he allowed the attack to happen because he wanted Mark dead? No, Beth shook her head. That was ridiculous. From all she'd seen, dogs seemed pre-programmed to give slavish devotion to their families. She couldn't remember a single instance when a dog had really been a dog in the manger. So, why on earth would Colin stand – or sit – by and let someone kill his best friend? Wouldn't he protect Mark?

Unless, thought Beth suddenly – a glimmer of an idea breaking upon her – unless he knew the person who was approaching. And then didn't act until it was too late. And was then simply scared away by the flashing of the knife. That was quite possible. Had Colin known Mark's killer?

Then Beth had another brainwave. 'Wait a minute. If Rebecca knew Colin and instantly recognised him, and she usually walks here in the park, then that means that lots of other people might spot him and we'll be able to find out all about this Mark, his owner. If he always took his "postprandial walk" here, or whatever.'

Beth personally thought that sounded a bit pretentious, but

any clue to the dead man's personality was going to be vital. She couldn't believe this had been a random killing by a maniac on the loose who'd just happened across the victim and his dog by chance. And if she was right, there had to be a good reason why the man was dead. Or, in light of her recent experiences, perhaps she should amend that to say a reason that made sense to the person on the other end of the knife. If she'd learnt anything recently, it was that murder was rarely rational.

Katie gave Beth a withering look. 'Haven't you been listening to what I've been saying? I'm *persona non grata* in this place nowadays. And Teddy is definitely *dog non grata*. The sooner I leave the better.' With that, she swigged down the last of her cooling coffee and prepared to haul Teddy home.

'Oh, Katie, no! You're not going to let yourself be beaten, are you? Probably half the dog owners here have had, um, unfortunate incidents with their dogs back when they were puppies. It's all part of a dog's transition to adulthood, isn't it? Just youthful exuberance?' Beth glanced at Teddy, only to see that he was now enthusiastically humping the table leg. He clearly had a lot to get out of his system. In all ways.

'Look, however full of, um, beans he is, we're here now and he's going to be a lot better behaved at home if we've had a good walk around. You can't argue with that,' said Beth. 'Perhaps you might want to think about getting him, erm, *done*? I'm not sure what age they need to be to have the op, but that would definitely sort out his hormones, I should think. Even a dachshund isn't going to look that irresistible if you've had your danglers cut off, I dare say.'

'I'd take him tomorrow, if I could,' admitted Katie. 'The trouble is, Michael is completely against it. Says it's an outrage, emasculating him in his prime, it's barbaric... Honestly, you'd have thought I was trying to give *him* the snip, he was so incensed.'

'Well, I do sort of agree that it's a bit medieval, if you think about how we used to do it to all those poor castratos, just for their voices. But in Teddy's case, to save your blushes, I'd definitely make an exception. I suppose Michael's at a delicate age – maybe he's worried about his own manhood,' said Beth, slanting a glance at Katie, who gave her friend a good-natured shove.

'No worries on that score, thank you very much. Just because Harry's that little bit younger.'

'Ten years,' said Beth, a little smugly. 'But then, that makes you a child bride, doesn't it? Whereas Harry's two years younger than me, so I'll end up looking like his granny. Assuming we ever get to that stage. But back to Teddy. I do think Michael is being a bit unfair. He doesn't have to take Teddy round Dulwich Park with all these saucy little dachshunds asking for a seeing-to, does he? Maybe you should get him to take Teddy for loads of walks at weekends, see how he likes being in charge of a serial rapist?'

'I did ask him at the weekend, but then he took Charlie along and I ended up going, too. I couldn't bear to think of how it might all end up, and I knew Michael wouldn't be able to cope if it all really kicked off. The absolute worst of the lot are the pro dog walkers. They tend to have a smaller dog or two and then a couple of really big ones, all on a bunch of leads. Teddy will just plunge in after a nice juicy little Westie. It's a total nightmare. You can imagine the tangle. The leads are completely knotted, all the dogs are going nuts, and Teddy's loving it and getting more and more excited by the second.

'He's absolutely fearless too. You'd think he'd be terrified of the great big dogs, but no. There's a teenage girl who walks four dogs every afternoon – I think she's at the College School and making a bit of extra pocket money – and Teddy just made a habit of going straight for the cockapoo in her bunch every time. I've had to stop taking him for a walk with Charlie after getting back from school, it's just too embarrassing. And then what's the point of having him? The whole idea was that Charlie would have lots of lovely healthy exercise and get away from the screens for an extra hour after school. But I don't want to shove him in the car and take him to the Rye at pick-up time; it's bumper to bumper then, and would completely defeat the object. So, I'm ending up getting two extra solo walks a day myself, which means I've had to cut down on my yoga classes and get shunned by every dog owner in Dulwich, while Charlie doesn't walk him at all. Honestly, I'm so fed up.'

Beth looked at Katie's miserable face and couldn't help cursing young Teddy. All right, he was an adorable scamp who was currently snuggled up with Colin and looking like a poster boy for well-behaved puppies. But anyone who upset her friend like this had Beth to reckon with.

'What about dog-training classes? They must have them here somewhere,' she suggested gently.

'Michael's totally against those as well. He had dogs as a boy and he's convinced he knows exactly what to do.' Katie sighed as Teddy, from looking as though he was about to have a snooze, suddenly leapt up on all four paws, ears pricked, and gazed off into the far distance. Without any warning, he was off, like an athlete who'd heard the starting pistol. And unfortunately, Katie – on the other end of his lead – was dragged along too.

'Teddy! *Teddy*,' she wailed. 'See you in a minute, Beth,' she called over her shoulder.

Colin, disturbed for a moment by Teddy's abrupt departure, looked up sleepily, sniffed the air, panted wisely, and subsided again onto soft paws. Beth patted his head gratefully. Perhaps there was quite a lot to be said for a tired old dog, after all. He was certainly beautifully trained, and even if he didn't have a great record as a bodyguard, he was still quite a reassuring presence. Beth was a bit worried that she might get too attached to him. After all, someone was bound to claim him, weren't they?

The man on the Rye was probably married or had a family, and they'd definitely want his dog.

Meanwhile, there were certain advantages to dog owner-ship, even on a temporary basis. Beth had already noticed that she was getting some polite acknowledgements from fellow dog walkers. She'd been trotting round Dulwich Park since she was a girl, and never remembered collecting quite such a bouquet of smiles before. Maybe some of these people actually knew Colin, but even if they didn't, they all seemed to approve of his docile ways and, by extension, of Beth herself. She rather liked her new incarnation as a respectable dog-owning type, even though it was based entirely on false pretences.

While Katie was getting the blame for having a sex-mad delinquent on her hands, Colin's staid ways were earning Beth entirely unjustified Brownie points. She'd had nothing at all to do with fostering his good behaviour. She was just, temporarily, on the other end of his lead. Still, it made her think.

Loosely attaching him to the leg of the table in case he made a totally out of character bid for freedom, Beth scampered off the bench and marched purposefully back to the café doors. She could get a refill of coffee for them both while poor Katie was being dragged to the far end of the park and back again. She might also be able to get some useful information.

Once inside the swish new space, Beth realised again how cold it was becoming outside. She peered through the window at Colin but, apart from seeming to arch an eyebrow at her – could dogs even do that? – he seemed pretty much oblivious to her absence. She turned to the blackboards, scanning quickly through all sorts of tempting snacks that she really shouldn't be succumbing to... But what harm could a couple of blackberry muffins do? They probably counted as one of her five a day, didn't they? And Katie really needed cheering up.

She was glad to see that the trays were still quite practical, despite the faux-farmhouse style of the café, and she slid a brace of muffins on one and waited patiently. After a few moments, she realised someone was trying to get her attention. She'd assumed they just had a frog in their throat, but no, the elderly lady in front of her in the queue had turned round and was coughing and valiantly endeavouring to catch her eye.

'Hi there,' said Beth expectantly.

'Colin's going to need his water, isn't he?' the lady prompted her.

'You know him?' Beth was astonished. This seemed too good to be true. Was there anyone in Dulwich, apart from her, who wasn't a long-standing friend of the elderly Lab?

'We all know lovely Col,' smiled the lady, who wore white hair in a tidy longish bob, which brushed the shoulders of her navy zip-up fleece. Her sensible jeans, too, screamed dog walker, but on her feet were bright red shiny Doc Marten boots, giving the lie to her suburban look. Beth was intrigued. Instinctively, she lowered her voice.

'I don't suppose you've heard what's happened to his owner?'

'Mark? What do you mean? Has something happened?' The woman was instantly alarmed.

Her friend, ahead of her in the queue, swung round. 'What's all this, Miriam?'

The fleece lady looked from Beth to her friend in consternation. 'Something's happened to Mark. Did you know?'

Just then, the assistant at the counter cut in. While they'd been busy, the queue had melted away, and the two elderly ladies were first in line. Both now, though, were thoroughly flustered. Beth stepped forward decisively. 'I'll have two cappuccinos and these muffins and two...?' she asked the women. 'Two more cappuccinos; four altogether. Then we'll go outside and have an, erm, chat,' she said. 'Or maybe you could go out now and stay with Colin?'

The ladies wandered outside and collected their own dog –

a rather cute little terrier with a raffish bedhead look to his salt and pepper coat.

Beth loaded up the tray, wincing a bit at the price of four of Dulwich's finest hot beverages, plus the muffins, and elbowed her way out into the cold again. She set the tray down carefully on the bench, noting that Katie wasn't back yet from her forced march with Teddy.

She slid a brimming cup over to each of the ladies, who'd sat down on either side of Colin, and took her own seat on the other side of the bench. She felt almost as though she was interviewing the women, positioned opposite them, and she took a steadying sip of the cappuccino to give herself a bit more thinking time, then opened her mouth to speak. But the older of the two women, wearing a shapeless purple coat, burst in first.

'Look here, I don't mean to be rude, but how come you've got Colin here? And where on earth is Mark?'

Beth took a breath. 'Well, that's the thing, you see. I'm afraid I've got some bad news.'

Just as she was about to launch into her sorry tale, there was a commotion, and a moving ball of black fur erupted onto the terrace, making straight for Colin and jumping on his back. Katie then appeared, huffing crossly.

'Honestly, that dog is going to be the death of me. Teddy, get off Colin! Now! This minute!'

Teddy, laughingly oblivious to his mistress's distress, continued to bound around the prone Colin, until, with great gravity, Colin lifted one paw and socked Teddy right on the nose. The little dog backed off, yelping piteously.

'I'm sorry, Teddy, but you had that coming,' said Beth, who'd been peering anxiously at the mêlée, while the two elderly ladies nodded sagely. Their own dog was sitting to attention, bristling and growling gently, but wisely holding back from entering the fray.

'*Teddy,*' sighed Katie, scooping up the wriggling puppy and trying her best to contain him on her lap while she took a steadying sip of her coffee. 'Christ, what a morning. And dog ownership is supposed to be so good for your health,' she said, with heavy irony.

As the dogs calmed down, even Teddy consenting to lie on Katie's lap in an uncomfortable-looking heap, Beth realised some introductions were in order. 'I'm sorry, I'm Beth, and this is my friend, Katie. We're, well, we're looking after Colin for a bit,' she said.

'Speak for yourself,' said Katie sharply. 'I've got about as much dog as I can handle right now.'

'Colin's no trouble, though, are you, Col?' said Beth, smiling over the bench at the old boy. He obligingly batted the ground with his tail.

'But I don't understand why you've got him at all?' said the woman in the purple coat.

Her friend butted in. 'I'm sorry, Jules is quite upset about all this. We're old friends of Mark Smeaton's – I'm Miriam, this is Jules. Has he gone on holiday or something? But I don't understand why he wouldn't have told us? We could have looked after Colin.'

'Now, come on, Miriam, you know Liquorice would have hated that,' said Jules firmly.

Mark *Smeaton*, thought Beth. Now she knew the victim's full name. But she just said, 'Liquorice? Oh, is that your dog?' looking under the bench at the little wiry-haired creature, who was still keeping his distance from Colin and Teddy.

'Yes, after liquorice allsorts, you know. He's a Heinz.'

'Is that a German breed?' Beth asked. There was so much she didn't know about Colin and his canine ilk.

'It means fifty-seven varieties – a mixture,' said Katie, with the weariness of the long-time dog owner, while Teddy tried to lick her face.

'He's very cute,' said Beth dutifully, looking at Liquorice

doubtfully. She supposed it was like being presented with other people's babies. No matter how much they resembled Winston Churchill sucking a lemon, you were still obliged to say how utterly gorgeous they were.

'We're straying from the point,' said Jules rather forcefully. Her iron-grey hair was cut in a blunter, less flattering version of Miriam's bob, and her battered purple coat looked decades old.

'You know, it's quite difficult,' said Beth, hunching her shoulders a little. Why must she always be the bearer of bad news? She'd already told that other woman – what was her name? *Rebecca Grey*. Now she'd have to break it to these two as well. She sighed inwardly. But, as she always said to Jake, better to get unpleasant tasks over quickly. Naturally, saying that to your child didn't guarantee that you followed through in your own life, but this time, she saw she was just going to have to.

'Something awful's happened to Mark. I've got some very bad news.'

FIVE

Beth looked back later on that half-hour as one of the most uncomfortable of her life. All the cappuccinos in Dulwich Park couldn't have soothed the two women as they came to terms with the sudden death of a dear friend. They took it in very different ways. Miriam melted into quiet, persistent tears, necessitating all of Katie's stock of kitchen roll, which had been jammed into her poor, abused bag to cope with Teddy's messes. Jules blustered and raged, venting her disbelief, shock and grief on the two hapless women in front of her.

Katie, exhausted by running after Teddy and demoralised by the strains of dog ownership, seemed to be letting the tirade wash over her. But Beth was getting increasingly annoyed. Eventually, she called a halt.

'That's enough,' she said firmly. 'We are not responsible for what's happened to Mark. You need to get hold of yourself and stop shouting at us. If you want to help us, you could start thinking about people who might have had a grudge against Mark, a reason for doing this. How well did you actually know him, anyway?'

Jules took a massive breath in outrage at this and was about to let fly again, when Miriam put a gentle hand on her arm and spoke at last, after blowing her nose luxuriantly on the soggy kitchen towel.

'Forgive us, please. This has been the most awful shock. Jules and Mark were very close. We're all artists, you see. We've worked together for years. Not exactly collaborators, but kindred spirits, you know?'

'Artists? I see,' said Beth, who transparently didn't see at all.

She thought back to the scene in the copse on the Rye. Was there anything that gave a clue to Mark's profession there? She didn't think so. But then, he'd hardly have been lugging an easel and paintbrushes around with him, would he?

'What sort of artist was Mark? Was his work controversial?'

Jules and Miriam looked at each other. It didn't take an investigative genius to work out that they were weighing up, very carefully, how much they should say next.

At home later, with a cup of tea steaming in front of her and a clean sheet of A4 on the kitchen table along with a couple of well-chewed biros, Beth was deep in thought. Jake was already safely collected from school, and had assured her, as usual, that any homework that had been discussed during lessons had been mooted on a strictly voluntary basis only. And guess what? He wasn't volunteering.

On another day, Beth might well have remonstrated with him. After all, Year 7, its long shadow already almost touching Jake's shoes, was going to be a very different story. There'd be homework aplenty and all of it would be compulsory, no matter which school he ended up attending. And if he managed to make Beth's dearest dreams come true and wriggle through the portals of Wyatt's, he'd be up to his little neck in the stuff.

On the one hand, this made her more inclined to turn a blind eye to his reluctance to go the extra mile now. Make hay while the sun shines, and all that. But there was an opposing school of thought which said he should get used to the whole process straight away. Then it would be less of a horrible shock when he was expected to toil for at least forty minutes a night after school, for the next seven years.

Today, however, Beth had too much on her own mind to worry about what might or, more likely, might not be going on in Jake's head. It was times like this that she blessed his PlayStation, devil's work though it most assuredly was.

On the sheet of paper in front of her she was going to write a list of the facts about Mark Smeaton. She hadn't thought of many yet, but she had her laptop fired up and was already delving into a surprisingly full Wikipedia page devoted to the late artist.

He'd been quite a phenomenon. From what she had seen of him yesterday, sprawled across the Rye in a pool of his own blood, he hadn't really looked an impressive figure at all. There was nothing like sudden death to strip you of all human dignity, as Beth had unfortunately discovered. But reading through what amounted to the man's CV now, she couldn't help but be impressed.

He was a Dulwich boy through and through. He'd been to Wyatt's – always a massive plus in Beth's book – and then on to the cream of the London art schools for a foundation course and then a Fine Art degree. Unlike most artists, who finished with high hopes only to be sucked into designing ads for margarine, Mark Smeaton had been noticed at his graduation show and had promptly become one of the talents to watch in the art scene. His entire output had been bought up, very publicly, by Baz Benson. Benson, the thuggish king-maker of the British art scene, had a huge gallery in Whitechapel, was married to an eminent and telegenic marine biologist, and lived in a massive Docklands mansion with wrap-around views of the Thames. But he looked like the kind of low-life who'd have minded the Kray twins' coats, back in the day.

Huge success at the tender age of twenty-three didn't seem to have corrupted Smeaton, but nor did it seem to have led to the stratospheric heights one might have expected. He had apparently carried on working away and had not, visibly at least, fallen into any of the traps associated with such fast fame and fortune. He hadn't been papped too often falling drunkenly out of nightclubs; he'd never acquired a string of status-hungry girlfriends. Instead, he popped up on highbrow TV shows, discussing that vital question, 'Whither art?' where he'd let fly with trenchant views. And his comments were sought by the broadsheets whenever creativity was discussed.

He'd seemingly shunned the cheap stunts that so many artists used to up their profiles, and appeared to have trodden an exemplary line, with no sign of the fallout that often partnered such Faustian pacts with glory. Yet, after the glorious blaze of his first show, there was little to show, in terms of art, for his years of work. It was a little curious.

Beth felt retrospectively embarrassed that she had known scarcely anything about him. She certainly could have passed him a million times in Dulwich Village without knowing that he'd been, briefly, one of the most accomplished and feted artists of this generation, or many previous ones, and was still a respected commentator.

Now she was studying the face that topped his Wikipedia entry, it was recognisably the one she'd seen prone on the scrubby ground of the little grove of trees. The photo, taken probably ten years ago, showed a pleasant young man, half-smiling, standing in front of a huge blobby canvas that she imagined must be one of his own works. If they were all like that, she wasn't sure she could quite see what all the fuss was about.

She was peering into features that looked, understandably, an awful lot livelier than the still form she'd come across only yesterday. Smeaton had been a reasonably attractive man, but not one you'd whip round to gawp at in the street, Beth decided, leaving aside the fact that she'd never really been the type to have her head turned. True, she'd felt a bit funny that time when Harry York had come through the door at Wyatt's, his distinctive stride and that big coat signalling a presence that was impossible to ignore. But again, she'd been terribly off-balance that day. It had affected her judgement, she reckoned. Would she have felt the same if Harry had come in on an ordinary Tuesday when she hadn't just found a bleeding corpse? She paused for a moment, thought hard, and realised she would.

Anyway, she wasn't here, with her blank sheet of A4, to think about Harry. He'd been such a grump when they'd met on the Rye that she hadn't really forgiven him. But she needed to shove all thoughts of him from her mind.

As soon as she'd thought this, she reached automatically for her phone. She'd just look to see whether he'd texted, then she'd get right back to the job in hand. She scrolled through her messages, then peered at WhatsApp and her emails too. Nothing. There were so many ways of being ignored these days. Voicemail, perhaps? But not a sausage there, either.

She tutted. She had to stop letting herself get so distracted by this nonsense. She wasn't a teenager, waiting for a first date. She was a grown woman, and if she wanted to contact Harry and short circuit all this pointless waiting for him to do the right thing, she could. Except, that would give him the upper hand, wouldn't it? And a chance to ignore her even more. And she really didn't want that.

Beth sighed and stuck her phone behind her open laptop, where she couldn't see it, and glanced again at the snowy white emptiness of the sheet in front of her. She grabbed a pen, pulled the paper towards her and started to write. At the top, under-lined and in her neatest writing, she put 'Mark Smeaton', then a one-sentence synopsis of where and how she'd stumbled across him.

Underneath, she wrote a few more words – the names of all those so far who'd wandered into the frame just by knowing Mark. Assuming this wasn't some sort of crazy, random killing, the murderer had to be someone who knew the artist. After all, Colin hadn't protected his master. Beth didn't know much about dogs – though in the last twenty-four hours she felt she'd been on a bit of a crash course – but she hoped Colin wouldn't really let a stranger stab his master multiple times and do absolutely nothing at all.

She took a quick look at him, under the table, snoozing comfortingly near her feet, and she realised he probably would. Particularly if the assailant had a Bonio about his person. It wasn't much of a comfort. Why did people love dogs so much, if they didn't perform one of the most basic services for those that fed and loved them?

Magpie, who'd been in high dudgeon ever since Colin's arrival, would run straight for her cat flap without asking many questions if anyone attacked Beth in front of her, she was pretty sure. If she was sitting on someone's lap, though, and that someone attacked Beth, then the cat might well bite, or worse – but mostly because she didn't like her pillows to move around of their own accord. A judicious application of a razor-sharp paw usually reminded everyone of their place in the scheme of things.

Magpie was attached to the house and to her food bowl, but was there any more to it than that? When they'd been burgled, a while ago, Beth had finally found Magpie in the garden, up a tree. She definitely hadn't hung around to remonstrate with the thief or protect her territory. Cats were unknowable creatures. Dogs were supposed to be so much simpler, so much more loyal, truly attached to their humans... but then look at Colin, who'd apparently done nothing at all to protect Smeaton. Maybe dogs were just better actors than cats?

In some ways, Beth preferred the straightforward transactional nature of her relationship with Magpie. There was no messing, no pretence of undying feline love. But then Harry had once told her a ghastly tale about an old lady lying dead for weeks, and her enormously fat tabby who'd been shut up in the flat with the body... Would Magpie? Could she? Would Beth even taste as good as the premium nuggets Magpie insisted upon? Ending up as substandard cat food was surely a fate worse than death. Beth didn't want to go there, in any sense. She turned back to her sheet of paper.

So, someone on this list might be the murderer. All she had to do was find a motive. Ha. That was a laugh. Teasing out the reasons for people's actions was every bit as tricky as trying to predict the behaviour of her cat. But she wasn't going to let a little thing like an impossible task put her off. She ran her eye down the very short roster of names again. There'd be more she'd be adding, for sure. In the meantime, though, she needed to delve into those she had here, and see what their connections to Mark Smeaton really meant. It was easy enough saying the artist was an old and dear friend, as the women at the café had this morning, but he wasn't around to contradict anyone now. Maybe they'd been at daggers drawn, and had all hated each other? It was hard to imagine, but not impossible.

Things could definitely get complicated in Dulwich, that much Beth knew for sure. And there was something else she was certain of too. It was up to her to find out the truth.

SIX

Baz Benson stood in the immense white space of his gallery. A burly figure, more like a car salesman than a specialist in fine art, he had a pronounced paunch, a thick thatch of prematurely white hair, an insincere smile that was always playing at the corners of his mouth – and a devious glint in his eye. In the far corner of the hanger-like space, a scarlet canvas throbbed with vicious colour. Opposite that, a hundred paces away, was a fiercely architectural desk. At it sat a blonde girl in her twenties, her sheet of hair as straight as a plumb line. Her head was bent over a pad of paper.

Benson was pretty sure the paper was blank, but he couldn't be bothered to stride over to find out. The place itself was empty; that was bad enough. Was it her fault? No, but she was around, so she was definitely getting the blame.

'Magenta! Come here,' he shouted. The sound bounced off the white walls and the girl skittered to her feet. Her heels, sharp enough to lance a boil, made her long, pale legs stagger across the blinding floor like Bambi on ice. Benson found himself tutting even as he leered at the shortness of her skirt and pertness of her breasts.

'What's wrong with this picture, Magenta?' he hissed as she approached.

'Picture? What picture?' she stuttered, turning to take in the three blank walls and the one red canvas. 'That one?' she said eventually, pointing.

'Not that one, you idiot. Why is this gallery empty, that's what I'm asking?'

Magenta looked at him, her startled eyes the velvet brown of a teddy bear's paw. The combination of those eyes with that hair was what had attracted Benson and saved her CV from the bin. Every week, another sheaf of applications came in. The Russell Group universities churned out girls like her ceaselessly: 2.1s in Art History; bright; hopeful; full of promise; desperate to make their mark. Six months making less than the minimum wage as a gallery slave, or nothing at all as an unpaid intern, usually sorted out the sheep from the goats. Unless they had a trust fund to fall back on, few could keep themselves in flat whites and high heels beyond that point.

Well, it certainly hadn't been this one's towering intellect he'd employed her for, Benson thought, raking her body with a hot glance. And, to his disappointment, she was reluctant to stay late, open up early, or in any other way risk being alone with him. Anyone would think she didn't want to get on in the profession. He'd have to get rid of her. And soon.

'You're supposed to get people into the gallery. Where are the crowds? Where are Mummy and Daddy's friends? Where are *your* friends?' he hissed.

'But they've seen the painting. Last week, at the opening.'

Benson's eyes flicked crossly to the pulsating canvas. On one level, it was fair enough. He knew how they felt. He'd definitely seen enough of the thing. But one of them should have bought it. Then he could replace it with another. That was the way he worked. And bloody Magenta should have known that.

He had a strong urge to slap her, but those days were dead

and gone, his lawyer had informed him in no uncertain terms. He satisfied himself with shouting instead.

'Well, don't just stand there. Get Slope on the phone. Now!'

'Slope?' Magenta looked confused.

'Yes, *Slope*. You have heard of him, haven't you?' Spittle flew from his mouth. He was pleased when she flinched away.

'I rang him twice yesterday, like you said. Hasn't he called you back?'

Benson sighed theatrically. 'If he had, do you think I'd be wasting my time calling him again?'

Magenta looked at him, bafflement apparent in those chocolate eyes. She didn't quite shrug her shoulders at him, but it was clear she felt she'd done as much as she could to expedite matters.

'All right then, coffee. Get me a coffee. Surely you can manage that?' he snarled. 'And be quick about it!'

Magenta looked him up and down, then reached behind the desk and grabbed her coat and bag. Sauntering as best she could on her perilous heels, she closed the door as he shrieked, 'Wait! I haven't told you what kind of coffee yet. Get back here *now*.'

Once she was safely outside and in full view of the bustling street, Magenta paused in the middle of the huge window onto the gallery, made sure she had Benson's full attention, then extended her elegantly long middle finger up at him, before swaying away in her shoes.

Benson, ducking from the curious glances of passers-by, kicked the wastepaper basket as he strode away from the preposterous desk. The day was not going well. Why the hell was Slope playing hard to get? And now he'd have to find a new girl as well. A stream of obscenities turned the expensive white space of his gallery to blue.

SEVEN

The next day Beth spent tied to her desk at Wyatt's, renewing her acquaintance with her in-tray. She was still in the thick of planning the next exhibition on the life and times of naughty old Thomas Wyatt, the swashbuckling founder of the Dulwich schools who, as she'd discovered, had been up to his massive ruff in the slave trade. With its customary aplomb, Wyatt's School had turned this appalling discovery into a talking point and a reason to endow an institute looking into the issue, which Beth was now heading up.

After the exhibition, her next project was to try and get a book on Wyatt's dark history up and running. It would be part biography, part study on the iniquitous trade he'd made his money in, and would encompass a historical examination of the man's life and times, as well as an understanding of the economic world he lived in. To say that Beth was daunted by the idea was an understatement. It was her brainchild, and played to her great love of history and her dogged research skills. But she was already beginning to think she'd bitten off far more than was reasonably chewable, even by Colin himself, who suddenly seemed to want to nibble on anything that didn't move away fast enough.

She looked over at him from her desk. He had his chops around the table leg over in the corner of the room. She could have sworn it looked a little thinner than it had the day before. She'd have to invest in some of those rubber chicken toys or something, otherwise he'd wear out all the furniture with his slobbering. She'd thought only human babies had teething issues, but elderly Labs seemed just as prone to put absolutely everything in their mouths. She wondered, with a sudden pang, whether it was an anxiety thing. Was he wondering where on earth his master had gone, and compensating by gnawing everything? It was a bit odd, but then she didn't pretend to understand dog psychology. She had enough trouble trying to work out small boys, big tall men and wayward cats.

One good thing was that, so far, she seemed to have got away with bringing Colin to work. She certainly couldn't leave him at home all day with only Magpie for company. She wasn't quite sure what she'd come back to if she did, but she knew it wouldn't be pretty. In theory, Colin had quite a size advantage over the black and white moggy, but Magpie had all the smarts.

It was nearly three by the time Beth had finished. She was glowing with virtue after spending almost a full day on the work she was supposed to be doing, allowing only for a quick lunch with her friend, Nina, and a brief trip out to the playing fields with Colin when he'd felt a pressing need. Ten minutes delving into Mark Smeaton after all that good behaviour really wouldn't be too terrible, would it?

But she'd exhausted Wikipedia and was at a bit of a loss as to where artists hung out on the internet. Maybe a general googling would bring up a chunk of gossip or a thread that she could follow? Or, wait a minute, had Smeaton ever been married or involved with anyone else? Was there a love interest in his background, someone who either had a reason to do him harm, or would want to help Beth find those who had? After all, as she now knew only too well, the secret to a murder often lay very close to home.

She quickly clicked her way to the biography section of Smeaton's Wikipedia page. But there was nothing there, bar a passing mention of his parents. She looked at the names, but they meant nothing to her. Suddenly she had a thought. There was one person she knew who was of the right generation, more or less, who had an encyclopaedic knowledge of Dulwich connections and might well have encountered Smeaton's parents – particularly if either one of them played Bridge.

It was with some trepidation that Beth picked up the phone to her mother, Wendy. Now in her fifties, Wendy's lifestyle was that of a much older woman, involving Bridge, little teas, tremendous enthusiasm for fiddly types of crochet and embroidery, and the occasional sedate walk in Dulwich Park with one of her long-time confidantes. Beth sometimes wondered how she'd grown to adulthood with such a light hand on the parental tiller. Her father had always been at work. She remembered trying to get into the garage, as a small girl, as that was the place her father disappeared to every morning and the spot he emerged from every night. With her child's logic, she assumed he spent his days shut away in there, and already she could see why he might want to. She'd even tried turning the hands of the kitchen clock forward, one day, to hasten him home. But despite her best efforts, the hours had dragged, and she and her older brother, Josh, had amused themselves in their own ways.

Josh had loved drawing and taking photos, while she had always had her nose in a book. Then Josh had discovered the opposite sex and taken to roaming the nearby park with a succession of girls from the College School, as today's Dulwich teenagers still did, but he'd always kept a protective eye out for his sister. Their somewhat isolated childhood had made them quite a team; the two of them against the world.

Times had been different then. There had been much less watchfulness over the business of being a child. She and her friends had later roamed freely after school in Dulwich Park, too, trailing home only as dusk fell and the park wardens rattled the gates. She'd always been the one urging her friends to leave, terrified of being locked in all night. Others had dragged their feet. There had been so much less to do at home – no computer games, no computers at all; children's telly limited to a couple of hours an evening; nothing for older kids and teenagers, and all usually finished by the time she got in anyway. It was no wonder she'd taken refuge in books from such an early age.

Sometimes Beth looked at Jake hunched over his console, and wondered if he'd ever take pleasure in a written world the way she had always done. Reading had been such a solace to her. Though she'd had friends aplenty at the junior school, secondary had been much trickier. But she was never lonely when she had companions like Nancy Mitford waiting for her in the Hons' cupboard, or Dr Watson, eagerly waiting to explain how his eccentric friend had arrived at another astonishing conclusion.

Josh, in his lazy, affectionate way, had been there for her when they were at junior school. But when he was eleven, off he went to Wyatt's. She, two years younger, waited for the moment when she'd go to the girls' equivalent in Dulwich, the College School. But it was not to be. It was then that one of the major crises of Beth's life had struck, with the death of her father.

There were repercussions for all of them. Josh, perhaps, lost a steadying influence that could have shown him there were worse things than commitment. Wendy was locked into (or embraced) a solo path, which became narrower and narrower with every passing year. And Beth's confidence that life would carry her through blithely took a knock she had never really recovered from. She'd been about to sit her exam for the College School when her father died and, to no one's surprise, in the circumstances it didn't go well. Instead, she found herself packed off to the second-best school in the area, which had been fine, but perhaps hadn't stretched her as much as she'd needed. She sometimes wondered whether it was this that kept her focusing so relentlessly on Wyatt's for her Jake.

With all she now knew about the stresses and strains on girls at academic hothouses like the College School, Beth was sure she'd actually had a lucky escape years ago. And she'd done very well for herself, there was no doubt of that. Her financial worries were caused by her lack of a partner and the relentless downturn in the fields of research and journalism that had always appealed to her so strongly, nothing else. And at her school, she'd managed to be a surprisingly big fish for such a little person, because the pond was comparatively titchy, while even years ago, the College School had been bursting with piranhas.

Josh, meanwhile, who must have passed his own Wyatt's interview when no one had really been looking, had never done anything much with his top-notch education. You didn't need a fistful of A levels or a university degree to hold a camera. True, though, he was a clever chap who'd carved out a niche for himself without appearing to try one iota, which was a hard trick to pull off.

Beth wasn't unhappy with her lot, however. Having landed the job at Wyatt's, and then managed to bump it up into something much more substantial, she was doing surprisingly well. Wendy too thoroughly enjoyed her life once she didn't have to keep breaking off her activities to iron a husband's shirt or nod along to his anecdotes, though for some time the little trio kept up the fiction that she was heartbroken. She certainly never looked at another man, but Beth, from her current vantage point, saw that more as her mother washing her hands of the entire sex as a bad job that might interrupt her Bridge schedule, rather than pining forever over her hard-working, kindly father.

When Beth had found to her horror that history had repeated itself and snatched her own husband away, she was determined not to follow her mother's path. She sometimes worried she had leant too far the other way and made Jake too much the focus of her life. That could be just as unhealthy as the benign neglect of her own childhood years. Katie had once said as much to her and, while she'd been furious at the time, she now saw the justice of the statement.

She'd redressed the balance a little with her relationship, such as it was, with Harry York. But even here she was beginning to suspect that Jake got more out of it than she did. It was great for her son to have a man about the place, not laying down the law exactly, but showing a different side of life. And, of course, he showed much greater aptitude with the PlayStation controller than Beth ever could. Isn't that what the psychologists said boys needed growing up?

But what was she getting out of it? York was perpetually cross with her, and she was always infuriated with him. Was this what love was supposed to be about? And, not to take too big a leaf out of Prince Charles's book, but what was love anyway? She wasn't sure it was the feeling she'd had lately about the big policeman. That might be better described as red-blooded anger.

One thing was for sure, though. Wendy adored him. She'd fussed over him as though he was a visiting dignitary on the few occasions Beth had towed him along for a Sunday lunch or an awkward tea. And true, his presence did somewhat lighten the atmosphere which, once again, was good for Jake.

Beth sighed and picked up the phone. Her mother meant well. And she might actually come in handy over this Rye business.

The phone rang five or six times before it was answered.

Wendy's nervous voice quavered, 'Hello?' as though certain she was about to be bombarded with exhortations to double glaze her windows or swap to an incomprehensible electricity tariff. Beth sighed again. She'd offered to get her mother caller ID to save her this anxiety, but Wendy had resisted, insisting it was all far too much trouble.

'It's me, Mum. Just wanted to ask you something. You know everyone on the Bridge circuit, right?'

As ever, when put on the spot, her mother started to prevaricate. Beth could just imagine her, standing in her over-furnished hall, surrounded by the fancy plates hanging on the wall and the porcelain statuettes on the console table. According to her mother, they were all worth a fortune. Every single one required loads of painstaking dusting, done by a long-suffering cleaner and most emphatically not by the lady of the house.

Her mother was like a beautiful piece of Dresden herself. Not quite as short as her daughter – and who was, Beth thought sourly – Wendy was still a tiny woman, delicately built, and with a shepherdess prettiness that had scarcely faded with the passing years. She favoured pastel shades, flouncy florals, trailing scarves and dainty little heels, despite her tottering steps. Beth sometimes thought a little crossly that she was a broken hip waiting to happen. Her hair was already snowy white. She maintained this had happened the moment her husband had had his heart attack, though the family album told a different story. Not entirely by coincidence, the colour was a perfect foil for her blue eyes and clear complexion. Indeed, her hair looked just like the eighteenth-century wigs sported by so many of her favourite ornaments.

As usual, she was acting as though Beth had trained an interrogator's spotlight on her and was trying to get her to admit to something incriminating. Her ingrained response was to equivocate for all she was worth. 'I wouldn't say that, dear, oh no.'

'Well, you've been playing for thirty-odd years, haven't you? And living in Dulwich for close to forty?'

'Don't remind me, dear. Are you trying to make me feel my age?'

Beth noted the asperity in her mother's tone and tried a new tack. 'You've got such a fantastic memory, I just wondered if I could run some names by you...'

This was much more successful. 'Of course, dear, any time. You know I always like to help where I can. Though I don't quite understand what you want, and anyway, I'm running a bit late. I should have left already; I only stopped because of the dratted phone. Oh, that was you.'

Beth frowned savagely, safe in the knowledge her mother couldn't see any of the range of grimaces she kept specially for their phone conversations.

'Right. Well, I'd hate to hold you up. But could we maybe meet? I could show you the names, see if you know them?'

'Well, if you really think it would be useful, dear, though I don't quite see how I could possibly... Of course, I'm quite busy... But who are these people, and why do you want to know about them?'

Wendy wasn't the only one who could descend into impenetrable vagueness when it suited her. 'Oh, I just wondered, that's all, we can chat about it when I see you,' said Beth airily. 'Shall we say tomorrow, then, at Aurora in the village?'

'Aurora? That place with the dreadful coffee? I don't know why you'd want to go there, dear. And I definitely can't do *tomorrow*.'

Beth kicked herself. Of course, Wendy wouldn't be able to meet so spontaneously. Anyone else might squeeze their daughter in with twenty-four hours' notice, but Wendy was so rigid in her habits she made the average straitjacket look like a Lycra catsuit.

'I'm just getting my diary,' said Wendy, and Beth waited in fuming silence as her mother pottered around audibly. Beth could see her all too clearly in her mind's eye, fluttering between this drawer and that, ineffectually faffing over notebooks and poncey pens adorned with silk tassels, before finally tracking down her appointments book. When she eventually got back to the phone, she was out of breath and flustered. 'This is making me terribly late, Beth. But, oh well, if you insist, let's pencil in something for next week. Perhaps we could meet on—'

'If you can't do tomorrow, how about the day after?' Beth asked. As she had a job and a child to manage single-handedly, she was willing to bet she was a tiny bit busier than a woman who'd never worked in her life. But no, as usual, the last word went to Wendy.

'I was going to say Monday. At two thirty. That's the earliest I can do it, and even then, well, it's not going to be easy. But I suppose I'll just have time before Bridge at St Barnabas,' Wendy twittered. 'I must go now, dear, I'm *terribly* late,' she added, putting the phone down without further ado, and certainly without checking to see whether Beth was also free. Beth smiled serenely as she replaced the receiver. Although her mother had managed to push the appointment as far away as she could, she had still agreed to a meeting, and Beth was a little surprised. She'd thought a lot more excuses would be deployed before a suggestion was trotted out that they got together next April. A delay of only a few days felt like a bit of a victory. OK, it might not seem like a major step forward to anyone else, but making Wendy drink a dishwater cuppa while doing something helpful was quite enough progress for Beth this afternoon.

She'd just have to contain herself until Monday and, who knew, by then she might have an even longer list of suspects to question her mother about. She quickly cleared her desk and collected Colin. He got up like a stiff old gentleman and shook himself thoroughly, before being hauled down the road as fast as both their stumpy legs would go, to pick up Jake.

It was a crisp, clear afternoon, the sky not yet tinging into the indigo of darkness. Colin panted heavily as they chugged along the chilly street. The days were drawing out and, though there was nothing yet on the twiggy trees to suggest spring was waiting in the wings, there was just the suspicion of a relaxation in winter's grip. Beth was glad to feel it, though it reminded her that the Wyatt's interviews were looming ever closer.

She suddenly realised that she'd probably have to get Jake an outfit. This was going to be tricky. There was no real problem in persuading him to be chatty and confident with adults. As an only child, he'd been used to bearing the full brunt of parental attention and was good with grown-ups. He wasn't at all keen on getting dressed up, though. There could be a major battle looming.

Luckily, at the school gates she bumped into Katie, who was listening with a slight smile as Belinda McKenzie regaled the playground with the latest crimes committed by her au pair, who, like a very difficult trigonometry problem, just wasn't working out.

'I simply asked her to get a little light lunch together for six or seven friends and their kids, and she actually rolled her eyes at me. Can you believe it?' shrilled Belinda, clocking Beth with a brief cold stare and then ignoring her completely.

Beth nudged Katie and they wandered a little away from Belinda's orbit, Colin collapsing at their feet after his hectic walk down the hill. Teddy, thank goodness, was nowhere in evidence – probably chewing Michael's expensive loafers back in Court Lane.

'Listen, I've just thought. Are you getting Charlie something smart to wear for the interviews? Jake will go nuts if I try and put him in a tie or something.'

'No, why bother? I was thinking that their uniform would be fine. After all, they'll be going back to school after they've been seen, won't they?' said Katie. 'Unless you're planning to get him some chinos or something... You're not, though, are you?' she added anxiously.

'No, uniform would be brilliant. I was wondering how I'd persuade Jake into a proper shirt. He's been wearing the school tracksuit bottoms and sweatshirt for so long, I don't think he could cope. Which might be a problem next year, but we'll get to that when we have to.' Beth sighed.

Although she had now seen shoals of hopefuls touring Wyatt's for the various entry points at Year 7, Year 9 and Year 12, she'd never taken much notice of what they were wearing. It was always different when it came to your own turn. And taking Katie's tip of sticking to the uniform would save Beth a fortune.

However, when the boys erupted into the playground minutes later, Beth did slightly shudder at the sight of Jake's sweatshirt. Once upon a time it had had the Village Primary's little crest emblazoned on it in white flock, but now there was a balding grey mess in place of the logo. She wondered if there was time to order another before the interviews. As he got closer, she grabbed his top unceremoniously and stared at the design. Then she scratched at it with a finger. Thank goodness, the grey was coming off.

On closer, and revolting, inspection, it turned out to be largely caused by matted black and white hairs from Magpie, which seemed to have stuck fast on the raised surface. Beth flushed a little guiltily, while Jake, affronted, tugged out of her clutches and ran on ahead with Charlie. Jake had been wearing the sweatshirt like this for months. She'd been washing it, yes, but she now realised she hadn't been studying it very closely.

She hoped Katie hadn't noticed. But, shooting a glance over at Charlie, she could see his uniform wasn't exactly pristine either. And, if she wasn't mistaken, his book bag bore distinct signs of having been enthusiastically chewed.

'Where is Teddy today?' she asked Katie as they started out of the gates. Her friend gave her what looked like a very guilty glance.

'Oh Beth, I've done something I'm not proud of,' she said, faltering.

'What on earth do you mean?' Beth asked.

'Well, look at you and Colin,' said Katie evasively. 'You've just taken to dog ownership like a duck to water, and you didn't even *want* Colin. He adores you and does everything you say.'

'Hang on, Katie. First, I don't own Colin. I'm just looking after him for today, maybe for tomorrow, but *very soon* he's going somewhere else, definitely. And second, he's not really doing anything I say, he's just too blooming knackered to disagree.' They both looked down at his smooth head, and Colin looked up, tongue lolling out of his mouth as he plodded calmly along.

'God, I can't wait for Teddy to grow up. He's so naughty all the time, and Charlie doesn't even seem that bothered about him any more. I thought they'd be best friends. You know I've always felt guilty about him being a lonely only. But Teddy ate his PlayStation console yesterday and Charlie actually shouted at him. I think if I said I was going to give him back to the breeder, he'd be quite pleased.'

'No, surely not? Charlie will forgive him, won't he?' asked Beth, though secretly she wondered what her Jake would say when he found out about the controller. Losing a bit of kit like that was a major calamity in a boy's life. And, of course, if Charlie only had one controller, how could they play all their games? 'You won't really give him back, will you?'

'I can't. What on earth would that say to Charlie about sticking to decisions? And also, Michael is still dotty about Teddy – because he spends the least time with him.'

'Look, Katie, obviously I know nothing about dogs, but age seems to be a big factor. I bet even Colin here was a terror when he was Teddy's age. I think if you're super patient and try to stick it out, then he'll settle down and really become part of the family.'

They came to a halt at the junction of Pickwick Road. 'Listen, do you want to come back to ours for a cup of tea? Might give you a chance to get some Teddy-hate off your chest before you have to go back to him. And we still have two controllers. Colin here prefers table legs.'

Katie thought for a moment, then looked at Charlie's hopeful little face. It was amazing how the boys, able to tune out so much of grown-up conversation, always zeroed in on anything to their own advantage.

'Oh, that would be lovely. But we can't be too long. We've got to get back to the monster,' Katie said out of the corner of her mouth as the boys raced ahead.

'What have you done with him? He won't be eating the house, will he?'

'That's what I was getting round to telling you. Trouble is, I feel so bad about it I don't really want to say it out loud. But here goes. I've bought him a cage,' Katie said, peering down at Beth to judge her reaction.

'A cage?' Beth was a little stunned.

'It's not quite as awful as it sounds. Apparently, it makes them feel more secure. And it definitely makes my house feel a lot more secure, that's for sure.'

Beth paused for thought. She wanted to be supportive, and what did she know about bringing up dogs, anyway? She found boys hard enough. But it really did sound a bit Guantánamo Bay. She had a sudden vision of Teddy crammed into an orange jumpsuit, but suppressed it hurriedly.

'Well, if it gives him a bit of a refuge, then it's probably a really good idea,' she managed eventually. She jingled Colin's lead and the old dog turned to her and gave her a big Labrador smile, ninety per cent tooth and fifteen per cent drool, which thankfully hit the pavement rather than her shoes. She might never have expected to be in charge of a dog for more than five minutes, but life with Colin was working out a lot better than she'd expected.

Or so she thought, until she swung open the front door at home and discovered that, in her absence, Magpie had knocked over a vase in the hall and left what looked suspiciously like the remains of half a mouse in the kitchen. Magpie was a very sporadic huntress, scarcely bothering with stalking anything more active than her bowl of disgracefully expensive cat pellets. So, the rodent offering, so hard on the tiny claws of the last victim to be laid out on these very tiles the other morning, was puzzling.

Beth sent Katie, Charlie and Jake into the sitting room while she whisked round with the Flash spray and kitchen roll. Wrapping the remains in an enormous swaddling of paper towels, she rushed out into the garden to perform a cut-price funeral service by hurling the poor old creature into the nearest wheelie bin. She then had a quick pang, wondering if it should go into the food caddy as organic waste. But confronting a mouldering carcass every time she disposed of a teabag was far too disgusting an idea to contemplate.

When she got back inside, Katie was sloshing boiling water into two mugs. 'I wonder if Magpie meant that mouse for you as a special present to say she's forgiven you for bringing Colin home?'

Beth snorted. 'That just shows your lovely nature, Katie. I reckon it means, "Why do you need that mangy dog when you've got me and this delicious snack?" Or something along those lines. There's no fathoming Magpie, really. Colin is easier to work out.'

Colin, snoozing in the corner of the kitchen, whacked his

tail against the tiles in automatic response to his name, but otherwise looked as though he was embarking on a long recovery process from a very full day's work.

'You're getting really attached to Colin, aren't you? I think you're going to be pretty heartbroken when he finds a new home.'

'Hmm,' said Beth, through narrowed eyes. 'It's true that he's a lot less bother than I thought he'd be, and so far they don't seem to mind him being in my office at the school. But I don't think I'm really cut out for dog ownership long term. Well, it's a lot to take on, isn't it?'

Katie sighed. 'You're telling me. I don't suppose you'd do a swap, would you? Teddy for Colin?'

'I think Michael would have something to say about that,' said Beth, not quite answering the question but privately thinking there would have to be an interconnecting system of skating rinks in hell before she contemplated that deal for even one second.

Just then, with a glint of green eyes, Magpie exploded through the cat flap, took a long look around the kitchen, glared hard at Beth – and even harder at Colin and Katie – whipped round, and jumped out again.

'She's in such a mood.' Beth sighed. 'I'm not sure what she expects me to do with half a mouse, but I'm guessing a quick interment in the bin is not nearly appreciative enough for her. Mind you, having Colin around is really keeping her fit. I haven't seen her moving so fast for ages.'

'I've nearly had it with Ted, I tell you. These animals,' said Katie in uncharacteristic gloom, stirring her tea thoughtfully.

'I know Michael's against it, so I wouldn't normally suggest it, but what about my idea of signing up with a dog whisperer? You could do it on the sly? Or at least have another go at trying to talk Michael round. I'm sure if he had any idea how upset you are he'd be the first one to put Teddy's name down. There are probably loads of clever ways to cope with puppies; you just need a few techniques, I expect. After all, you're not the first person with a bit of a scamp on your hands,' said Beth.

'You're right, I'll have to talk to Michael again. I know it's silly, but I sort of feel I'm letting him down by needing more help. He's convinced that everyone is just born with these dog skills that I haven't got at all. We didn't have dogs when I was growing up. It's making me feel a bit inadequate.'

To Beth's horror, Katie's beautiful blue eyes filled with tears, but she fanned her face rapidly with her hands and that glazed, over-bright look receded. A big swallow and she was a close approximation of her usual chirpy self again.

'Don't mind me, Beth. I promise I won't sit blubbing in your kitchen, I know how you hate that. I'll sort out some dog control people. I'm sure Belinda will know someone – she knows everybody, after all. I've got to get on with that. At the moment, just getting through the day with the little, erm, chap is taking all my concentration. But what about you? Are you still looking into that business, you know?'

From Katie's shuffling in her seat, and her evident discomfort, Beth deduced she was talking about the mysterious death of Mark Smeaton. It was odd that her friend was taking the conversation in this direction, but maybe anything was better than the subject of Teddy and his dreadful manners.

'Well, I am. I'm going to ask my mother if she knows those two friends of Mark's we bumped into in the park, or even his parents. Or that woman, Rebecca Grey. You were pretending you weren't there, but she said her son, John, was a friend of his, remember? Then I'm not sure where to take it next. Any ideas?'

'I have been giving it some thought...'

This time Beth was so astonished, she couldn't help breaking in. 'That's not like you, Katie. You're usually trying to tell me to drop stuff like this like a stone and pretend it's not happening. Don't tell me you're finally getting the detecting bug?'

'No, I am not! Certainly not,' said Katie vigorously. 'Michael would never forgive me if I did anything more dangerous than a really tricky yoga move, you know him. It's just that, I suppose I must admit, thinking about it has distracted me a bit from the whole Teddy business. I can see why you get so into it. It's like having a crossword to solve, or a really big jigsaw or something.'

Beth, who still bore a scar from the stitches she'd had after being hit over the head not so long ago, and who had grown sickeningly used to very unpleasant surprises, contented herself with a gentle, 'Hmm.' But far be it for her to decry the merits of displacement activities. Her whole life was based around them, after all. She managed a gentle smile.

'Have you got any leads then, Miss Marple?'

'Well, I know we should both be focusing on the boys' interviews, or even our jobs or whatever, but it did strike me that Michael's got quite a big friend in the art world.'

'Has he? Who's that?' asked Beth, deciding she'd pretend she hadn't heard the list of things they both ought to be getting on with.

'It's Andy Kuragin. You know, the guy who owns the only edgy gallery in Cork Street, the Red Square.'

'The man who specialises in all the uber-trendy British artists?'

'Yep. And he's coming to lunch tomorrow. Want to join?'

'Oooh, yes please.'

Beth was delighted. A lovely long Saturday lunch with Katie meant many fewer hours than usual kicking a football around in the park with Jake. It was also the promise of a meal that was neither sourced, prepared, cooked or washed up by her, which was a massive treat in itself. Knowing Katie, it would be delicious into the bargain, although frankly Beth sometimes felt she would eat a battered bathmat if she hadn't had to grill it herself. Ten years into her job as head chef for one unadventurous small boy, and any interest Beth had ever had in nutrition was long gone, beyond ensuring they didn't both get scurvy. Better still, Jake would have a lovely time. And best yet, Beth herself might well be able to make a bit of progress on the Smeaton business.

'Have you met Kuragin before? What's he like?'

'I've seen him at a few gallery openings and things,' said Katie casually. As usual, Beth marvelled at the way everyone except her seemed to go out all the time, to exciting parties and soirees that just weren't on her radar at all. She upbraided herself for getting so set in her ways and resolved to try harder to make use of London, right on her doorstep, and filled with as much cultural promise as an overflowing jewellery box. She could always ring Zoe Bentinck next door and ask her to babysit. Zoe loved the extra pocket money and got on really well with Jake. And her big sister had just graduated from uni and was looking for work – she'd be happy to help if Zoe had too much schoolwork.

But Beth needed someone to go to these events with. Was Harry really going to enjoy exhibitions and shows? Would he ever have the time, even if he did have the inclination? And if he did, would he then be called away by a last-minute crisis, leaving her twiddling her thumbs with an empty seat next to her, feeling like a spare part yet again in a sea of couples? She felt a little glum at the all-too-familiar mental picture. But Katie was still musing about this Kuragin bloke.

'He's very Russian, if you know what I mean. The accent, the sense that he'd say really deep things, if he just knew our language a bit better. That feeling that he's been ripped away from his homeland and yearns for the frozen Steppes...'

Beth looked at Katie. 'Are you sure you're not reading a lot into things?'

'I probably am, but just wait until you meet him and tell me you're not immediately thinking about horse-drawn sledges and velvet ball gowns. It's something about those cheekbones. Honestly, you could slice cheese on them. A really hard Parmesan. And the way he bends over your hand and kisses it. It's like something out of *War and Peace*.'

'Is it now?' Beth smiled. 'I'm surprised Michael hasn't challenged him to a duel.'

Katie nudged Beth's arm affectionately. 'It's not like that. And talking of love interests...'

'Which, apparently, we weren't?' Beth raised her eyebrows. And wondered a little if Katie had been reading her previous thoughts.

'...what about Harry? Are you at the "invite one, get two" stage, or do you want to casually see whether he's free, or should I ring him? Not sure where we've got to yet. I mean, are you a couple or not?'

Immediately Beth's face fell. 'That makes two of us, Katie. I don't know either. I haven't spoken to him since we found the, er, well, Mark Smeaton.'

'Really?' Katie was clearly a bit taken aback, but she regrouped quickly. 'Well, let's face it, he must be busy. Something like that is going to tie him up for ages, isn't it?'

'Well yes, of course. But not even a text? I mean, come on. I'm sure Michael would find the time to fling you one line, even if he were in the middle of the biggest publishing deal of all time.'

'Ah yes, but Michael's perfect, isn't he?' Katie was a little smug. 'Apart from the cheekbones.' It was Beth's turn to give her friend a little nudge, and they were still giggling like naughty schoolgirls when the boys came in loudly complaining that they were on the brink of starvation.

Beth was suddenly stricken. She whizzed over to the freezer but, apart from a few escaped orange crumbs, the fish finger section was horribly bare. She knew that if they'd gone to Katie's, Jake would be enjoying – well, possibly that wasn't the word, but at least he would have been *offered* – an entirely organic, ethically sourced, brassica-rich plate of extremely expensive veggies. She turned guiltily to her friend.

'How about beans on toast? Just this once? I think I might have the low-salt sort...'

'Beans! Yum,' shouted Charlie, who'd been cruelly deprived of this childhood staple thanks to his mother's anxieties about food colouring, added sugars, and virtually everything else contained in each enticing turquoise tin.

Beth fished a can out of the cupboard, looked at it quickly, then turned the label so that Katie couldn't see it definitely wasn't the low-salt variety, and sloshed the cheerily coloured contents into a pan without further ado. If it had just been her and Jake to feed, she probably would have nuked the beans in the microwave. So, in a way she was providing quite a deluxe service by cooking them the old-fashioned way on the hob. She was pretty sure Katie thought microwaves were the root of all evil, along with much else that made family food quick and easy.

Delving into the bread bin, she made the unwelcome discovery that she only had white sliced, which she was pretty sure Katie equated with crack cocaine. More horrifying still, one slice had a tiny fleck of blue on one edge. Mould! Hastily chopping off all the crusts and hurling them in the bin dealt with that problem. Penicillin was good for you, right? Inwardly, though, she was chastising herself. She only had the two of them to look after – and Harry as an occasional third when they were on speaking terms. For heaven's sake, why couldn't she just learn to get the basics of life under control? No one expected her, at this point, to morph effortlessly into Katie and source cruelty-free samphire at the drop of a hat, but staples like their daily bread? That really shouldn't be beyond her, as a responsible adult in charge of a growing child.

Once the bread had been toasted to a golden brown, piled with beans, and had a scattering of hastily grated cheddar cheese on top for good measure, Beth felt a tiny bit better about her mothering skills. She slid the plates in front of the expectant boys, and both dug in happily.

'Some for you, Katie? Or another tea?'

To Katie's credit, there was no evidence of the shudder that Beth was pretty sure she was suppressing at the thought of eating beans, and she agreed gracefully to more tea instead.

'I'm so glad you'll be coming tomorrow,' said Katie. 'Though Kuragin is madly, um, interesting,' she said hurriedly, as the boys downed forks for a second and listened in, 'he's quite intimidating. I'll be glad to have you there for support.'

Beth, still feeling bad about the blue bread and watching the boys rather anxiously as they chomped away, was very touched. 'That's lovely to hear, Katie. You know I'm always on your side. Any time. But you'd be absolutely fine without me there, you know that really.'

Katie smiled. 'And now, boys, while we've got you here, let's practise a bit of general knowledge.'

Charlie immediately hunched over his plate but Jake, unsuspecting, put his head on one side. 'Is that about war and things?'

Katie looked baffled, but Beth smiled quickly. 'No, love. Nothing to do with soldiers, it's not that sort of general. It's more, erm, things you should know about the world.'

'I think I know everything I need to know, thanks,' said Jake, turning back to his beans. Charlie gave him an admiring glance. But as he seemed to realise all too well, this part of his mother's dinnertime patter wasn't optional.

'What do you think about Vladimir Putin then, Jake?' said Katie brightly.

'Um, I think he might be quite good in goal,' mumbled Jake.

Beth suppressed a smirk. She was pretty sure he did know what Katie was on about and was just trying to deflect her. At least, she sincerely hoped so.

'What about President Biden, how do you think he's doing?' Katie leant forward earnestly.

'Uncle Josh calls him "President Bidet." A bidet is something you wash your bottom in,' Jake said brightly, and both boys erupted.

'You don't pronounce bidet like that. And I'll be having a word with your Uncle Josh when I next see him,' said Beth.

'Why, Mum? You laughed so much when he was telling us that tea came out of your nose,' Jake pointed out helpfully. Beth decided to fall back on the timeless strategy of speaking very loudly and pretending she hadn't heard what her darling boy had said.

'Right then, everyone. There'll be ice cream for people who've finished up everything and help take their plates to the sink,' she said, then took a swift look at Katie's face and added, 'with lovely bits of fruit on top.'

Beth took the least wizened apples from the bowl on the table, peeled and chopped them quickly and studded them over the chocolate chip ice cream in what she hoped was a healthy and responsible way. She crossed her fingers Katie wasn't too horrified at this appalling blip in Charlie's nutritional programme. She was probably giving him all kinds of omega 3 supplements to make sure his synapses were firing correctly for the interviews, so maybe they'd counteract the effects of this little smattering of junk. To give her friend credit, she was sitting there calmly and watching Charlie ingesting it all with a patient smile on her face.

'What are you cooking for lunch tomorrow? How are you going to get round your usual conundrum?' Beth asked, raising her eyebrows at her friend.

Katie had evolved an elaborate and time-consuming way of feeding the two demanding men in her life – one who would willingly eat no vegetable matter at all; and the other who had no choice but to eat mounds of the stuff, at least until he moved out at eighteen.

'Oh, I'll just do my *MasterChef* trick – balance the meat on the veg. Works with Michael every time,' said Katie calmly, slightly out of the corner of her mouth in case Charlie cottoned on. Beth got the hint and changed the subject a little.

'And what do Russians eat, anyway?'

'He's not an alien, Beth. I expect he'll be fine with anything.'

'You're not cooking borscht or something, in his honour?'

'I hadn't thought of that, but it does involve loads of beet-root. Maybe I should,' said Katie, brightening up until she heard a very audible groan from Charlie.

'Not beetroot, please, Mum.'

'I'll give it some thought,' Katie said with a sweet smile at her son, and Beth knew that soup would not be on the menu tomorrow after all. Her friend might be on a mission to improve her boy in every possible way, but she had a heart softer than the ripest organic avocado.

Once Katie and Charlie had left, and Beth had done the minimal tidying up required by such a low-effort meal, she settled down at the freshly swabbed kitchen table. Jake was allegedly brushing his teeth and getting into pyjamas, but was almost certainly reading one of the gaming magazines her brother had brought over on his last visit. They saw Josh so infrequently that she didn't like to remonstrate with him too much over his dodgy choices for a ten-year-old. At least he wasn't bringing him *Playboy* yet – though, knowing Josh, it wouldn't be long.

Opening up her laptop and looking in a desultory way at the freelance projects piling up inexorably in their folder, like mountains of washing begging for the machine or the crumpled arms of shirts drooping from the ironing basket, Beth immediately found her mind wandering.

Her first worry was Harry. She still hadn't heard a word from him since they'd parted ways on Peckham Rye. Was it normal for a relationship to be this bitty, to have no real continuity, and to exist in a series of blips and dips caused by catastrophic rows? Was she enjoying it at all?

She thought hard about it and, unbidden, a picture of Harry in his perpetual peacoat sprung into her mind. The coat, which he seemed welded into at times – and at other times, excitingly not – summed him up. It was rugged, the material was stiff, it was uncompromising, heavy… rigid, restrictive, unyielding. But inside, she knew there was an unexpectedly lovely, quilted satin lining, soft and comfortable, and immensely warm. Sometimes she snuggled up under it on the sofa and felt she had come home.

She could see why he was upset that she had become a bit of a murder magnet. No one wanted their girlfriend, or boyfriend for that matter, to be hanging out with corpses the whole time. But he did, and she was fine with it. Mind you, he had official status, and she'd always known what he did for a living, from the moment he'd breezed into Wyatt's on what had seemed like the worst morning of her life. Nowadays, of course, there were the memories of other dark events clamouring to overtake it.

Beth shook her head. There was nothing she could do about Harry and his views. She knew from experience that probably the best thing was to leave him to stew for a bit. Depending on how angry he was, he'd either lie low for a few days, or appear at her doorstep to shout at her a bit more, which could sometimes turn into an equally passionate, but slightly quieter, encounter upstairs. With that thought, she checked her phone one last time just in case she'd somehow missed a text. This was very unlikely. When they were rowing, her ears became supernaturally attuned to her phone's alerts, and she knew nothing had come in for a long, long time.

Oh well. She wouldn't think about it. Work was much too boring, so her mind turned to Jake. A smile tugged at the corners of her mouth as she thought back fondly to the way he'd deflected Katie over the supper table. If he didn't get into Wyatt's, maybe a career in stand-up comedy beckoned? Or maybe, given the school's fantastic theatre and drama staff, he'd flourish even within Wyatt's fiercely academic system.

She wondered if there was anything she could do to brush up on his knowledge levels without making him want to slam on the brakes any more than he already had over their beans. Maybe some sort of interactive quiz? There must be a website that catered for this – and if there wasn't, maybe she should make her fortune creating one. She had a desultory look online but couldn't find anything that wouldn't leave both of them slumbering peacefully through the entire interview process.

Instead, she decided to look up this Kuragin that she'd be meeting tomorrow. That way, she'd be ready to ask some vaguely competent questions about the art market, and perhaps worm a bit of information out of him about poor Mark Smeaton – what sort of person he was, and, of course, why on earth anyone would have wanted to stab him so many times in broad daylight.

Thinking of Smeaton reminded her suddenly of something the man had left behind – Colin. She looked up from the Wikipedia page on Kuragin which was just loading. The dog had been quiet for ages. If he'd been Jake, she'd have said he was much, much too quiet. Did that go for elderly Labradors, too? Was dormancy a sign of quietly nefarious behaviour that would need a major telling-off and hours to put right?

She got up quickly and ran into the sitting room, expecting to see signs of canine havoc. But when she paused for breath in the doorway, she was rewarded by a spectacle she'd never thought she'd see. Colin and Magpie were on the sofa together. At opposite ends, but with every appearance of accord. All right, neither of them was technically allowed on the furniture – though that was a battle Beth lost with Magpie on a daily, almost hourly basis – but it was still a very sweet little tableau. Colin, giving her a bit of a hangdog look, seemed to know he'd transgressed, but convinced her with his sad brown eyes that he was much too tired and old to move. Magpie, though, acted as if she'd been caught in flagrante, and leapt off her cushion like a cartoon cat being electrocuted and careered down the hallway. The last thing Beth heard was the resounding crash of the cat flap as the moggy threw herself out into the crisp Dulwich night.

'Right, missy. So that's the end of you pretending I've done you a terrible wrong by inviting Colin into the house,' said Beth in the general direction of the cat flap, while patting the dog's head fondly. If he could worm his way under Magpie's impressive strategic defences, then there was surely no fortress impregnable to this gentle old chap.

But that didn't mean he was maintenance-free. Even as she looked at him, he started wriggling in a way she recognised. There had been days when Jake would swear blind for hours he didn't need the loo, only to find – once they were nowhere near any – that one of them was right, and one was very, very wrong. Jake hadn't done this for years, of course, and she was hoping it was a one-off from Colin, too. All she needed was a dog with prostate issues. She fetched his lead and slipped on her boots. Up to the end of the road and back would have to suffice. She didn't want to leave Jake alone for too long. Nothing would happen, she was pretty sure, but if he woke for any reason – a rare but not totally unknown phenomenon – she didn't want him to feel he'd been abandoned.

Colin made it as far as the gatepost before taking his first comfort stop. Beth tried to avert her eyes, and was hoping he was marking his territory rather than the distance his bladder could now travel, when she saw a familiar figure sauntering up the road towards her.

'What are you doing out at this time of night?' said a gruff voice with just the faintest twang of an Irish accent.

'Oh, I thought I'd abandon my son and run off into the sunset – with this dog you lumbered me with,' said Beth acerbically.

'Don't be like that, darl. It's been a tough old day, I can tell you,' said Harry York, his arms coming round and all but engulfing her.

Beth slid her hands under his coat, feeling its silky lining and breathing in the scent of tired male. How come this was now the only place in the world where she felt really safe? She breathed in again, and with her exhalation, all her doubts and fears seemed to evaporate on the night breeze. Here was one of the few people in London who could legitimately say their job had been murder. And, despite his exhaustion, he'd come home – to her. She buried her cheek in the rough navy wool and hugged harder.

EIGHT

Beth's first call of the morning, after a solid eight hours in bed – if not asleep – was to Katie.

'You know you were asking whether I'd be bringing Harry today?' she asked, feeling that she was sidling up to her friend like a cold-caller on commission.

'Oh, is he coming? That's great,' said Katie, as usual making Beth's life much easier.

'Are you sure you don't mind? We can bring anything you like, if you haven't got enough...'

'Absolutely not. When have I ever under-catered? Just bring yourselves. Looking forward to seeing you.'

Beth put the phone down with a happy smile. Katie was a constant reminder of the right way to do things – with a cheerful acceptance and a firm belief that things were going to go her way. That wasn't to say that Katie, or her life, were perfect. Her recent troubles with the awful Teddy were testament to the fact that a fly could land in even the most perfect ointment. But once she'd got round Michael enough to sign the puppy up for boot camp, Beth was sure Katie would swat even that pesky threat to her equanimity.

When the little trio turned up at the imposing door on Court Lane, though, Beth realised she'd been rather optimistic. As the chimes of the bell died away, all she could hear was an increasingly frantic barking and, if she was not mistaken, Michael's deep voice raised in what had to be anger. In all her long acquaintance with the family, she'd never heard this sound before, and it was quite impressive.

She exchanged glances with York. He was trying to look as off-duty as possible in some rather rumpled chinos that he'd left at Beth's on a previous unscheduled stopover, and his shirt from yesterday, topped off, of course, by the peacoat. A long shower had done much to soothe away his stresses from the day before and reinvigorate him after a surprisingly busy night. Beth smiled up at him fondly. It was just as well that she wasn't into snappy dressers. But then she couldn't talk.

As usual, she was in jeans, jumper and a jacket, with her pixie boots, and her old faithful handbag slung over her shoulder. Jake was probably the smartest of them all, though his newish trackie bottoms were looking short already. That was another thing Beth had to sort out before the dreaded interview, which was looming so close now that she could almost feel it breathing down her neck.

The moments passed, gradually stretching to seem more like hours, as the three of them looked at each other, eyebrows beginning to rise. Beth was glad they'd decided not to bring Colin with them. He'd been slumbering so peacefully on the sitting room rug that they hadn't had the heart to drag him along. Maybe he and Magpie would continue to develop their clandestine friendship away from the gaze of interested human eyes. And Colin had definitely seemed too tired to cope with Teddy's exuberance today.

Actually, Beth felt pretty much the same way. Inside, the barking continued, and Beth's heart sank a little. Teddy was just about OK in a park, but in Katie's house, during a nice meal?

This wasn't quite going to be the relaxed Saturday lunch she'd been hoping for.

A shout came again from the recesses of the house, though this time it sounded a little further away. Beth had her finger on the bell, ready to press again and for longer this time, when suddenly it was wrenched open and Katie stood on the threshold, her blonde hair standing up like a halo all round her head. It was obviously going to take her a lot of yoga to get into her calm place today. There was a strong smell of burning wafting ominously from the kitchen, where all the doors had been flung open, despite the chilly day.

From the doorstep, Beth could see right into the garden, where a figure at the far end seemed to be shaking a fist at a black ball, which she was willing to bet was Teddy, doing his best impression of a contrite puppy. It lasted about a second, and then he was jumping up and down again as though on springs.

Katie looked at them all a little blankly for a moment, as though she'd forgotten why she'd even opened the door. Then she snapped into hostess mode and stepped forward to hug each of them very briefly, then make a palaver out of taking scarves and gloves and bags, and hanging them up. Beth automatically started taking her boots off – Katie was fussy about her floors – but her friend shook her head at her.

'No need. We'll probably be out in the garden at some point,' she said in a rather downbeat way.

At that moment, the door of Katie's very grown-up sitting room swung open. This room was permanently off-limits to Charlie and Jake, and was so smart that even Beth always felt like a wobbly toddler let loose with a beaker of Ribena on the few occasions she'd set foot in it. The lilac damask sofas and silky Persian rugs were terrifyingly beautiful, not to mention the astrakhan and sheepskin cushions, the glass and marble coffee tables, and the shelves of priceless first editions. It was

Michael's room, really, and wasn't compatible with small boys –
and *definitely* not with dogs. It was the kind of room that Beth
partly envied and partly shied away from, knowing she would
never have the space or budget to create such a rarefied sanc-
tuary and could never live up to the décor even if she did.

Then a man strolled out as though he owned the place, his
energetic pace and the light behind him giving him the illusion
of youth. As he approached, Beth was surprised to see he was
well into his fifties, if not older. He had carefully brushed salt
and pepper hair that looked blond until you studied it, coming
to a widow's peak on a high forehead. A mobile, tanned face
was enlivened by green eyes that would give Magpie a run for
her money. His firm hand was outstretched first to Harry, then
equally ceremoniously to Jake, then he reached out for Beth's
little paw and pressed it to his lips with a flourish, bowing low –
very low, thanks to her height – over it, before straightening up
with just a twinge of difficulty.

Beth felt for him. Maybe people had all been shorter in
the days when such gestures were de rigueur? She'd recently
towed Jake round the National Maritime Museum in Green-
wich, and had marvelled at Lord Nelson's tiny little coat,
worn at the battle of Trafalgar. It would have fitted her beautifully, and she quite fancied the epaulettes – though she
wasn't so keen on the bullet hole left by the French sharp-
shooter who'd done for the admiral. After seeing this – in her
mind, at least – she liked to picture everyone in 1805 as her
height or smaller. But the very tall man right beside her
brought her back to the present day, by stiffening noticeably
at this theatrical gesture. When she risked a glance up at
Harry's face, she saw it had that wooden look that meant he
was Not Happy.

Beth tutted inwardly at men's territorial ways, but she did
wonder what Michael made of this courtly chap who was doing
such a good impression of the man of the house, offering them a

gracious welcome and, he no doubt hoped, getting female hearts to flutter with his olde worlde charm.

'Andy, Andy Kuragin,' he said, his English charmingly accented with Russian. 'What a pleasure.'

Even if Beth hadn't already known his name, and been fore-warned of his ways by Katie, she would have suspected he was Russian, just because of the indefinable beauty of all the angles of his face. If everything Beth had read about this man was true, then she couldn't really imagine why he'd find it such a pleasure to meet a simple London copper (albeit an inspector, to give Harry his due) and a single-mum-cum-archivist, let alone a ten-year-old whose hands, Beth suddenly realised, were probably still quite sticky after breakfast. But she couldn't fault Kuragin's impeccable manners, and he was certainly doing an impression of someone whose dreams had all come true thanks to meeting little old them. Beth immediately set her inner dial to 'mistrust', though she ticked herself off for doing it.

'Come on in, let's see where Michael's got to,' said Katie abruptly. Beth wondered if she was enjoying this man oozing his charm so thoroughly over her house and everything in it.

'I might just go upstairs, see if I can find Charlie?' Jake said hopefully, looking in Katie's direction.

'Course you can. You know where to go,' she said, ruffling his hair as he passed. They wouldn't be able to do that to each other's boys for much longer, Beth realised with a shock. Already, even Jake was shooting up. In the next few years, they'd reach their full adult heights – probably not towering, if Jake took after her at all, but certainly taller than his mum. And their little boy selves would have vanished, as surely as all their *Postman Pat* books had been consigned to the attic.

'Let me get you a drink,' said Katie, leading the way into the magnificent sweeping kitchen. Here, there were the first real signs that things were awry. Normally, Katie would have done the grunt work of preparation long before her guests had arrived, and the only way they'd be able to tell she'd been slaving would be when she opened the oven door and brought forth some amazing dish.

Today, there was a chopping board out, bearing some bits of chorizo that looked seriously mauled. And if Beth wasn't mistaken, that was an actual badly charred chicken leg lying abandoned on the floor near the bin. She picked it up and, after checking wordlessly with Katie, tucked it carefully into the rubbish. On the top, inside the bin, she was startled to see more chunks of incinerated chicken, plus several tell-tale empty cardboard sleeves from Frost – the tremendously swish frozen food shop that had recently opened in the village, and was now doing a roaring trade with all those too posh to prep.

Beth kept her face bland but resolved to ask Katie quite a few questions when an appropriately quiet moment arose. She washed her hands quickly at the sink to get the black bits of scorched chicken off, while her friend poured what surely were much more enormous quantities of wine than usual. Before even handing them round, Katie took quite a hefty swig from her own glass.

'Let's pop into the garden for a second, catch up with Michael,' said Katie in an over-bright way, and with a smile that didn't get within fifty feet of her eyes.

Beth nodded, put her arm round Katie's waist and gave her a squeeze, then wandered out in her wake. With anger in every stride, Katie marched over to Michael, who was at the far end of the garden. She made it long before Beth, with her short legs, and even Harry and Kuragin, who were making the desultory polite conversation of strangers who are rapidly discovering they have nothing at all in common.

By the time they'd caught up with Katie, she had clearly said what she'd needed to say to Michael, who was looking a little chastened – not unlike Teddy, who was lying at his feet in a bundle of silky black fluffiness, a bit like one of Katie's fancy cushions. Unlike them, however, Teddy had a mind of his own, as they saw a moment later when he jumped to all four of his feet and took a flying leap at Andy Kuragin.

To give him credit, the older man simply rapped out the word, 'Down!' and Teddy dropped like a stone, sitting panting on the grass, gazing at the older man as though he'd been at dog obedience classes all his life.

Harry and Michael exchanged a brief glance that Beth couldn't quite decode, while Katie declared brightly, 'Well, you certainly seem to have the touch. Now, isn't it lovely to be getting a bit of air in the garden, already? You can really feel that spring is coming, can't you?'

Beth agreed enthusiastically, though she was giving the game away by wrapping her arms around her middle and even sticking her cold hands into the sleeves of her sweater. She was regretting having left her jacket in the hall, and wondered what Katie was playing at. Yes, Teddy was quite capable of being an utter pain, but surely they could just shut him out in the garden? Did they all have to suffer with him?

Possibly Michael felt the same way, as he suddenly said, 'I'll just go and check I've opened the red wine...'

'Oh no, you won't,' said Katie firmly. 'It's fine, I did it earlier. Let's just enjoy the lovely blue sky for a while, shall we?'

Beth looked up obligingly. The sky was, indeed, the same piercing blue as Harry's eyes. But the lack of cloud cover meant the chill was all the more ferocious for it. If she stood outside for much longer, she'd be an icicle.

'Forgive me, my dear Katharine, but my old bones... this reminds me a little too much of my beloved Siberia,' said Kuragin with a laugh. 'Might we admire the day through your wonderfully large windows for a while?'

Everyone nodded enthusiastically, apart from Katie, who just looked resigned. A minute later, Kuragin was shepherding the ladies back to the house. At the last minute, Michael and

Harry stayed put, toughing it out, or possibly just avoiding the Russian. And Teddy, clearly hesitating over whether to follow Kuragin or keep lolling with his master, settled for some random high-pitched barking and pointless running about before collapsing again near Michael.

Katie snapped the doors shut and instantly Beth could feel sensation returning to her numb fingers as the warmth of the kitchen enfolded them. She looked at Kuragin speculatively. Might as well dart in a few questions while Harry was occupied.

'I understand you're an art dealer, Andy,' she started.

'Oh, some people call it that,' said Kuragin expansively.

'What do you call it then?' Beth was puzzled.

'It could be a metier, or some might say a calling. I like to think I'm nurturing talent,' Kuragin said, looking down modestly.

Inwardly, Beth thought he seemed to have done quite well out of his 'nurturing', which he clearly felt was as selfless a calling as being a nurse or a nun, and should be given commensurate praise. His jumper was cashmere, his shoes were the sort of soft and supple leather that even she, no connoisseur of footwear, knew cost an absolute bomb. And she was willing to bet that the huge bottle-green Jaguar parked outside Katie's house, which Harry had wistfully said was brand new, was his, too.

'I wondered if you might actually know someone we, erm, came across recently,' Beth ploughed on. Behind her, Katie dropped the colander into the sink with an almighty clatter.

'Oh? And who would that be, Miss Elizabeth?'

'It's Beth,' she said shortly. Katie might not mind all this 'Katharine' palaver, but Beth hadn't been called Elizabeth since she was being told off for filching a Twix from her parsimonious paternal grandmother's store cupboard, and she didn't warm to it at all.

'I'm so sorry, *Beth*, please excuse my old Russian habits. We are used to at least three versions of our names in my home country. Here, I'm known as Andy, but I also answer to Anatoly, Anatole and even Sunny. My name means sunrise, you see.'

Despite her desire to crack on with her questioning as quickly as possible while Harry was out of the way, this was the sort of irrelevant detail that Beth adored. And before she knew it, she was becoming quite side-tracked, asking the meaning of loads of Russian names that had always intrigued her. There'd been a girl at school called Svetlana, always unfortunately nick-named Sweaty, and it was fascinating to discover her name actually meant 'Northern Star'.

It wasn't until she saw Harry and Michael finally walking slowly towards the kitchen, seriously hampered by Teddy bouncing around between them as though he was on his own personal trampoline, that she realised she had to get on with it.

'Mark Smeaton. That's the name of the person we, er, met, isn't it, Katie?'

Katie, still with her back to them and busy with the washing-up, paused for a moment before replying. 'Um, yes. I think so. That is, I think you know more about all that than I do.'

As Katie was clutching a tea towel at the time and refusing to look round, it wasn't hard for Beth to decide that she was literally washing her hands of the whole thing. But it was too good an opportunity to pass up, and Michael and Harry were getting ever nearer, despite Teddy's best efforts to trip them up.

'Did you know him, Andy?'

'*Did* I? Or do I? Your language is so confusing sometimes. Well, I *do* know him. Of course. All of us in the art world know Mark. A talent I can only describe as... ferocious,' said Kuragin, his face creasing in what Beth would later remember as a sneer.

'That's quite a word to use,' said Beth, thinking back to her research on the artist. After his initial, searing debut show, there didn't seem to be much in his career that justified the epithet. 'Didn't, er, don't you like him? I thought you'd had some sort of collaboration?'

She frowned, trying to remember everything she'd read in that Wikipedia page. Or what the ladies at the café had said about Smeaton. Her memory was getting worse and worse these days.

'How much do you know about Smeaton?' asked Kuragin, unconsciously echoing her thoughts. His eyes, cold green slits, focused on Beth intently. Suddenly she knew that beneath the charm, there was pure steel. She tried for the airy approach.

'Oh, not so much. We just bumped into some friends of his recently, you know how you do. It's a very small place, Dulwich.'

'Yes, I'm beginning to see, I think. And you met Smeaton in Dulwich?'

'Erm, no,' said Beth, realising a little too late that her disastrous habit of telling the truth was going to trip her up. 'We met him, um, on Peckham Rye.'

'Peckham Rye? Was he exhibiting there?'

'Well, no. I mean yes, in a way...' said Beth.

Katie swung round from the sink, clearly having heard enough of Beth's bumbling, and proffered the wine. 'Let me top you up,' she said with a smile, filling Kuragin's glass to the brim.

Maybe she was hoping that if he was sozzled, he wouldn't take exception to Beth's questions. Then she performed the same trick with Beth's glass, to the extent that Beth had to take an immediate sip to stop the delicious wine slopping over the rim. Was Katie hoping that getting Beth tipsy would stop her interrogation? In that case, she didn't know her friend as well as she thought.

Beth was just drawing a breath to come out and tell Kuragin the true situation with Smeaton, when there was a bang at the glass doors, as Teddy hurled himself against them, ricocheted

off, and paused to renew his assault. Meanwhile, Michael and
Harry were still deep in conversation not far from the gate to
Dulwich Park which made this such a coveted property, and
paying absolutely no attention to the frantic hound. Beth tutted
under her breath. She knew, of old, how talented Harry could
be at ignoring situations he didn't want to get involved in. It
looked as though he'd met a fellow exponent of the art in
Michael.

Teddy thudded against the window again, so hard that it
must have really hurt the silly creature. Beth wondered if this
was one of his new games, and the reason why Katie had had
them all standing around in the garden earlier. But they
couldn't do that all through lunch, unless she was planning to
serve sandwiches, and it was definitely not the weather for a
picnic.

Harry, she supposed, was hardened by spending so much
time on the streets – plus, he had somehow hung onto his jacket
while Beth had surrendered hers at the door. She was willing to
bet Michael was freezing, but it seemed he preferred that to
spending too much time with Kuragin. Curious, as Katie had
said they were friends.

Beth wandered down the long room to let the dog in, but
Katie bustled past her, muttering out of the corner of her mouth,
'I'll have to shove Teddy in the cage. Keep Kuragin talking!'

Poor Katie. A moment ago, she'd been trying to stop Beth
chatting to – or, if you preferred, cross-questioning – her guest.
But Teddy's wilfulness had trumped her own good manners.
No wonder she was so fed up with the mutt. Beth turned
around and trotted back to Kuragin, who was watching her with
a strange sort of concentration.

'I'm just wondering where I've seen you before,' he said
easily, seeing her raised eyebrows at his prolonged scrutiny. 'Are
you an art enthusiast?'

'Well, only in an amateur way. I love Wyatt's Picture

Gallery, just round the corner. I don't know whether you know it?'

'But of course! Anneka Baker is a dear, dear friend. And her mother! What a ballerina, in her day,' he sighed.

Beth mentally rolled her eyes, then realised she was being unfair. She hadn't even met Drusilla Baker, the famous former Royal Ballet star whose daughter, Anneka, was the chair of the gallery's board of trustees. But Beth wasn't a big fan of Anneka's, that was for sure. The woman hadn't exactly been obstructive during Beth's investigation into the poisoning of a teenage girl, but given the circumstances, anyone who was less than wholeheartedly helpful was a monster in Beth's book. Who wouldn't want to do everything they could, faced with such a crime? And on a much more trivial note, Beth was honest enough to admit that the other woman's effortless elegance had made her feel like a total bumpkin.

Kuragin had the same quality. He was suave, and he'd been attentive, yet he had something about him which suggested that, if they'd met at a cocktail party, he'd definitely be the type to keep peeking over Beth's shoulder – never difficult at the best of times – ready to dump her like a shot for anyone who'd be more use to him socially, financially or sexually. But maybe Beth was letting her prejudices run away with her. She resolved to give him the benefit of the doubt. After all, if she avoided everyone who was wealthy, stylish and well connected, she'd have absolutely no one left to talk to in Dulwich.

'How would you describe Smeaton's art?' Beth asked, trying to hold his attention. Suddenly, it looked as though she'd hit on the right tack.

'Is it possible that you don't know?' Kuragin said, leaning towards her with his eyes narrowed again.

'Know what?' Beth opened her eyes wide. But Kuragin didn't say what she was expecting at all.

'Slope!' he said, with a self-satisfied smirk.

'Sorry, what?' Beth was baffled.

'You have heard of the artist, Slope? Who leaves these so-witty graffiti around with his little spray can that sell for millions? The terrorist throwing a birthday cake instead of a Molotov cocktail? The man painting out the twelfth star on the EU flag after Brexit with red paint, that drips down like your country's lifeblood?'

Beth stared at him, wide-eyed. 'You're not saying...?'

'Yes, Slope and Mark Smeaton are one and the same.'

'Really? Are you sure?' Beth was staggered.

The man she had seen had scarcely looked like the most celebrated graffiti artist of this, or any other, generation. True, no one looked their best when dead, and perhaps particularly not when they'd been stabbed a great many times. But then, he'd been wearing those posh-boy red chinos. How did that fit with being an edgy, incognito street artist? And hadn't he gone to Wyatt's School? It wasn't exactly an identikit portrait of a rebel.

Yet the more Beth thought about it, the more she realised that could be a perfect disguise. Didn't the Establishment always breed its fiercest critics from within? The Soviet spies, Blunt, Philby and Maclean, had all gone to public schools before being recruited at Cambridge. Tom Driberg, the vociferous Labour MP, had spent large chunks of his life working on the true-blue *Daily Express*, where he'd started up the wickedly snobbish William Hickey column. Even the writers PG Wodehouse and Raymond Chandler, who'd gone to a school only a shade less renowned than Wyatt's in Dulwich itself, had both turned on their backgrounds to some extent. Wodehouse's comic soufflés were tainted by his naïve dealings with Germany during the Second World War, while Chandler's coruscating prose dripped glamour onto a vicious way of life that he'd certainly not seen for himself in Dulwich Village. Being put into a privileged system as a child didn't mean you were guaranteed to come out the other end as a supporter.

'You are shocked. It's not the image of this place, is it?' Kuragin gestured round the beautiful kitchen and, by extension, the placid and prosperous environs of Dulwich itself. 'But what can you expect? The bourgeoisie exists to create friction, no?'

For the second time in their short conversation, Beth felt a possibly unwarranted irritation rising. Though she often felt as if she was on the outside of all that was so comfortable about Dulwich life, that didn't mean that she didn't love and value everything she very much hoped the area was going to do for her son. And she certainly wasn't going to stand around while someone stuck her best friends – and Kuragin's hosts – into a category he seemed to have nothing but contempt for. How rude.

There was another reason why his comment had riled her. If the *friction* he spoke of so lightly led to a violent death, then she was even more against it. She felt like turning on her heel and joining Harry and Michael outside, where they were loitering quite determinedly. On the other hand, she was finally gleaning some useful information about the murder victim, and that had to mean it was worth continuing to winkle what she could out of Kuragin.

She also had to be honest with herself and admit that she found it annoying that Kuragin had been able to wrong-foot her like this. She'd certainly noticed the anomaly that Smeaton hadn't seemed to produce much art since that stunning debut show, yet had managed to remain a darling of the art world, but she hadn't twigged at all that he might have had an alter ego. His Wikipedia page hadn't whispered a word of the secret. So, he was the talent behind Slope! What an extraordinary thing.

She hated the fact that Kuragin had got one over on her. He was quite visibly preening now, thrilled at her ignorance. But who, living in Dulwich, would have made that connection? She comforted herself that there was nothing in the frankly smug, well-heeled world Smeaton moved in which suggested for one moment that he would make his living at the extreme edge of left-wing political grandstanding. It was not only biting the hand that fed him, it was garnishing it with sage and onion stuffing before chomping it down whole.

She wondered whether Harry had found this out about Smeaton yet. The idea of getting a march on him was very appealing, she had to admit. He'd been such a crosspatch lately. Though he'd atoned last night – quite thoroughly, she remembered with a half-smile – it would still be deeply satisfying to get her hands on lots of juicy information if she could. And Kuragin might be in a confiding mood, now that he thought he was so damned clever. She leant forward and widened her eyes at him.

'You're a dealer, did you do much business with Smeaton yourself?'

Immediately the shutters came down. Kuragin sat back, took a sip of his wine and let his glance flit about the room. He was clearly trying to find something to comment on that would turn the conversation, but he was failing. Maybe Katie's lovely kitchen was too bourgeois for him, Beth thought crossly.

'Oh, but come to think of it, I suppose his works were probably a bit too valuable for you,' she said innocently. She took a cocktail sausage from the dish on the counter, and then slightly ruined her nonchalant act by eating it in one bite, and then had to chew very fast to rid herself of bulging hamster cheeks. Somehow, she managed it, while watching Kuragin carefully.

As soon as her mouth was empty and her eyes had stopped watering, she was back on the attack. 'You probably don't have that sort of gallery, do you? I've heard Slope's stuff changed hands for absolute fortunes. Not many people could handle that sort of deal, I suppose.'

Sure enough, Kuragin's vanity was piqued. 'On the

contrary, I handle many works that are much in excess of any price Smeaton may have attracted,' the man barked.

'*May have?*' Beth pounced.

'I'm sorry?' Kuragin raised his eyebrows.

'You said "may have", in the past tense. Why was that, I wonder?' Beth took a step nearer.

The Russian was starting to look very uncomfortable. He put his wine glass down with a snap, endangering the delicate stem in a way that would have had Katie wincing if she'd been with them. Beth wondered briefly what was keeping her friend; surely she must have shoved Teddy into his cage by now? But she needed to focus on Kuragin.

'Do you know something about Smeaton, about where he is?' she asked slowly.

At that moment, there was a blast of cold air as Michael and Harry tramped back into the kitchen. Inwardly, Beth groaned. It was terrible timing. Kuragin immediately broke away from Beth's gaze and hailed Michael like a long-lost friend.

'Let me top up your glass,' he said, grabbing the bottle and striding away from Beth as though she were radioactive.

Having for once wiped the mud and grass off his shoes, not something he was so punctilious about in her house, Harry wandered over to her side. 'Everything OK?' he asked, smiling down at her.

'Did you know that Mark Smeaton is actually Slope, the artist?' Beth said with no preamble.

Harry tutted and turned his head away, shook it slightly, then directed a chilly blue gaze right at her. 'Really? You want to do this now, at lunch with your friends?'

Immediately, Beth felt terrible. She didn't want to ruin poor Katie's lunch party. Yes, she wanted to find out as much as she could about Smeaton; of course she did. She'd found the man's poor broken body and she owed him that much. And as she'd now somehow also acquired his dog, she felt they were tied together in a strange and unexpected way. Colin had wagged his way into her heart, with his uncomplaining gentle nature.

She worried briefly about how he was managing at home with only Magpie for company, then dismissed the thought. He'd been asleep when they left to come over to Katie's, and doubtless he'd be asleep when they got back.

Though she wouldn't trust Colin an inch as a guard dog, having seen the appalling scene on the Rye where he must have unaccountably stood by while murder was done, or maybe even taken one of his extended naps, she had now become very fond of him. If she could find out who'd killed his master, she would. But yes, maybe Harry was right. This wasn't the moment to get the thumbscrews out.

Chastened, she pressed his hand. 'You're right, I suppose. Listen, I'll just see what Katie's up to. I'm getting peckish and I bet everyone else is too.'

Beth wandered out into the hall and looked around her. Katie must have taken Teddy off into the utility room. In Beth's own house, the 'utility room' was the top of the washing machine, upon which perched everything from the washing basket – permanently overflowing like the magic porridge pot in the story – to the ultra-strong stain remover spray, which was Beth's secret weapon against Jake's one-boy campaign to destroy all his clothes. Right at the bottom of the basket was a strange string bag she'd bought on a whim for delicate items, before she'd realised they didn't have any.

Katie, meanwhile, had an entire room, roughly the size of Beth's sitting room, devoted to her laundry procedure. It wasn't quite floor-to-ceiling marble, like her kitchen, but it was still very swanky.

Or had been. As Beth opened the door, she saw that Teddy had wreaked his familiar havoc here. The floor was littered with toys that had already been loved to death. There, in the corner, was the large cage, which was really more of a bijou wire-mesh bed – a cube that stood nearly as tall as Beth. The idea, presumably, was that this was Teddy's retreat from the world, where he would curl up on a gorgeously squashy-looking fleecy bed, in a womb-like environment, forget his troubles, and drift off into peaceful doggy slumbers, dreaming of delicious cotton-tailed rabbits.

Unfortunately, this wasn't going to happen today. The cage was already occupied. Teddy was sitting disconsolately outside, with the ruins of a particularly pricey-looking astrakhan cushion at his feet. And inside the cage, huddled up in a position that even years of yoga couldn't possibly have made comfortable, was Katie. Her head was buried between her knees, her arms hugging her legs into her chest, reminding Beth strongly of a painting of Prometheus she had once admired.

'Katie!' Beth was shocked. She hadn't realised things had got this bad, despite the evidence of the charred chicken, the frozen food and the chopping board. Not only was their lunch seriously at risk, but, much more worryingly, it looked as though her friend was having a mental health meltdown of epic proportions.

'Katie, come out, please,' said Beth, trying not to raise her voice too much. She didn't want to alert Charlie or Jake to the crisis, or have anyone else seeing this distressing scene. 'Things can't be as bad as all this, surely?'

There was silence, apart from Teddy slobbering gently on a corner of the very dead cushion, and a faint sniffing emanating from Katie. Beth had never seen her friend like this before, and it was a seismic revelation. Katie was her rock. Whatever Kuragin said about his own name – and she couldn't imagine anyone who was less like a ray of sunshine – Katie had always been the one to bring light, warmth and joy into Beth's life. There had been so many times when she'd felt she couldn't go on, when even thinking about Katie and her generous, optimistic nature had been enough to convince her that her troubles would lessen if she just persisted for another minute, hour or day. Now Katie herself had been brought to this pass. Was it all about Teddy, or was there a lot more going on?

Beth couldn't help giving the dog a very cross glance as she edged past him to the door of the cage, which was still open. She pushed it all the way back until she was close to Katie, and it was a little as though they had just chosen to sit together for a chat, although in a very uncomfortable fashion. Beth leant against the cage, and put a hand in to pat Katie's arm in what she hoped was a comforting way. She was so bad at all this tactile stuff.

For a moment, she considered abandoning ship and going to fetch Michael, but she knew that was pure cowardice. After all Katie had done for her over the years, the least she could do was share her friend's misery for a while. And besides, it had been clear since the moment they'd arrived that things weren't going at all well between Katie and Michael. No prizes for guessing what the cause of the problem was. Beth flicked another cross glance towards the puppy, who was entirely oblivious, now happily licking the source of many of his wilder urges.

They sat there in silence, Beth stroking Katie's arm ineffectually, Teddy drooling with little guttural sounds of rather revolting pleasure, while Beth tried to formulate some sort of sentence that would express total solidarity with Katie's suffering, yet uplift her enough to get her out of the cage, and possibly the room. Then Beth's stomach suddenly rumbled loudly. It was enough to break the tense atmosphere, and both women giggled a little.

'Oops, sorry about that,' said Beth. 'Look, I know you're feeling awful and I completely sympathise. But I think everyone's getting to starvation point. Well, apart from Teddy,' she added, averting her gaze from his busy tongue. 'I know I am, so the boys are probably really hungry. Is there anything I can do to get lunch going? Or would you like me to just sit with you for a while? What's the best thing I can do?' she asked.

Katie sighed, her head still buried in her knees, then finally she turned her head to the side. Her fine blonde hair had stuck to her face a little. While it had been cold in the garden, in this airless room it was getting quite warm with three stressed bodies grappling with a lot of emotions – or in Teddy's case, with cushion remnants and other things that Beth didn't even want to think about.

'I'll have to come out, won't I?' Katie said sadly. To her horror, Beth saw that her friend's blue eyes had that sheen which meant tears were less than a blink away. She nodded gently, but didn't risk saying anything in case she got it wrong and the floodgates opened.

'The irony is that I've been trying to persuade Teddy that it's great sleeping in his cage, really comfy and safe and lovely. He won't have anything to do with it. But now I know for sure it is actually super-comfortable, even scrunched up like this. I could stay here all day.'

'Please don't.' Beth's eyes widened in alarm. 'It really doesn't look at all relaxing, with your elbows virtually up your nose. You're going to get cramp,' she said, more confidently than she felt. Yoga teachers probably never got cramp, since they were made pretty much entirely out of elastic and rubber. But how on earth would it go down with Kuragin, let alone with Michael, if Beth breezed out into the kitchen and announced Katie wouldn't be joining them as she was having more fun in a cage? Would Kuragin find that this was the kind of *bourgeois friction* he enjoyed so much?

Katie sighed again. 'I suppose I can't stay here all day, can I?' Beth shook her head. 'Has Michael even noticed I'm missing?'

Beth searched her memory of the kitchen, then had to shrug. 'To be fair to him, he's been outside all the time with

Harry. I thought he and Kuragin were friends, but he seems to be avoiding him. Am I imagining that?'

Katie took a deep breath and Beth thought she was going to sigh for a third time, but instead she started to unfurl herself and wriggle out of the cage. Teddy, of course, thought this was the most marvellous game. He dropped his investigations to come sniffing around his mistress's head and arms instead, making her extraction process all the more difficult and probably not at all hygienic.

Just when Beth thought she'd have to grab a limb, either canine or human, and give it a hearty pull, Katie emerged fully, looking really only slightly flustered considering she'd been jammed in a pet cage for some considerable time. She scraped the hair off her face, rubbed her eyes with the palms of her hands and asked Beth, 'How do I look?'

Beth surveyed her for a moment and could say, with hand on heart, 'Really much better than anyone has a right to, after hiding in a cage.' Now that Katie had emerged, she felt she could risk a question or two. 'What on earth is going on, Katie? I know Teddy can be a nightmare, but this is, um, a little extreme.'

Katie, now sitting effortlessly cross-legged by the cage with Teddy's adoring head in her lap, looked at her friend ruefully. Beth tried and failed to achieve anything like Katie's serene lotus position with her short legs, tight hamstrings and hips that didn't want to give an inch, and settled for curling up any old how, hoping they'd be getting up very soon.

Meanwhile, Katie murmured, 'You won't believe it, but it's this damned dog again.'

'I have absolutely no trouble at all in believing it. Is he just driving you round the bend?'

'Well yes,' said Katie, stroking Teddy's ears while he gazed at her in ecstasy. 'But it's much worse than that. He's done something really bad.'

For a second, Beth looked at her friend in wordless alarm, a bewildering series of possibilities rushing through her mind in a frightening slide show. But then she shook the visions away. This was Katie, and a puppy. It really couldn't be as catastrophic as it seemed. 'Honestly, Katie, whatever it is, you'll feel better if you talk about it. Just tell me. Please.'

'It's dreadful. I feel so terrible about it. He's only gone and eaten the memory stick with Kuragin's book on it. It was such bad luck, really, just before Kuragin arrived. The stick was on the desk in Michael's study. Teddy jumped up the way he does, and two seconds later it was gone, and Teddy was looking a bit like he had indigestion. And now Michael's got to break it to the man. That's why he's being so weird with me. Well, not just me, but Teddy and Kuragin as well. The only person he wants to be around at the moment is Charlie, and all Charlie wants to do is play with Jake.'

Despite her faith in her friend, Beth had been expecting all this to have been a bit of a fuss over nothing. But destroying someone's book? She had to admit that wasn't great. Kuragin would have a legitimate reason for going nuts. And so did Michael.

'Oh, Katie, I'm so sorry,' Beth said immediately. 'This is a pickle, isn't it? I can see why Michael is cross, I really can – but it's not your fault, is it? Listen, we don't have to stay. Particularly not if Jake is monopolising Charlie, and Charlie is the only one who can get Michael to calm down. I'll get him out of your hair...' She made to get up, but Katie lunged for her arm.

'Don't you dare move! You've got to stay. Protect me from Michael. And Kuragin. *And* this blooming dog as well.'

Beth couldn't help laughing, but looking at Katie's stricken face, she realised it was too soon. Much too soon. She tried to make Katie see sense.

'Listen, you don't need to take the blame for Teddy eating the memory stick. It's hard enough to stop him eating the whole house, let alone a tiny bit of plastic. And surely Kuragin will have another copy of this book? Or a backup on his laptop, or something? Who only has one copy of an important document these days? Only a total idiot, surely.'

Katie smiled, and though it was a tentative shadow of her usual beam, it was still like the sun coming out on a dreary, overcast day. 'You're right. He must have a duplicate. We've been working ourselves up over nothing. Come on, I'd better get out there, face the music. I know I didn't eat the stick personally, but Michael is treating me as though I did.'

'That's so unfair! He must have noticed Teddy's a bit of an omnivore,' said Beth, glancing over at the puppy who was now taking a few exploratory nips at the laundry basket. As it was made of plastic, it seemed to be resisting his gnawing. So far. She wasn't sure if the little dog was just breaking in new teeth, or whether he had a boundless appetite and hollow legs. But if he kept on eating at this rate, he'd be bigger than Katie's enormous house in a month or two.

Beth scrambled to her knees, planning to help Katie up, but Katie effortlessly unwound herself to her full height while Beth was still struggling, and graciously held out a hand to her friend.

'How come you've spent the last I-don't-know-how-long stuck in that thing, and yet I'm the one who looks like they've been dragged through a hedge backwards?' Beth muttered. She smoothed down her jeans, which had picked up a fair sprinkling of Teddy's hairs, a bit of cushion stuffing and a generous tuft or two of pale blue fluff from Katie's tumble drier.

'Ah, the many advantages of doing your sun salutations regularly,' said Katie. For a moment, Beth braced herself for more of a spiel on the merits of yoga, but her friend had other things on her mind. 'Let's face the music, shall we?' said Katie, giving Beth a somewhat grim smile.

They trooped out of the utility room together, with Teddy leaping up and down at them as they walked, as though it was normal practice to skulk in there during a lunch party. They paused for a moment in the kitchen doorway, then Katie bravely breezed straight over to Michael, who was looking slightly hunted as he uncorked yet another bottle of wine.

Beth realised that the fact there wasn't a screw top in sight was now the giveaway sign of a very highfalutin party indeed, with a true connoisseur in charge. She couldn't remember how long it had been since she'd had to tangle with a cork. The Chardonnay she lugged home in bulk under cover of darkness from the small Sainsbury's in Herne Hill certainly didn't require such niceties.

After pecking Michael on the cheek, Katie turned to the bank of ovens discreetly set into the long sweep of pristine marble. If Beth'd been forced to fry a bit of bacon at gunpoint in Katie's kitchen, she would have been flummoxed. There was no outward sign of any knobs or dials, but in seconds Katie had everything going and various pans were bubbling away like there was no tomorrow. Hey presto, lunch was back on track, and with no sign of the giveaway Frost aluminium tins to reveal that the meal wasn't all Katie's own work. The hungry men relaxed visibly.

Then Katie turned back to the little group. 'I think you were going to tell Andy something, weren't you, Michael?' she prompted.

Michael went puce and gave her a look which didn't require over ten years of marriage to interpret. But he accepted the conversational baton Katie had hurled his way, and cleared his throat. 'The thing is, Andy... Well, it's like this...'

It was excruciating. Beth was no stranger to prevarication herself. In fact, she liked to dally for a good long while *before* she put things off. But watching someone else do the same was hard work. She flicked her fringe out of her eyes anxiously and saw Harry glance at her. Fringe-fiddling was one of her 'tells', a sure-fire sign she was ill at ease.

Harry now looked with renewed interest at the scene between Michael and Katie. Kuragin, meanwhile, was glugging back his wine, apparently impervious to undercurrents which were currently making the room about as relaxing as total immersion in a Jacuzzi with all your clothes on. Beth was rather glad to see how much of the delicious Chablis he was putting away – with any luck it would act as an anaesthetic against the news he was just about to get.

'Look, Andy, there's no easy way to tell you this, but the puppy – Teddy here – has a bit of a bad habit... He's at that stage, you know? Everything goes in his mouth.'

'Ah yes,' said Kuragin, though he looked a little mystified. 'Like a baby. I remember my own Natasha when she was two... This is a while ago now, you understand,' he added, as though the assembled audience couldn't have worked that out.

As Beth was revising Kuragin's age upwards every time she saw his face catch the light, she wouldn't have been at all surprised to hear that Natasha now had children – possibly even grandchildren – of her own.

'Well, yes, indeed. Notwithstanding that, and be that as it may...' said Michael, reverting to a slightly pompous work persona that Beth had never really seen before. It was a measure of how flustered he was, and how much he was dreading breaking the bad news to Kuragin. It seemed as though Katie was finding it equally unbearable, as she was twisting a tea towel between her hands, but as usual she did the right thing when it became clear Michael was just going to take refuge in executive-speak.

'Look, Andy, what Michael's trying to say is that the dog has basically eaten your memory stick. He just chews up everything at the moment, and the stick was lying around on the table in Michael's study...'

'Where the door *should* have been shut,' Michael added pointedly.

'Yes, where Michael should have kept the door shut,' Katie added with all the appearance of wifely compliance, yet without admitting any culpability.

During this tense scene between husband and wife, Kuragin had been switching his attention from one to another with the well-bred but disengaged interest of the Duchess of Cambridge watching the men's final on the Centre Court at Wimbledon. Yes, there might have been tennis fans there who'd been queuing since dawn, or who had applied for tickets at birth, but for her it was just another public engagement at which to display a jaunty hat and a polite smile.

Kuragin still looked a little baffled, but not seriously perturbed. Beth wondered whether it was a language thing, or whether the dreadful penny was yet to drop.

Three seconds later, gravity got the better of it. The man suddenly paled and, as the colour leached out of his cheeks, he looked every one of his many years. Beth felt for him, though she took a step backwards as a rush of blood and anger rushed in to fill the void of his obvious shock and disappointment, and his face became as red as an NHS poster warning of the dangers of hypertension.

'Are you telling me my book has been eaten by that creature?' he thundered, gesturing at Teddy, who squirmed with pleasure at being addressed and was now so used to shouty voices raised in his direction that he seemed to positively relish the attention.

Katie nimbly stood in front of Teddy to protect him from Kuragin's wrath, and Beth realised for the umpteenth time what a gem her friend was. Despite her own ambivalence towards the pooch, to the extent that she had just shut herself in a cage to distance herself from all the problems he'd caused, she had fearlessly sheltered him from the wrath of a really rather frightening man, who was now towering over her and spitting with rage.

Michael, despite his clear annoyance at the whole memory

stick debacle, which he seemed to lay squarely (and unfairly, in Beth's view) at Katie's door, also had no hesitation about throwing himself into the fray. He was immediately in front of Katie, so there was now a little queue being threatened by one angry Russian. Beth was agog, but before the situation could escalate, Harry was calming things down.

'Kuragin, can I top up your glass?' he said smoothly, taking the man's arm and leading him a little way from the cooker, where the bubbling of the pans and Teddy's sudden yapping were only serving to overheat the situation further.

As they walked the short distance over to the dining table, Beth was relieved to see Katie's arms sneak round Michael's back for a quick cuddle, and his hands go up to pat his wife's reassuringly. He might not be thrilled that Teddy had ingested Kuragin's golden prose – and what publisher would be? – but protecting his wife was a higher priority. Beth raised her glass to both of them and took a tiny sip.

At the dining table, Harry was handing a shell-shocked Kuragin yet another brimming glass of Chablis.

'But what am I to do now? All those months, years... all wasted,' he said, darting a glance of pure venom at Teddy, who was peeping out from behind the marble island where Katie was now putting something into bowls.

The sooner we start to eat, the better, thought Beth, as her stomach rumbled again. A lot of hungry, stressed adults, and a dog with a bottomless ability to get into trouble, did not make for an easy situation when tempers were running high.

Harry was continuing to be a large, reassuring presence – the only one amongst them who wasn't visibly on edge. 'You'll presumably have backed it up somewhere?' he said casually.

Kuragin thought for a moment. 'You know, I need to ask my secretary. She takes care of all that sort of thing,' he said, with a glimmer of a return to the expansive, aristocratic demeanour that he usually affected. This potentially miraculous solution to his travails had clearly not occurred to him at all. 'I will pop to the garden and call her,' he said, gliding out through the unlocked doors.

As soon as he'd left the room, Beth turned to Katie and Michael, who were grinning with relief. 'Phew! Let's hope his secretary's a bit more on the case with technology than he is,' Beth said brightly.

Michael made a pantomime of wiping sweat from his brow and turned to Harry. 'Thanks for calming that down, mate. It was getting a bit nasty.'

Harry smiled modestly. 'As luck would have it, I had a terrorism refresher course last week. He's a lot easier to deal with than a suicide bomber, I'll tell you that.'

Beth couldn't resist giving him a hug. It was at times like this that it really was handy to have a policeman around. Harry smiled back at her, and her heart took a sudden leap. Yes, he'd been grumpy earlier (again!) when she'd been trying to get somewhere with the Smeaton case, but he was basically on her side. On *their* side, she realised rather proudly, as both Katie and Michael beamed at him in delight.

The mood had cheered up so much that even Kuragin coming back in and announcing in a crestfallen way that he couldn't get hold of his secretary didn't put too big a dent in things. Beth had every sympathy with the woman. Why should she be available to take calls from her employer at 1 p.m. on a Saturday, for goodness' sake? She remembered dimly from a long-ago Russian history module at uni that serfdom had been abolished in 1861. Maybe Kuragin, who definitely seemed to be behind the times, hadn't got the memo yet.

Now that frayed tempers had been knitted up a little, Katie snapped back into hostess mode and bustled over to the ovens, sliding out several beautiful Italian earthenware dishes. Each one contained a Frost lasagne. Golden brown on top and bubbling seductively, they managed to look authentically home-made, but in the best possible way. Beth's own lasagnes, as rare as hen's teeth, suffered from either too much or too little béchamel sauce, leaving the pasta alternately bone dry and crispy, or water-logged. Her last effort had seen the liquid cascading out during the cooking process, to sizzle away happily on the bottom of the oven until it vaporised into an indelible sooty stain.

These triumphant lasagnes suffered from only one problem – they were too irresistible. Everyone crowded round and made it difficult for Beth and Katie to plonk down bowls containing a delicious-looking salad, some new potatoes that had been flown halfway round the world to join them via the nearest Waitrose, and an intriguing-looking beetroot and quinoa dish that she was absolutely certain Jake would shun.

The boys thundered downstairs at the first time of asking and took their places without any prompting, and everyone else followed suit. Katie passed the beetroot first to Kuragin, saying, 'I thought you'd recognise this dish, I looked it up, so I know it's a special Russian staple.'

He gave every appearance of delight, but Beth sensed a reserve in the man. She supposed if she were to be served a full English breakfast at every meal, in honour of her country's supposed traditions, she might get a bit fed up, too. She noticed Harry taking a microscopic portion.

Once everyone had full plates, Kuragin turned politely to Harry. 'And what is it that you do? Are you involved in publishing, too?'

Harry laughed. 'I'm a detective with the Metropolitan Police,' he said, seeming to brace his broad shoulders for a response.

Beth was sympathetic. In such a huge and bustling city, everyone had a tale of woe about a missing bike or a picked pocket. It was a bit like being a doctor at a party, she decided. People bombarded you with their symptoms and expected not a diagnosis, but in this case an instant arrest. To her surprise, though, Kuragin didn't immediately expect Harry to sort his life out.

'You must be investigating the Smeaton murder, then?' he said, glancing shrewdly over at Beth.

She fumed inwardly. He must have known her game all along. All her delicate questioning had elicited nothing and, even more gallingly, the damned man had known about the killing right from the start. He must have been enjoying her efforts to find out what and how much he knew, laughing at her down his long, aristocratic nose. Inwardly, she harrumphed, but she schooled herself not to show her annoyance. She could still chisel some information out of him, she knew she could.

'And how did you hear about it? There's been nothing in the media about it yet,' Beth said, not even trying to stop herself.

Harry, Katie and Michael were now staring at her hard, while Jake and Charlie looked up from plates that were suspiciously untroubled by beetroot.

'News travels so fast in the art world,' said Kuragin expansively. 'For example, did you know that his last works – or those of Slope, I should more properly say – are already doubling in value?'

'I've never quite understood why that happens,' said Katie, trying to plop some beetroot onto Charlie's plate but missing when he yanked it out of the way at the last moment. She frowned at him until he placed his napkin over the rich red splatter and refused to meet her eyes. It wasn't until he'd taken a compensatory mouthful of green salad instead that she refocused on Kuragin.

The art dealer sat back a little from the table and took a breath. He was clearly preparing to deliver a lecture. Beth resigned herself. Though she found listening to overprivileged, opinionated, middle-aged (or older) men delivering their opinions about as enjoyable as performing a pedicure with her teeth, she had to concede that at least this was an area Kuragin did actually know something about. He wouldn't just be chuntering on for the joy of listening to his own voice, as some of the old buffers' brigade seemed to. She might even learn something, as long as she didn't get too angry and bored to listen.

Idly, she watched Charlie flick the splotch of beetroot onto the floor by his feet. As if at a prearranged signal, Teddy bounded forward, tail wagging furiously, and sniffed at the little mound. Immediately, his ears went down, and he looked up at his beloved master with troubled, even hurt, eyes. If he'd been able to speak, he'd have been saying, 'Seriously? What the hell is this?' Beth suppressed a smile.

'You find my explanation amusing?' Kuragin broke into her thoughts.

She swivelled to look at him, feeling chastened but fighting it. She'd done nothing wrong. He'd been droning on; she'd been zoning out. This wasn't school, and she didn't owe him her attention.

'Definitely not amusing, no,' she said frankly, hoping she was staying on the right side of rudeness. However obnoxious she was beginning to find the man, he was still Katie and Michael's guest.

'You weren't interested in my explanation?'

'Scarcity value pushes up prices. The fact that Smeaton, or Slope, won't be producing any more work means that there is a limited pool of his pieces available. Therefore, while there is a market, the price of each work will grow exponentially,' said Beth, summing up Kuragin's fifteen-minute exposition succinctly. 'I'd love another helping of the delicious lasagne, if I may?' she turned to Katie, who was trying to hide her own smile.

As they cleared the table later, Katie turned to Beth and whispered, 'You know, I've just thought of someone else we should talk to, you know, about that business?'

'We?' Beth asked, a little taken aback.

'Well, if you'll have me. Yes, why not. After all, I saw the poor man, too. And I sort of have this feeling...'

'Yes?' Beth was agog.

'Why should it all be down to the men? You know, Michael didn't sort out the memory stick issue. Or get me out of the cage. And Harry hasn't exactly been pushing forward with the Smeaton business, though I suppose he couldn't over lunch. But what I mean is, why are we waiting for them to sort anything out? Look at them,' Katie said, pausing to gesture over to the lunch table, where the men sat, surrounded by remnants of the meal, stacks of dirty plates, empty dishes and napkins tossed here and there, ignoring the mess with the ease of long practice. 'They won't clear that lot up on their own, unless we put a bomb under them. Why should we assume they'd be any better at sorting out the really important stuff?'

Beth looked at Katie, astonished. She didn't know whether to laugh, cry or hug her friend. She settled for just nodding her head. About a hundred times. 'Katie, you're on. Let's do this. I thought you were just going to give me another lecture on how dangerous it all is.'

'Well, it is,' said Katie, immediately looking doubtful again. 'But as long as you promise we won't get hurt, then I think we should get on with it. It feels like it's been ages now, and nothing at all has happened...'

Beth paused for a moment and looked seriously at her friend, then quickly checked over her shoulder. The men were still intent on their own chatter and were paying no attention to them. She spoke in a low, careful voice, hoping against hope that her friend would understand what she was about to say.

'I completely get how you feel. I feel the same way. But I can't promise it won't be dangerous, you know I can't. People don't like giving up their secrets. And someone violent is behind all this. Someone who was angry enough to stab Smeaton all those times. You saw him, you know it wasn't one clean, quick twist of the knife. That would have been bad enough, for goodness' sake. He would still have been dead. But this is what Harry would call *overkill*. It was hatred, pure and simple. That's a nasty person out there on the loose. And look at what's happened to me over the past few months. I've been hit on the head, my house has been burgled, my office has been broken into – and a really, really weird woman did a wee in my loo that one time and didn't even flush.'

Katie laughed, and Beth smiled, too, but then she said more seriously, 'I mean it, Katie. There's a murderer out there. A bona fide bad person. And people get even more ruthless when they're under threat.'

Katie was silent for a moment. 'I hear what you're saying. For a moment, I'd just forgotten all that stuff, but you're right. It's serious. I need to think about this.'

Just then, Michael called over, 'Katie, love, any chance of some coffees? And, um, a bit of space on the table would be great, you know? We can hardly move our elbows here.'

Katie widened her eyes at Beth, and inside Beth hugged herself. Thanks to Michael's timely display of drone-like laziness, there was more than an outside chance that Katie would actually help her out this time. And they'd be an unstoppable team, they really would.

'OK then, let's give it a go,' said Katie, her sudden smile illuminating her face.

Beth felt excitement bubbling up, then realised this was not an appropriate reaction to a murder investigation at all. What they were doing would be complicated hard work, and staying out of trouble would probably be the most difficult thing about it. But she couldn't help it, she was thrilled. Yes, she'd become something of an accidental veteran at these matters over the past few months. But she'd been ploughing a lonely furrow. Harry had never been backward at telling her how much he hated her getting involved. Now, to have not only the support but the active encouragement and participation of her best friend – it was a prize she'd never been expecting to receive. And they were always the best kind.

'You're on.' Beth could have said much, much more, but those two words summed up a new accord. All of a sudden, she couldn't wait to get going. And it looked as though Katie felt the same.

'What's our first move?' her friend asked, leaning forward over the worktop in her eagerness.

Beth thought for a moment. 'I thought you said you'd remembered someone we should talk to?'

'Oh that,' said Katie, seeming a bit bashful. 'Well, now that I think about it, I'm not sure... You've got more experience of these things than I have. What do you think we should do next?'

Beth pondered for a moment. She wasn't going to let Katie get away with taking a back seat. But she did have her own agenda that she'd been aching to pursue. And having Katie along was going to make it all so much easier. Probably. 'How are you fixed for Monday morning? I think we need to go back to the Rye. See if this doggy can find a bone.'

'A bone?' Katie wrinkled her brow, then her face cleared. 'Oh, I see! A clue. Yes, absolutely. Let's do it.'

Beth smiled, but inwardly she felt the first twinges of anxiety clutch at her stomach. Maybe she had been overestimating her friend's potential usefulness? Goodness knew, Katie was not exactly Philip Marlowe material. She wasn't even as hardcore as Nancy Drew, for heaven's sake. And this was a serious business. What on earth were they letting themselves in for?

NINE

Magenta wasn't normally prone to nerves, but rocking up to Andy Kuragin's gallery that morning at what felt like the crack of dawn, she was a lot less confident than she looked. It was in a nicer part of town than Benson's, though, which was a good start. Whitechapel might be achingly trendy, but the cobbles there had played havoc with her heels and she was instinctively more at ease in the wide and reassuringly expensive streets of Mayfair. No bearded hipsters here, selling ironic breakfast cereal. They simply couldn't afford the rents. She wasn't sure how Kuragin could – and she certainly didn't want to find out. Like Benson, he rarely sold a canvas, but when he did, it was for big bucks.

She looked around quickly as she pressed the discreet buzzer. There was a sharp click as the heavy front door released and she pushed it with both hands before stepping elegantly into the vestibule. Maybe Kuragin was expecting a ram raid? She knew they'd happened in Mayfair before – determined thieves would drive their cars through the plate-glass windows of jewellers and galleries and make off with whatever they could grab. Or maybe Kuragin was just worried about the Russian Mafia.

With a slight shiver, Magenta looked around her. The vestibule was kitted out with everything you'd expect. A pristine floor, buffed to a shine that made it seem very unlikely that anyone had ever walked over it before. A discreet bank of lifts at the end of the corridor that hinted at more floors just off-stage, as swanky as this one. And right in front of her, a marble console table that would have looked at home in any stately pile, bearing an enormous vase full of aggressively twisted driftwood, interleaved with the comically cheery heads of orange gerberas. Above the arrangement, stage-lit, was a long horizontal canvas.

If she wasn't mistaken, it was an early Slope – an interwoven riot of separate strands of aerosol paint. She leant forward until the tip of her nose was as close as she could get to the signature. It was the famous poodle, but not quite the stylised cottage loaf two-balls-of-scribble-with-a-nose-and-ears that had become so familiar and distinctive. This looked like a cruder, clumsier version. And, although it seemed to be defecating a globe, in the trademark Slope style, the drawing was more tentative than other versions she'd seen. That could just mean it was a really, really early work and thus had tremendous scarcity value. Graffiti juvenilia, after all, was often buried under layers of municipal paint as soon as it was completed, and that was the best-case scenario. Mostly, it was scrubbed off by earnest council workers or reluctant community service teams, reduced to rubble when walls or buildings came down, or bleached, crushed and whitewashed, if it was on railway land.

Magenta was just wondering if she could get even closer still without climbing into the artwork, when there was a discreet cough at her elbow. She'd been so intent on the picture that she hadn't noticed Kuragin, fleet-footed as a cat, creeping down the corridor towards her. Had he come from the lifts, or from the door right at the end? Whichever, she was thoroughly startled, which was no doubt what he intended. Silly of her, really, she realised. He'd known she was here – he, or an underling, must have buzzed her in, and the place would be rigged up with CCTV everywhere. While gallery owners often made a pretence of allowing their clients to wander freely and view their works in lonely splendour, every movement was in fact being tracked. If, as Kuragin did, you only displayed works with a value of over six figures, it was a sensible precaution.

Magenta tried to cover her discomfiture with an airy smile, revealing her perfect white teeth. 'Andy,' she cooed, kissing the dapper figure on both cheeks.

'Always such a pleasure, Miss Magenta. Or should I call you Madge?'

'Naughty! You know you mustn't,' she cooed, then walked into the main gallery with just a suspicion of a swing to her hips. She knew that would have him mesmerised.

Sure enough, he was right behind her and, when she turned again to meet his eyes, the speculative look had been replaced with one she knew a lot better – sheer, naked lust. She danced out of reach on her high heels, coming to a stop in front of a Slope canvas that she immediately identified as a later work. Sure enough, the scatological poodle motif was a simplified yet strident flourish here, the crossed eyes of the dog adding the final touch of contemptuous humour. And even better, for her, it was in full view of the enormous glass windows onto the street.

It was still relatively early. There were few people coming and going outside, but a council street cleaner looked in interest at the tableau the couple made as Kuragin came up behind her. Beauty and the beast, she was willing to bet, was not far from his mind. The man gave her a crooked grin and hefted a mighty brush from his wheeled trolley, and set to on the gutters. Though the council had the money to keep him out on the streets every day, in truth this was one of his quieter patches.

Those who strolled in Mayfair tended not to drop much on his pavements, but he still patrolled as slowly as possible. Oxford Street was too much like hard work, and Regent Street? Well, you couldn't move for tourists. Whereas here, sometimes you could pick up tips looking after someone's car while the traffic wardens prowled. Or see a story playing out, like in this here gallery.

Inside, emboldened by her audience, Magenta turned to face Kuragin and, from her square stance and unflirtatious glance, tried to make it perfectly clear that it was going to be all business from now on.

Kuragin looked her up and down before he spoke, then shrugged his shoulders and seemed to accept the changed situation. 'I take it things went well with that idiot, Benson,' he said tersely.

'Yes, exactly as expected. He does have an early Slope – but not as early as yours.'

'Of course not,' said Kuragin smugly. 'And did you have any trouble with him?' he asked, over his shoulder, as he strode towards a discreet white counter to the side of the gallery.

'Just the usual,' said Magenta. It was her turn to shrug.

'Nothing you couldn't handle; I take it?' Kuragin seemed keen for the details. She wasn't that surprised; he had a reputation for prurience. Magenta thought back to the little scene that had played out in Whitechapel. In truth, it had gone too far for her liking, and she somewhat blamed herself for misjudging the situation. But there was no reason why Kuragin should have all the ins and outs.

'You know me so well.' It wasn't quite an answer, but Magenta was banking on Kuragin's curiosity being rapidly exhausted. Anything that wasn't strictly related to business could always be relied upon to tire him quickly. And, whatever he might say, he didn't really care about her at all, she knew that.

It was one of the many reasons why Magenta was coming to the conclusion that the art world wasn't for her. Maybe it was time to look into that law conversion course instead? She could pick up plenty of interim work at home to tide her over till term started. There were loads of people she knew who needed little jobs doing. She'd ask around. And the best thing about that, as well as not having to mix with jerks like Benson and Kuragin? She wouldn't have to wear these bloody high heels ever again.

TEN

'Look, in the end, Mark didn't really care about us at all. I'm telling you, Mum.'

Rebecca Grey turned away from her son. He might be edging towards his forties, but in his voice she sometimes still detected traces of the whiny child he'd once been. Very large traces, today.

'I don't think we should be here. And we definitely shouldn't be doing this,' he said again, coming up to her and holding her arms. They were standing in Mark Smeaton's four-storey townhouse in Dulwich Village, the sheet-glass floor-to-ceiling window forming the fourth side of the drawing room, facing onto the wide grass verges and white picket fences sweeping towards Wyatt's Museum of Art. The blood red velvet sofa and the glass and chrome coffee table were strewn with old newspapers, coffee cups and a pile of junk mail. The bottle-green velvet armchairs opposite were similarly laden, and in the small galley kitchen behind them the sink was full of dirty dishes. Mark might have been the most successful artist of his generation, but he was not immune from the stresses of Dulwich life, and his cleaner had quit the week before. Even in SE21, you just couldn't get the staff these days.

'Don't be silly, John,' said Rebecca, freeing herself from her son's clammy hands with some difficulty. 'We're just here to make sure everything's in order for poor Mark, before the police get here and go over everything. You know Rosita left last week, you've heard me discussing it with Mark on the phone. I know you're not interested in cleaning, but Mark would have hated leaving everything like this, you know he would. You were as keen as me to come here, so I don't know why you're so eager to leave all of a sudden.'

John looked uncomfortable and just gestured again at the huge canvas on the wall behind them.

'You see? That's what he thought of us. Of everything we do,' said John, his voice tinged with that pleading note.

Rebecca averted her gaze from the mess of angry reds and blacks that screamed across the creamy background. She didn't pretend to be political; she didn't even know much about art. But it was true that the massive outline of a dog straining to excrete was not a pleasant sight. How Mark could have lived with it, she really didn't know. And poor Colin. Though she supposed he wouldn't have known what he was looking at.

She much preferred Mark's other work from his long-ago graduation show. He'd been such a talent, as a boy. She still had a sketch he'd done of her over supper one night after school. He'd picked up a pen and just caught her so brilliantly, effortlessly, inconsequentially almost. Yet those few lines managed to be more telling, more alive, than all the photos of her that had ever been taken. But drawing per se wasn't enough – he'd had to develop an angle, be political, controversial, to make himself stand out. Well, it had worked. Too well, it seemed.

She thought back to the early days again. Her John had showed such promise then. He'd really been better than Mark. Well, almost. And of course, poor Simon Bude, who had actu-

ally been the best of all three. What were the chances of having
three such talents in one class? There'd been less gifted boys,
too, like that lad who'd been so into photography. But John,
Mark and Simon had been amazing. And somehow it had all
turned out – like this.

At least John had kept up with his creativity, branching out
into woodwork. A smile flickered briefly into life on her worried
face at her accidental joke. Mark could never compete on that
front – he'd only excelled in two dimensions.

She sighed sadly, looking around. She supposed Mark's
little sketch of her would be worth a fortune now. As would all
these other works. And who would it go to? They'd had a desultory look for a will but found nothing. Mark's parents were long
gone and, like her John, he'd never managed to keep a girlfriend
for long. But she hadn't come to pick through his affairs. She'd
just wanted the place to be tidy. Mark had been snatched away
so suddenly. He had no one else to look out for him, poor boy.
What if the police had got here and found the place a tip? He
was so proud. He'd have been mortified. And this was the least
she could do for him.

He'd been part of their family for years now. Since that day,
how long ago was it? When all three of them had slipped away
in the night. She'd always been such a light sleeper. If only she'd
woken. But no. That had been the one time when she'd heard
nothing. Well, never again. For years now, she'd stirred at the
slightest noise. It wasn't surprising.

She remembered the call she'd got. Three, or four, was it, in
the morning? From some police station or other. Saying that
John had been arrested. Arrested! Her boy. And with him was
Mark.

'A serious matter,' they'd said. Down at Loughborough
Junction. There must be some mistake, she'd told them. Her boy
had no business there in the middle of the night. What on earth
could all this be about? She'd woken her husband, who'd blus-

tered and thundered and then finally done something useful for once in his life and called their solicitor.

It had all come out, gradually, in one of those grim interview rooms. She'd had no idea. None. Oh, she'd known the three of them – her John, Mark Smeaton and Simon Bude – were inseparable; had been since day one at Wyatt's. They'd had so much promise. John had loved to draw – superheroes, dinosaurs – when he was little. Mark had that brilliant knack of capturing faces. And Simon, such a talent, creating whole comic books of characters. So funny, and so satirical. That one based on his pets had been hilarious. He'd had something special. But she'd known nothing of their other ventures. She blamed Simon, she did. Though he'd paid the price.

She'd always understood that Mark's signature on his anonymous art had been that little dog. Rather sweet, as a tribute to his long-dead friend. And cute, as long as you didn't look at the world at its back legs and realise where that had come from. But this massive version really wasn't to her taste at all. And a poodle! *Their* dogs. They'd always bred them. She did sympathise with John. It was hard not to be cross. But her son had always been sensitive. He shouldn't take things to heart the way he did. She adopted the conciliatory tone she often – too often – used with John.

'I'm not sure what Mark was trying to say with this picture, and I understand that you weren't a fan, but you can't take it as an attack, John. Don't be silly. Mark loved you. Loved us, and everything we do. Look, he's got one of your bookcases here, hasn't he?' she said, gesturing towards the hulking shelves John had made his friend.

Carpentry had always been his special thing, and it was wonderful how he made a living out of it, even though he produced so few pieces. He was a craftsman; she was proud of her son. Always would be, whatever anyone said. Even his father, who was always so hard on him, had a soft spot for John's 'bits and pieces', as he called them. They only put them in the garage because there was so little space in the house.

She took a last quick look at the shelves and the picture, then turned back to John, who had a hand stuffed in his pocket and was looking a little edgy. For a second, she scrutinised him through half-closed lids. It was the expression he'd had as a child when he'd pulled one of the dogs' tails or trodden on the cat's paw. Malice, and guilt.

Then the sight of all the papers and cups distracted her, and she started to tidy up in earnest. 'Come on, John. The sooner you give me a hand, the sooner we can be out of here, and that's what you want, isn't it? Don't worry about that picture any more. I'm not. It's just a symbol, love.'

'Symbol my arse. *That dog's* arse,' John muttered sourly, staring at the poodle's fathomless black eyes as it arched its curly back forever. 'Haven't you realised yet? Mark always knew exactly what he was doing.'

ELEVEN

Sunday was spent recovering from the ructions of Katie's lunch, but Beth was up bright and early on Monday. It was day one of their joint investigation. She'd taken the day off work and was feeling energised and optimistic – until she saw Katie's outfit. Gone was the 'I'm not with this puppy' hoody, gone too was her usual yoga-guru Sweaty Betty ensemble. In its place, Katie was wearing – apparently without any sort of irony – a raincoat with a turned-up collar, despite the cloudless day. If she'd started talking out of the corner of her mouth about 'broads' and demanding hard liquor, Beth wouldn't have been surprised.

'I think you've forgotten to wear your homburg with that little getup,' Beth said with what she decided was admirable restraint, as she clambered into Katie's car on Court Lane.

'My what?' Katie looked blank.

'Your 1940s gangster titfer,' Beth said, eyes going briefly skyward.

'You can't talk. What was your first job of the day?' Katie laughed.

'Um?'

'Don't tell me you haven't just tailed Jake to school, Ms Gumshoe?'

'Well, since I was meeting you anyway... And now he won't walk to school with me, even if I'm going that way. It's ridiculous.' Beth crossed her arms over the seatbelt.

'I'm just teasing,' Katie said, pulling out into the stream of SUVs now heading away from the schools. 'I'd totally be the same if Charlie was walking to school. And yes, before you ask, he will be. Next year. Just as soon as we know where he's actually going.'

Katie, unlike Beth, had lashed out in a big way on the school applications process. Every time you put a child into a private school exam, you had to pay. That meant Beth was only trying Wyatt's, plus the two very good state schools in the area. Katie, on the other hand, had cast her net wide, and thrown her wallet open to the four corners of London. Charlie was going to have a very busy interview season, being chauffeured here, there and everywhere – ironically missing a lot of school in the process.

'So, boss, what exactly are we going to be doing on the Rye today?'

Beth glanced over at Katie, but her face looked serious as she concentrated on the aggressive mummy traffic zooming up towards the Horniman Museum. Beth always felt a tiny pang when she passed the building's curiously rounded clock tower, standing proud over the Tesco garage and the traffic snaking up to Sydenham. The Horniman, which was still exhibiting the same stuffed walrus that had simultaneously repelled and fascinated her as a child, had been the scene of her dear friend Jen's second wedding.

She determinedly turned her thoughts towards the present day, though once again sudden death dominated her plans. How had she got herself into this position? There'd been nothing in her thirty-something previously blameless years on the planet which had even hinted that she'd ever become some sort of investigator. Maybe just as well, or she'd probably have run screaming from her fate. But at least she now had Katie on side.

'I thought we'd do a sort of reconstruction...'

'You mean like in those TV shows, where they get actors to play all the parts?' There was no mistaking Katie's eagerness. And yes, even Beth did feel that it might be quite jolly to do a bit of role-play on the Rye. But she had to clamp down on that. This was no game.

'This isn't fun, Katie. We won't be asking all the local actors, like James Nesbitt and Jo Brand, to make a quick sitcom, for heaven's sake. We're trying to jog people's memories. I'm hoping someone will recognise Colin, remember seeing Smeaton on his last walk...'

'Yes, and it's a lovely day,' said Katie absent-mindedly. Her mood not dented at all, she swung the big steering wheel to overtake some hapless wannabe yummy mummy in a far smaller car.

Beth tutted a bit, but knew she was kidding herself. It was glorious to be outside; Katie was quite right. Why shouldn't they enjoy that? It didn't mean their investigation was any the less serious if they relished the fact that the sky was an untroubled turquoise and, even though it was cold, the wind had forgotten to blow.

Once they'd parked and started walking, their cheeks soon pinked up in the brisk, fresh air. The dogs were loving it, too. Teddy, of course, was running about like an Olympic athlete who'd escaped the dope tests, and even Colin was sniffing the air appreciatively and pulling slightly on his lead.

'Look, he knows where he's going,' marvelled Beth, as the big dog towed her inexorably forward.

'You'd better let him have his head, see where he takes us,' said Katie, trying to untangle Teddy, who was busily wrapping his lead around her legs.

'I don't dare take him off the leash, though,' Beth said.

'Why not? I would,' said Katie.

'I know you would. That's how we got into this mess in the first place,' said Beth tersely.

'Oh, come on, Beth. Have a heart. Look at Colin. I haven't seen him this full of beans – well, ever.'

It was true; Colin was rejuvenated, tugging her forward, even letting out the odd husky bark. Beth struggled with the sensible side of her nature for a little longer, then gave in to the impulse and slipped the hook on his collar. 'There you are then, boy. Off you go.'

Colin looked round at her, his tongue dangling in what she interpreted as a sincere thank you, then off he lolloped, surprising them all with his turn of speed. His ears flapped comically on either side of his head, and his thick tail moved from side to side like a rudder in stormy waters as he galloped forwards across the scrubby grass of the Rye. Beth looked at him fondly – then realised he was going to be out of sight unless she got a major wiggle on.

'Here! Hang on, Colin, wait for me!' she said, launching herself after him and realising with a clutch of dread that this was an action replay of the other morning – except with Colin in the surprising role of runaway instead of naughty little Teddy.

Katie stayed where she was for a second, giggling, then she was being dragged along, too, as Teddy put on a spurt of speed and started following his chum at breakneck pace.

Beth, already out of breath and trying to brush her fringe out of her eyes with her hand, was tiring of this game very rapidly. Colin was still going, though he was slowing up. Unfortunately, it was becoming all too clear where he was headed – the copse of trees where his master had so recently met his end. Beth realised with a sinking heart that the poor dog probably thought he was heading for a tender reunion with Smeaton. She couldn't let him bound into those trees all on his own and face the inevitable disappointment. She put on a last, desperate turn of speed and managed to catch hold of his tail.

It said a lot for Colin's equable temperament that he didn't immediately turn and snarl at Beth, as many dogs would have done. She knew that Magpie, certainly, was massively protective of her tail and would still whisk it out of Jake's way whenever he came anywhere near her, in memory of terrible times when he was crawling and his main aim in life had been to grab and hold onto it. Colin, luckily, was a lot less highly strung. He looked around in surprise, saw his temporary carer puce in the face and puffing in a way that would have alarmed a less tranquil dog, and obligingly slowed down a little. Beth, panting heavily, managed to snap the lead onto his collar just at the moment they entered the small stand of trees.

Immediately, it was as though they had left central London far behind. Hard to imagine now the ring of traffic that rumbled almost continuously around the Rye, with its trundling red buses, tooting mothers in Range Rovers, and the occasional blare of a police siren as life in south London continued on its urgent way. In the copse, the pace of life seemed to slow almost to a standstill. Even the light changed. Outside, the day had been as crisp as a Granny Smith apple. Here, with the tangle of branches up overhead, there were enough deciduous trees, tall yews and conifers to filter out the brightness and make the place a glade of mysterious dappled shadow.

Despite herself, Beth shivered in her jacket. She knew that, realistically, lightning wasn't going to strike twice. There wouldn't be another body in the clearing – surely there couldn't be? Fate wouldn't be that nuts. But she realised why she'd felt such a sense of foreboding only a few days before. This spot had an atmosphere all its own. Murky, muffled, it felt full of secrets.

Colin snuffled the ground. Beth wasn't sure if he was trying to pick up the scent of Smeaton, or if he was just doing normal dog stuff. As he promptly cocked his leg against a sapling, she decided it had to be the latter. He then looked questioningly up at her.

'Don't ask me, Colin. You brought me here. What would you like to do next?' He just peered back at her with what appeared to be doggy devotion. All of a sudden, he seemed to have run out of steam.

Maybe he was as beset with doubts as she usually was, Beth thought. Maybe now that they were on the threshold of the murder scene, he didn't quite want to go any further, afraid of what he might see – or not see. If Smeaton wasn't there after all, where did that leave Colin? Bereft again, surely.

Beth sighed and grasped his lead a bit more firmly. She was going to have to step up, be the bigger person (well, the only person; Colin was a dog, she reminded herself), and get this bit over with. If he really wanted to revisit the scene of the crime, then that's what they would do.

Strangely, though, she felt Colin's resistance as she tugged on the lead. It seemed he didn't want to go into the clearing, but started to pull slightly to the left, off the beaten track. Beth, of course, had taken all the warnings in Red Riding Hood very much to heart but, despite a lifetime of anxiety, she was having more and more trouble lately staying on the straight and narrow. Now she plunged off the cinder path with the dog, her pixie boots crashing through the scrubby undergrowth of weeds tough enough to survive a London winter.

They wound through the trees for a few minutes, with Beth reminding herself desperately that, even though it felt like the deepest countryside, in fact they were still in Peckham, and the path, the South Circular, Katie and Teddy, and the Rye, were all within a large stone's throw. Finally, Colin brought her up to a thick old tree and sat down with a flump on a patch of flattened grass. Beth cast around quickly. They were still invisible from the Rye – in the thickest part of the copse now, she would say at a guess. From the condition of the ground, it seemed this place was well used, which was odd in itself.

Colin was now staring expectantly up at the tree, then back to Beth, then back to the tree. She watched him, perplexed. The odds seemed very slim indeed that he'd turn into Lassie and bark three times to tell her what the hell was going on. *'What's that you say, Lassie? The children are stuck down the mineshaft?'* On the other hand, he definitely did seem to be trying to communicate.

'Is it something to do with the tree?' she asked him, feeling ridiculous at even voicing the question. But Colin immediately thumped his tail and gazed at her, apparently more expectantly than ever. She sighed and stepped forward to inspect it.

As a native south Londoner, she couldn't have taken even the wildest guess at what type of tree it was. It was just a biggish, brownish one, with a lot of branches. Probably great for squirrels at some times of the year, but looking a bit naked now with denuded twigs poking upwards into the wintry sky. She raised an eyebrow at Colin, but he just stuck out his tongue at her and panted in that way that made him look as though he was smiling at a secret joke. A joke that seemed to be on her, at the moment. Beth put her hands on her hips and thought hard.

There were no convenient messages saying, 'Read me' tied to the tree with ribbon. There was no obvious sign of disturbance that led her eye anywhere in particular. There was no graffiti, for instance, which might have suggested Smeaton had a special interest in this place.

She still found it quite hard to believe that anyone so posh-looking could have really been much of a whizz with a spray can. Surely it was only teenage boys who did that sort of thing, the type of lads that hung out at railway stations after dark, daring each other to tag in more and more dangerous places? She'd read recently of a heartbreaking case where some boys had been killed on a railway line at night, doing exactly that. Her eyes had filled with tears as she'd scanned the paper over breakfast. She wished she hadn't seen the story when Jake had actually noticed for once and asked if she was all right. She'd had to insist that she was, though the lump of pain in her chest for the families involved gave her a tiny fore-taste of how she'd feel if anything like that ever happened closer to home. She'd been surprised at the raw jaggedness of her reaction – until she remembered there'd been a similar case, when her brother Josh had been at Wyatt's, years before, idling away his time before more or less running away with his camera. Maybe this modern story had reminded her of that tragedy?

Hadn't some kids in Josh's class been mixed up in some-thing up at Loughborough Junction? The hugely busy inter-change in the south-eastern rail network, not far from Dulwich, had trains whizzing through it at all hours of the day and night. There were rumours – always denied by those in authority – that nuclear waste was carried through this part of the system in the small hours, on its way to be treated somewhere or other. It was the kind of thing that had the inhabitants of SE21 grinding their expensive dental inlays in annoyance. Somehow, their side of the river was considered fine for such dangerous operations, while north London, where property prices tended to be even higher and where people enjoyed the inestimable boon of the Underground as well, was kept sacrosanct. This rankled far more in aspirational Dulwich than it did in places like Catford, which had long ago accepted their lot in life.

While the nuclear trains might be an urban myth, it was definitely true that freight and passenger lines used the junction constantly. For Beth, this made it the perfect place to avoid. But for teenage boys, intent on making their presence known, desperate for the thrill that comes with breaking the law and getting away with it, it must have been a magnet. Getting a tag on one of those suspicious engines chugging through the night, or marking a signal box or a more commonplace commuter train, would be quite a buzz, Beth could see that.

She was pretty sure that there'd been a death, and a bit of a scandal way back then, but the details escaped her.

She'd have to check up with Josh when he was next within reach of a phone signal. She wasn't even sure where he was at the moment, but since it was a chilly January in Dulwich, the chances were that he'd be somewhere warm, with a photogenic totalitarian regime to bring to justice. She often made light of his job and always disparaged his attitude to the women in his life, but it suddenly struck her that, in some ways, perhaps they weren't so different after all. Both trying to right wrongs where they could, in their own haphazard ways.

She batted such thoughts away and looked up at the smooth, unhelpful bark in front of her, and wondered what on earth the tree could tell her. And if it remained silent and unco-operative – which was highly likely, this side of Narnia – what glimmers of ideas could she dredge up from her silt-filled memory which might help her now?

Something was calling to her – a vague echo from her ill-fated stint moonlighting for the solicitor, Paul Potter, in Herne Hill. She'd been doing her bouncy friend, Nina, a favour – a very big favour, as it turned out. The office had been a sea of beige, except for her friend's desk. That had been crammed with lurid tombstone-sized paperbacks, bulging out of most of the drawers.

Beth hadn't had much time on her hands, as Potter had turned out to be a demon dictator of bogus reports, but in between bouts of furious typing she had to admit she'd dipped her toes into the murky world of trash espionage, written by Nina's favourite author, L.A. Teen. It was highly addictive stuff, all the more so as it came with that delicious frisson of naughtiness. She shouldn't have been wasting her time at the job, and she definitely shouldn't have been wasting it with this stuff. That, of course, made it utterly irresistible. Teen's hero, Jim Grasper, was always correctly interpreting signs and symbols in seconds flat, which made Beth feel a bit lacking. All the investigations she'd been involved in had required tons of careful thought and, if she were totally honest with herself, a lot of luck in there with the judgement. The fact Grasper was fictional did make it all a bit easier for him, she reasoned.

What would he make of this tree? Could she channel Jim Grasper's amazing deductive powers just when she needed them most? She looked up at the trunk, wrapping her jacket more tightly around her. Now that they'd stopped walking, the chill was really starting to sink in. She shook her head. Grasper was proving no inspiration. But she had read enough John Le Carré in her youth to know that dead letter drops were a definite spy thing.

She started to edge round the tree, looking closely at its bark. Colin signalled his approval with a short yap, and somewhere close at hand Beth heard Teddy yodelling back excitedly. Good, that meant Katie was nearby now and might be able to help.

Sure enough, there was a sudden crashing sound and Teddy exploded into sight, tail and both ears flying in his own slipstream. He was a spectacularly gorgeous doggy, thought Beth fondly, as he hurtled towards her. Then he crashed right into her and her thoughts became much less friendly.

'Ooof! Honestly, Teddy,' she remonstrated when she'd got her breath back. Teddy took that as massive encouragement and jumped up to lick her face, which wasn't that far away from him, unfortunately for Beth. She was holding him off with both hands and a leg, while Colin looked on in mild interest, when Katie finally caught him up.

'God, I'm sorry, Beth,' she said, ineffectually calling Teddy to heel, then giving up and simply manhandling him off her friend. 'But what are you doing here? I thought you'd make for that clearing where, you know...' she trailed off.

'I did too, but Colin had other ideas. He seems fixated on this tree. I haven't a clue what it's about, but I was just having a look around it when you came. Can't see anything out of the ordinary.'

Katie started to pace round the chunky trunk herself, carefully scrutinising its markings and knot-holes. Suddenly she stopped. 'Look. There's a sort of dip up there.' She pointed to a spot several feet above Beth's head.

'Where? I can't even see,' Beth wailed. Once she'd made sure she wasn't going to land on any doggies' tails, she started jumping up and down to see if that gave her a better view. But it was no good. Within seconds, she was scarlet in the face and she still couldn't even see what Katie was talking about, let alone get a proper look.

Katie stood on tiptoe, then on one leg, accidentally-on-purpose doing a perfect yoga 'tree' position while she was at it, stretching her arms high, high above her head, and bringing her palms together. Not for the first time, Beth envied her friend's extra inches, her grace, her long slender limbs – well, just everything, really. Then, round about the time when Beth decided she'd had enough and that her friend was merely showing off, Katie unfurled her hands and inched them along, high up on the trunk.

Beth took a step backwards to see if she could get a better view. Then took another, and another. Finally, standing on a small clump of weeds, she could just about see what Katie was up to.

Katie, meanwhile, had been feeling her way around the upper reaches of the trunk. She dipped one hand almost nonchalantly into a shadowy hollow and, with a sudden cry of surprise, brought something out. She was so astonished that her perfect tiptoe posture crumpled completely, and she fell back-

wards heavily onto Beth, who'd run forward to see what Katie
had found.

Beth, in turn, subsided heavily onto poor old Colin. The
dog let out a heartfelt whimper, then wriggled out of their way.
Despite the impact leaving them both breathless, they couldn't
help laughing. Teddy, never able to resist a prone grown-up,
pranced over to give them lavish kisses, which got them stumbling to their feet and wiping down their faces in disgust.

'Ugh! Sorry about him, Beth. He just can't help himself,
he's a big licky puppy, aren't you? Aren't you, Teddy-weddy?'
Katie bent to stroke the dog, who waggled his whole body in
ecstasy.

'Katie, that's enough of that, where's that thing you found in
the tree?'

Katie looked blank for a second, then both of them turned to
scrabble on the ground. Colin, meanwhile, patiently thumped
his tail on the floor. After a moment or two frantically scouring
the clumps of grass, Beth looked his way and realised the big
Lab had something in his mouth. In horror, she yelped to Katie,
and they both rushed forward to pull it out.

Not surprisingly, Colin quailed at this onslaught and got to
his feet, somewhat shakily, and prepared to do what for him
passed for a bolt. But Beth, with great presence of mind, put one
pixie boot firmly on his lead, and then slowed her pace and
signalled to Katie to step back. She approached him gently, and
patted his velvety head while murmuring soothing words to
him. For the first time, Colin gave her a very uncertain glance
out of his big chocolatey eyes, then he opened his mouth in his
characteristic huge grin, and the package dropped out. Beth
immediately pounced on it, though when she felt how wet it
was with copious amounts of Colin's slobber, she rather wished
she hadn't.

They both stared at the object in distaste. It was still identi-
fiable as a brown manila envelope, and made a thickish packet,

held closed by an elastic band. Beth looked at Katie and started to remove it, hoping it wasn't all going to disintegrate in her hands.

'Wait a minute,' Katie put her hand on Beth's wrist. 'Shouldn't we report this to the police? It could be evidence.'

'There's nothing to say it's connected to, you know, Smeaton,' objected Beth.

'What are the chances of us finding a weird envelope just a stroll away from the scene of a murder?' Katie's point was perfectly reasonable. But it wasn't what Beth wanted to hear.

She was curious, as always. And waiting for the police to get here – or worse, for Harry to come and tell her off for even walking near the little grove where Smeaton had been done to death – was a lot less attractive than simply having a good look and then making a decision. Beth suddenly realised that having Katie along as her partner was not all going to be plain sailing. She was used to making decisions as she went; by the seat of her pants, some might say. She certainly didn't want to have to run everything past Mrs Sensible.

'Look, it's falling apart anyway,' said Beth. And sure enough, she could pretty much peer right inside the package without actually removing the rubber band. What she saw gave her pause. She looked up at Katie.

'That's not...?'

'It is,' Beth whispered.

They were looking at a huge wodge of cash. For Beth, who lived perennially on the breadline, a bunch of £50 notes this large probably represented many months' money. Maybe even a year's worth? Enough for tutoring (not that they were doing that any more, but with this money she could force Jake to take up the violin), new sweatpants for his interview, as many sacks of fancy cat food as Magpie could chomp her way through – and that was saying a lot – as well as a bone for Colin. Every single day.

She was speechless.

Katie, a little less used to penury than her friend, was still staring in consternation at the envelope.

'That's a *lot* of money, Beth. We've got to report it.' Her voice sounded a little censorious, and immediately Beth's hackles rose.

'Well, I didn't put it there. And yes, I agree,' she said, the heat dying away as she thought things through. She fished out her phone with a bit of a sigh and dialled the familiar number. Just as familiarly, it went straight to voicemail.

'What do we do with it now?' Katie seemed horrified at the ramifications of their find. Despite herself, Beth was rather thrilled at the money and kept ticking off bills she could now theoretically pay, even though she knew in her heart of hearts that all this dosh was going straight to Harry as soon as she could hand it over.

'Can you shove it in your bag?' she asked hopefully.

Now it was Katie's turn to be shirty. 'Mine's full up with all Teddy's stuff,' she objected, patting the minimalist number that Michael had so fondly hoped would rival Belinda McKenzie's current It bag. He had reckoned without Teddy giving it a severe chewing and Katie using it to transport the pigs' ears and chew toys she needed to distract the puppy from whichever tiny dog he was finding sexually irresistible that day. It was already a sorry sight. 'What's wrong with yours?'

They both knew Beth's bag was also titchy, and also full of crap. Although her OCD tendencies meant there wasn't a surface in her house you couldn't see your reflection in – including the tops of the paint cans that had been in her hall for months, waiting for their moment – her bag was a grey area. A surprising number of Twix wrappers, Wispa packets and Haribo bags that she carried around 'for Jake', but which he didn't know existed and never got to sample, were perpetually in transit in Beth's bag.

She gave Katie a sour glance but gamely accepted defeat and started shoving the packet into her bag, squashing who-knew-what in the process. Finally, she'd tamped everything down enough to get the zip done up.

'I feel like everyone's going to know I've got hundreds of pounds on me, as though this is completely see-through,' Beth said, patting her handbag protectively and darting a glance around her as though purse-snatchers were lurking behind every bush.

'Even if it were transparent, I think there'd be enough camouflage in there to disguise that money.' Katie stooped to pick up a few stray sweet papers that had fallen out during Beth's struggles, and shoved them into her own pockets without comment.

'I suppose the bigger question is, what on earth was all this money doing in the tree? And is there anything else in there?' Beth wrinkled her forehead, and Katie sighed but obligingly stretched herself up again, and moved her hand around care-fully in the little cavity.

'Nope, nothing else in there apart from the odd dried-up leaf and a few things I couldn't really identify and don't want to think about.'

'Nothing man-made, though?'

'No, definitely not. Felt more like, you know, dead bugs, that sort of stuff,' said Katie with a delicate shudder.

'There are no identifying marks on the envelope. Nothing to tie it to Smeaton – or anyone else...' Beth ruminated quietly.

'Surely Harry will just test the banknotes for fingerprints?'

'Yes, but unless whoever's touched them is already known to the police, then they won't be in the database,' Beth pointed out. 'OK, well, that feels like all we can do here. There's nothing in the grass anywhere, is there?'

'Well, if there was, then Teddy's slobbered or peed on it, or Colin's eaten it,' said Katie, looking at the two dogs severely. 'I don't think they've got what it takes to be police sniffer dogs, let's put it that way.'

Teddy rolled over under their gaze, letting them have another eyeful of the reason for much of his misbehaviour, and Colin panted, his raspberry tongue hanging down like a wet bathmat. Beth and Katie both sighed a little. As sidekicks, the dogs so far left a lot to be desired.

'Let's go along to the, you know, *scene*, and see if there's anything there that we missed last time,' said Beth.

'To be fair, we weren't actually hunting around before. We just called the police and let them get on with it...'

'Like the great citizens we are.' Beth smiled. 'Yes. But there might be something that's just gone unnoticed.'

'I'm loving all that faith you have in Harry and his team.' Katie's voice was dry.

Beth gave her a sideways look. 'You know what I mean. A different perspective... they're always in such a rush anyway, and they're just looking for the obvious stuff – footprints, murder weapon... We can take things at a more oblique angle.'

'Oh, can we?' Katie seemed amused. 'Off we go then. Lead on, Sherlock. Do I need to get my magnifying glass out?'

Beth gave her friend a tiny playful shove, and they were giggling as they collected up both dogs' leads and walked on.

But when they got to the forlorn clearing just a few metres further towards the centre of the Rye, there was little to suggest that anything untoward had ever happened there, let alone a grisly murder. Apart from some tattered bits of yellow and black crime scene tape hanging from a branch, there didn't appear to be a single remnant left from the business, let alone a pile of helpful clues.

Beth and Katie were looking at each other in deep disappointment when a ghastly sound rent the air. It was Colin, who'd sat down on his haunches in the grass close to where

Smeaton had been lying and was letting rip with a bloodcurdling howl.

Feeling the hairs rise up on her arms at the horrible sound, Beth dashed forward to comfort the old Labrador. There might be nothing visible here to the naked eye, but the dog certainly knew his master had been here – and then had never been seen again.

Colin was beside himself now, nosing the ground, snuffling the air, turning round restlessly, while Beth tried to calm him. Next thing they knew, Teddy was becoming infected with the nervous skittering that was so uncharacteristic for the older dog but meat and drink to his hyperactive friend. Within seconds, the puppy was bouncing around on the spot, barking frantically, yanking at the lead, and generally being a total and utter Teddy.

Beth and Katie looked at each other. The situation was deteriorating fast and it was nigh on impossible to scrutinise the place more closely – even if there had seemed to be anything worth gleaning here. As far as they could both see, there was nothing around any more except for lots of flattened tussocks of grass – and two overwrought canines.

'Let's go, Katie, this isn't getting us any further. Besides, I've got all this money burning a hole in my bag. I need to get home and get rid of it.'

'Don't you mean, ring your nice boyfriend and ask him to take it off you?' Katie raised her eyebrows.

'Well... I *have* left him a message. Not my fault if he's too busy to call me back, is it? And besides, I just want to count it first.'

'Beth, no! We've got to just hand it over. What if there's "trace" on it, or whatever?'

Beth tutted. 'We're not in the FBI looking for serial killers. Well, at least I hope not.'

Katie looked around her anxiously, but apart from their own barking and whimpering dogs, the place was quiet. As quiet as the grave. Even the relentless passage of dog walkers across the Rye could have been happening on another planet. There was nothing stirring here, apart from naughty Teddy and tragic Colin, and they were stirring plenty.

'Anyway,' said Beth, realising she sounded shifty even to her own ears, 'I'm dying to know how much money is in the envelope. Aren't you?'

Katie met her eyes reluctantly. She nodded. 'I haven't seen that much cash in one place since... well, since ever really. It's like something out of James Bond.'

'Come on then, Miss Moneypenny,' said Beth, secretly thinking that her friend would be perfect as a Bond girl. Those luscious limbs and blonde tresses would fit the part perfectly. Of course, both of them were too modern and resourceful to have anything to do with such an outdated franchise, she told herself sternly. Especially as there never seemed to be parts for those who were a bit more on the five-foot-nothing side of things, unless she'd wanted to play an Odd Job-style villain, and she didn't fancy that, thank you very much.

They walked determinedly out of the copse, back onto the Rye proper. By this point, the dogs were calming down with every step, though Colin did keep looking back as though he couldn't quite believe he'd left his master behind again. It was very poignant.

Beth almost wished they could have stayed there and performed some sort of farewell ceremony for Colin, though she had no idea what form that would have taken. She knew that elephants mourned their dead, she knew that dogs could be steadfast, but she'd never seen with her own eyes an animal's purely heartbroken pain before. She knew pretty much for a fact that Magpie wouldn't spend more time at her graveside than it took to establish there was no premium cat food hidden in a handy urn. She'd have human mourners, she knew. But there was something impressive and peculiarly moving about what Colin had just been through.

It made her realise that although Smeaton had become a shadowy and somewhat ill-defined figure as the days had stretched by since his slaying, this posh-boy-cum-rebel artist had been a flesh and blood man with the sort of sterling qualities required to win the love of a pure soul like Colin. The knowledge made her all the more determined to find who had left him crumpled and dead, his lifeblood leaking into the Rye.

Once they'd put some distance between them and the copse, and they were out on the reassuringly open, slightly bleak heath again, Beth turned to Katie. 'Is it my imagination, or are people looking at me strangely?'

Katie looked her quizzically, then scrutinised the dots ahead of them which represented faraway dog walkers who, even if they were looking in their direction, wouldn't have been able to make out much at this distance without the assistance of binoculars. 'I think you're being a bit paranoid.'

'It's this money. It's weighing me down. I'd suggest going back to that café for a coffee, but we can't very well get it out there and start counting it, can we?'

Katie laughed. 'Not unless we want it to be the first item on Belinda McKenzie's lunchtime bulletin.'

Beth flinched instinctively and looked around again. 'She's not here, is she? Tell me she's not.'

'You're safe, don't worry,' Katie said reassuringly. 'She's too grand to walk the pooches, anyway. One of her "team" does that.'

'What is the point of having dogs if you don't walk them yourself?' Beth muttered, realising she was already sounding like a die-hard dog owner. Though new to the whole canine malarkey, she was already feeling a bit fitter, having had to escort Colin on his sedate perambulations. It somehow seemed like cheating to get someone to take the responsibility off your hands. But that was Belinda McKenzie all over.

Despite some moments of rapprochement recently, when Beth had almost thought they could be friendly some day, Belinda had taken the recent downfall of one of her acolytes very hard. True, it had been a shocking business, and had laid bare exactly how far some would go to preserve the outward appearances Dulwich held so dear. But it was clear that for Belinda at least, and for the many in SE21 who considered her pronouncements to be law, it was Beth herself who'd been culpable by exposing the true nature of the horrible crime to public comment. Normally Beth didn't care too much what Belinda and her ilk thought of her. But now that she was concealing a huge quantity of possibly stolen money about her person, she wanted to attract even less attention than usual.

'Listen, I think we should get back to my place as quickly as possible. I'm betting you don't want to be counting dodgy money in *your* kitchen?' Beth asked Katie quickly.

Though her friend had plunged with surprising enthusiasm into sleuthing, Beth was willing to bet Katie had thought it was just going to involve crossing suspects off a nice tidy list, not tramping through crime scenes and concealing evidence. A shake of her blonde head confirmed Beth's prognosis, and it wasn't long before they'd stuffed both dogs back in the car and were on their way back to Pickwick Road.

* * *

Watching them go, and taking a quick picture of Katie's car registration with his mobile phone once he was within range, was the man who had silently tailed them all the way from the copse. It wasn't difficult to merge in with all the rest of the dog walkers, he thought sourly. Particularly when the people you were following were dim-witted women who spent the whole time chatting to each other and seemed oblivious to anyone else. He'd been a bit worried that the Labrador might have spotted him, even if those harpies hadn't. But then that dog had always been stupid. Just as stupid as its dead owner.

* * *

Looking at each other a while later, over the piles of money, Beth and Katie shared the same round-eyed, slack-jawed astonishment. There was £30,000 on the kitchen table.

Beth couldn't believe how small a space such a fearsome sum took up. The pack, once they'd got it out of the slightly soggy, unmarked manila envelope, was about the thickness of a good page-turner – not a C.J. Sansom medieval whodunit, but certainly the size of an enjoyable Peter James police procedural. It wasn't as long or as wide, though. It was more like, Beth realised, a huge chunk of Monopoly money. Funny, that.

She squinted at it more closely, just to make sure it didn't have toy trains on it, but no, Queen Elizabeth's head was blushing at her from piles of russet and rose £50 notes, or staring with a gimlet eye from the glacial purply-blues of an equally unfeasible number of £20 notes.

Part of her couldn't help going off into a reverie about what one single mother could do with a windfall of £30,000. It represented a *lot* of PlayStation games. It would cover hundreds – Katie would probably say thousands – of new boots for her. Even a painter to come, finally, and redecorate her hall with those tins that had been hanging around forever. Or maybe she could dump her Homebase magnolia and get an almost identical Farrow & Ball shade of antique cream for three times the price. They could get a dishwasher. And there would be holidays, truly swanky ones like the skiing jaunt Katie herself had just been on.

For a few moments, Beth wondered what she would have

done if she'd laid hands on this money on her own – if Katie hadn't suddenly become her partner in crime and tagged along this morning. She could have sneaked it back to the house alone, tucked it under her mattress, and just enjoyed the feeling of being suddenly, unexpectedly and unwarrantedly rich.

But it was the unwarrantedness that she knew she would always balk at. This money wasn't hers and, however tempting it might be, she would never, could never, have kept it. No matter how many tracksuit bottoms it would have bought for her Jake, she would not have slept easy in her bed knowing she'd basically stolen it. It was annoying, it was inconvenient, it was downright unfair, but truth and honesty were written deep into each strand of her DNA. And she could no more take and spend this money than she could leave Colin homeless or turn her back on a mystery. She just wasn't that sort of person.

But where on earth had the money come from? Could it seriously be coincidence that a murder had taken place within yards of such a stash of cash? It seemed to stretch the bounds of credulity further than even the plots of Nina's paperbacks.

True, it might well not be Smeaton's; she couldn't say for sure that he'd been about to fish it out of its hidey-hole and that was the reason he'd been killed. It was equally possible that he'd put it in the tree himself, to be picked up by someone else. Or maybe his killer had expected him to have the money on him, then attacked him in a frenzy when Smeaton had disappointed him, reneged on the deal, or refused to hand the cash over?

Beth realised it was quite unlikely that they would ever know exactly what had happened. She loved it when an investigation was all tied up with pink ribbons and solved to her satisfaction. But she knew – because Harry was always telling her – that it was much more likely than not that the truth would never be unravelled. Mysteries, in an enormous city like London, were often destined to stay mysterious.

That didn't mean she couldn't try her hardest to solve them.

And now, with Katie at her side, she felt it was more likely than ever that she'd get to the bottom of this one. After all, she shouldn't lose sight of the fact that if it hadn't been for her flexible friend and those much-envied extra inches, the money would have stayed hidden in the tree – possibly permanently. Beth herself hadn't been able to see that there was a little hollow high up in the trunk. And if she had spotted it, she would never have managed to get to what had been secreted there, unless she'd stood on top of Colin. The jury was out on whether even such a placid dog would have allowed such a thing. So, if she'd gone out alone, she would almost certainly have come back alone... and empty-handed. She owed this enormous clue – or perhaps she should say thirty thousand of them – to Katie.

Beth didn't know whether Katie was having her own little fantasies about what she could do with the money. The difference between them was that Katie already had more than anyone could ever want. True, it wasn't precisely her own money; Michael was the breadwinner. But he was an open-handed man with perfect and justifiable faith in his wife, and they shared everything fifty-fifty, as per their marriage vows. If Katie wanted anything enough, he would have been only too pleased to buy it for her, though she would never demand diamonds and furs.

Katie could have worn the most expensive designer clothes and lived at the most palatial address, but she left that to the likes of Belinda McKenzie, who needed to prove something so much more than she did. Katie was happy with what she had. She might ostensibly steer clear of the more spiritual aspects of yoga, but she had already drunk deep of the message that materialism wasn't helpful. Admittedly, she'd done that from the cushiest of yoga mats while bedecked in the latest Lululemon outfits. But hey, this was Dulwich.

It was time for Beth to shut away her own little flight of fancy. She gathered together the notes, suddenly stricken by the thought that they now bore nothing but the sticky fingermarks left by her and Katie. But that was too bad. Surely no one, not even Harry, could expect them to find a chunk of money like this and not want to know how much they'd stumbled across? But now that she thought about it, when had Harry ever shown a relaxed understanding of any of her manifestations of insatiable curiosity? She frowned under her fringe.

'I'm wondering if we should have worn Marigolds while we were counting this?'

'I did say that! But it's a bit late now, isn't it? Anyway, it was all pretty much covered in doggy drool, wasn't it?' Katie looked up from the piles on the table, an uncharacteristic and matching frown appearing on her own forehead. She was still tanned from her recent ski jaunt, and her blonde hair, glowing skin and air of boundless health radiated through the kitchen and made Beth feel a little like a pit pony by comparison. These winter months were hard on those with her Celtic colouring. Mind you, the summers weren't easy either, with her milk bottle legs stubbornly refusing to change shade. And at least in the cold she could wear a big jumper and cover everything up, she thought, snuggling into her capacious sweater.

Just then, she looked up and spotted Colin, who was outside in the garden but panting up against the French window like a dog exiled from paradise. Teddy was bouncing around in the shrubs at the end of the little patch Beth called her own, over by the Bentincks' fence. She sincerely hoped he wasn't on the scent of poor old Magpie. She'd been so much better than they'd ever hoped about the arrival of the old Labrador, but Teddy could well prove to be a step too far – as he was for almost everyone.

'OK, well, we know how much is here now. We'd better ring Harry again, see what he wants to do about it.' Beth knew she was deriving a bit of solidarity from the 'we' here, and hoping it might shelter her from some of Harry's inevitable wrath. They were bound to have done something wrong, in his book. Whether it was going to be finding the money in the first place, or finding it and taking it away, or taking it away and then counting it was anyone's guess.

As before, the call went through to Harry's voicemail. But this time she left a quick précis of the situation, locking eyes with Katie as she did, so her friend could prompt her with any detail she'd forgotten. Katie, though, seemed happy enough with her version of events. Once she was off the phone, Beth looked again at the table – so many tins of Pedigree Chum; not that Colin was staying forever – and started to gather up the money with a sigh.

'The fact that it's a round £30,000 means it's definitely no accident,' she said, thinking slowly. 'If it was £29,875 or something, then it might just be someone's life savings they were taking to the bank...'

'...when they got waylaid by a tree?' Katie's eyebrows were up in her hairline.

'Well, true, but it would seem a bit less deliberate. To me, such an exact sum – it's a payment.'

'A ransom? Or blackmail?'

Beth shivered. Blackmail was such a horrible crime. She'd thought, once before, that she'd stumbled across it. It had turned out to be something else entirely, and she'd been glad.

'If it was a ransom, wouldn't we have heard about it? And maybe £30,000 is a bit low for a kidnapper?'

'It doesn't have to be a person, though. It could be anything. If Smeaton was this Slope – maybe it was a painting!' Katie chirped.

Beth looked levelly at her friend. She was all for her input, and she knew herself how great it was to have a eureka moment during an investigation. But she did hope Katie wouldn't be firing ideas out madly in all directions, especially if they then had to investigate each and every one. It could take them years to close the case.

'We need to know more about Smeaton. That's what this is all about – that man we found. The type of man he was should tell us what sort of crime we're looking at. Why the attack was so frenzied. And why anyone would be hiding money in trees right near the murder scene.'

Katie shuddered delicately. 'I hate that word, *murder*.'

'You'd better get used to it,' said Beth levelly. 'It's all part of the job.'

'The job, *ooh*,' said Katie. 'I can't help it; I do find it a bit exciting. More exciting than teaching stretch classes to Dulwich ladies, if I'm honest.'

'I thought you loved teaching yoga,' said Beth, aghast.

'I did. I do. But day in, day out, the same old things... It's nice to do something with a bit more variety. So, what's our next step?'

Beth suppressed a tiny smile. Katie might be all bushy-tailed now, but a bit of routine checking of alibis would soon have her yawning. She peered at her watch. 'I think we should have a sandwich,' she said.

Katie looked a little deflated. 'I thought you were going to say, "Grill some suspects" or something, well, really a bit more exciting.'

'Well, I suppose we could grill a sandwich, if you like. But the trouble is, we don't really have that many proper suspects yet, do we? There's Kuragin, who's such an oily charmer, he's totally the type to sell a double bed to the Pope. I'd take every word he said with a mine of salt. Then I'd also add in Baz Benson, the man who originally discovered Smeaton, or Slope – I've read about him on Wikipedia. Bit of bruiser; I bet he's got a sinister past. Or Rebecca Grey from the park. She's pretty mysterious. And what about the son, John, that she kept mentioning? He and Mark were supposed to be such great friends but, from what she said, they'd had a falling-out? Could there be something there, I wonder? And then there are those other two dog-walking ladies, Jules and Miriam. I'm hoping Mum'll know them at least in passing, they're the right sort of vintage. Not to mention Smeaton's parents. And there's that railway accident that happened while my brother Josh was at school... I keep coming back to that. Smeaton must have been at Wyatt's around that time. There could be a connection. Mum's promised me all the inside gen when we see her later.'

This wasn't true, of course. Wendy lived in a fog of impenetrable vagueness about everything except the game of Bridge, but Beth had promised *herself* that her mother was coming up with the goods.

'Ooh, Wendy, great. I haven't seen her for yonks,' said Katie.

Beth wished she could feel the same enthusiasm. She loved her mother, but families were complicated, that was for sure. Their relationship worked best when they had her blithe brother Josh between them as a buffer. His airy unconcern about absolutely everything acted as a balm: on Beth, who knew she fretted much too much; and on her mother, who seemed to find all her daughter's life choices bewildering, and open to second-guessing and passive-aggressive criticism, which she was by no means adept at hiding.

Beth eyed Katie speculatively. She'd left a quick message for Josh, hoping he'd remember that far-off incident with trains when he'd been at Wyatt's, but there was no telling when he'd pick it up or even if he'd get back to her. He was probably in the thick of one of his jaunts, though she supposed she shouldn't really call them that. He'd turned his hobby into a highly lucrative career, trawling the world's trouble spots and, so far, avoiding any injury or danger to himself in typical fashion. So, in the absence of her laid-back brother as protection from her mother, Katie would do nicely.

· · ·

An hour later, Beth was slightly revising her opinion. Yes, Katie was certainly keeping the conversation flowing beautifully. She was so clever at drawing people out on their interests, and listening in what seemed, and almost certainly was, rapt attention and even fascination. But they were no nearer to getting to the nub of the matter which was consuming so much of Beth's headspace. And Beth had heard more than enough about who'd played which card and why at the Bridge club last night.

'You see, if you bid one no trump, you're really saying you have a balanced hand. Now ACOL would put your high card points at twelve to fourteen, but if you're playing a strong no trump, then you'll have fifteen to sixteen. And, of course, Lydia had absolutely no such thing! So, down they went, like the *Titanic*. All hands on deck!' Wendy tittered gently, and Katie smiled in apparent enthusiasm.

'I'd love to start playing Bridge, wouldn't you, Beth?' She turned to her friend, eyes shining.

Beth looked at her in annoyance. She wasn't sure if it was because Katie had left Teddy locked in his cage at home, but her friend seemed ridiculously carefree this afternoon, and full of frankly batty notions.

'Maybe, in about three decades,' Beth muttered mulishly, knowing Wendy wouldn't bother to strain to hear her. Then she added more loudly, 'Now, about these ladies we met, I'm pretty sure you'll know them, Mum, won't she, Katie?'

'What?' Katie seemed to be deep in reveries about her and Michael sweeping all before them at the Bridge club. 'Oh, yes. Yes, we met these ladies who know someone we, erm, came across... We wondered if you'd bumped into them.'

'And why did you think I would?' Wendy wrinkled up her brow a little and peered across the table, stirring her cup of Earl Grey tea with a tremulous hand and hesitating over adding a second sugar lump in a way that drove Beth mad. There was always a pause while Wendy seemed to be deciding whether or not to stop at a single cube... but she always went on to have two. Without fail. Why not just plop in two, in the first place? Save all the fluttering and flummery? Beth fumed to herself.

She concentrated on taking deep breaths and waited for the irritation, which she knew was irrational and ridiculous, to subside. Why shouldn't her mother take two sugars in her tea? Or twenty-two, if she so wished? But it was the semi pretence that she only took one which got Beth's goat. A goat that, she had a feeling, was going to get a lot more ravaged as the afternoon progressed.

'Well, Wendy, Beth's always saying you know absolutely everyone in Dulwich... and as you know, she never exaggerates,' Katie said with a winning smile.

Wendy's mouth quirked up at the corners. There was something about Katie's approach that seemed to convince her that a gentle joke was being played on Beth. Beth wasn't at all surprised to find that her mother found that quite irresistible.

'Oh, you're too kind, my dear. Well, I've lived here quite some while now. I couldn't even begin to remember how many years it is—'

'Coming up to thirty-eight,' Beth mumbled.

'—and I suppose I have met a few people in my time, yes,' said Wendy, entirely ignoring Beth's interjection. 'Just tell me who you're thinking of and I'll let you know if I've come across them,' she said confidingly to Katie.

Despite herself, Beth smiled. Her friend had played this so much better than she ever would have, and it looked as though the softly-softly approach might just bear fruit. Katie turned to Beth with a wrinkled brow. 'What on earth were their names again?'

'Jules and Miriam. They're dog walkers, so you might well have come across them in the park, even if you don't know them from Bridge or from around and about...'

'Jules and Miriam? Hmm.' Wendy cupped her chin in her

hand, settled a gauzy cashmere scarf more fetchingly around her throat, and seemed to go into a daydream.

After a few moments, Beth started to fidget, but Katie darted a fierce look at her and she managed to still her rebellious hands and feet, trying to compose herself and refuse to allow any irritation to show. On the surface at least. She applied herself to her horrible cappuccino instead. Katie had tried to reroute their little meeting to Jane's instead of the original venue, Aurora, but Beth was pleased that she had prevailed. Though Jane's was well known to produce hands-down the best coffee in the area, Aurora was always deservedly half-empty. Wendy, though she had protested a little at coming here, wasn't much affected because she preferred tea anyway. And the fact they weren't being overheard by Belinda McKenzie or any of her spies was worth a thousand premium coffee beans to Beth.

Distract herself as best she might, Beth found her patience being stretched to its furthest limits as her mother fiddled with one of the innumerable necklaces strung about her neck like ribbons round a maypole. Wendy favoured the sort of outfits that even Barbara Cartland or the Queen Mother would have dismissed as hopelessly fussy, garlanded with extras like tinkling bracelets or today's cascade of beads. Beth cast a baleful eye at them and tutted inwardly.

Beth shifted in her seat, but to her surprise it was Katie who raked her chair back suddenly and fixed Wendy with a pointed look. 'Anything spring to mind?' she asked, stirring her cappuccino with unusual speed.

Wendy drew back a little and said, 'Oh!' in a tiny, high-pitched voice. Then, at last, she seemed to focus. 'Um, what were those names again?'

'Jules and Miriam!' chorused Beth and Katie.

'Yes, yes, Miriam and Jules, that was it. Well, I can't really say I've ever... not really...'

Beth and Katie exchanged looks, both downcast. Beth never

had terribly high hopes of Wendy coming up trumps – except in a Bridge game, of course – but Katie had clearly pinned a lot on this. Then, just as they were resigning themselves to getting nowhere at all, Wendy piped up again.

'Unless you mean Julia, Julia Winthrop? And she does always have a friend with her, I thought her name was Mary-Ann, but of course my hearing isn't what it was...'

Beth knew this was her cue to insist Wendy's hearing was pin-sharp, but she was too excited. 'You do know them, then?'

'Well, I wouldn't say I exactly *know* them, Beth dear, but yes, I've played Bridge with them.'

'You have? But that's wonderful. So, what can you tell us about them?' Katie was leaning forward again, but this time she was all smiles.

'Well,' Wendy said confidingly, 'I will say that Julia is the more reckless of the two. Quite like a man, she is, in the way she hurls an ace down on the table, as though she's challenging you to a duel. Mary-Ann, I suppose I should say Miriam if that's what her name is, is a quieter sort of player. Not as confident. She'll underbid, as often as not, and trumps on air, too.' Wendy pursed her lips up at this.

Katie couldn't help but let her disappointment show. 'But don't you know anything about them as people?'

Beth, meanwhile, was thinking. It wasn't a lot, but it did confirm the impression she'd had of the two women. Jules was the more ebullient of the two; Miriam was submissive. But that wasn't enough to go on.

'Do you know anything else about them? Where they live?'

Wendy went into brain-racking mode again, which meant fidgeting with her scarves, plucking at her necklaces and gazing vaguely around the café as though for inspiration. Again, just when both Beth and Katie had given up hope of more enlightenment, she spoke up. 'I've a feeling they live around Pond

Cottage way. You know, tucked behind the playing fields...' she drifted off.

'But that's literally round the corner from you, Mum. Surely you'd know if they were that close?'

Wendy lived in one of the smallest houses on College Road – the only toll road left in London. It was one of nefarious Thomas Wyatt's longest lasting money-making wheezes, raking in travellers' money relentlessly since 1789. It was currently charging cars £1.20 a time to pass through, every day except 25 December, and felt like a civilised form of highway robbery to those who simply wanted to get to Sydenham by the most direct route. But it successfully cut traffic on the road, as most people took the long way round, and Wendy had enjoyed many peaceful years in her little home there, bordering the golf course where her late husband had spent quality time with his clubs.

She looked baffled at the idea that she'd know all her neighbours. 'Oh, well, people do come and go, dear. And this Julia and Miriam, well, *not* the best Bridge players, if I'm brutally honest with you.'

The strong implication was that, if they had been card aces, Wendy would have been best buddies with them. Beth shook her head. Her mother was never going to change, that was for sure. And at least they now knew a little more about the women – and roughly where they lived. It was something to go on. Outside the café, footfall was increasing relentlessly as pick-up time approached. Beth checked her watch and saw Katie doing the same. It was that time of day again.

When she thought back to her pre-Jake life, she was amazed at all the time she'd once had at her beck and call, and despaired to think how little she'd crammed into it. Even now that Jake was getting such a big boy (relatively speaking), having him around in the afternoons seriously curtailed the amount of work she could get through, whether that was legitimate stuff she was paid for by Wyatt's, the freelance projects she still had going on

the side, or the investigations which had filled up so many cran-
nies of her life in recent months.

But even as Katie started gathering up her gloves and scarf,
Beth realised she had to press on. Josh might take forever to ring
her back about that train business years ago, but Wendy was
right here, right now.

'Mum, I don't suppose you remember something that
happened when Josh was at Wyatt's? When some boys got into
trouble at one of the stations, for spraying graffiti? I think it
might have been down at Loughborough Junction.'

Wendy, who'd been faffing around with her handbag,
sorting out some small change to leave as a tip – she'd made the
automatic assumption that Beth would pay for her tea – looked
up immediately. 'Of course, dear. Those poor boys! What were
their names? Mark... That was one of them I think...'

Katie dropped her gloves back on the table and Beth sat
forward. 'Was that... Mark Smeaton?'

'Yes, yes, well of course it was,' Wendy said, as though Beth
should have known that all along. 'I haven't thought about him
for a long time. Though I saw his name in the paper a few years
ago, some art show or something... Funny, as he wasn't really the
best in the class. But then, after what happened, I suppose it
made sense. He probably just improved, and of course there was
no one, really, to compare him with any more. The third boy
was a bit of an also-ran, from what I remember. Josh knew Mark
and the others, but thank goodness he wasn't involved. Too
sensible,' said Wendy smugly.

Beth blinked. Her mother was finally coming up with the
goods, though only she could have described Josh as sensible.
She imagined he just hadn't shared Mark's friends' interest in
graffiti. Thank goodness.

'So, you actually knew Smeaton! And his parents?'

'Oh, they died ages ago, some sort of accident abroad. I
mean, *really*,' said Wendy, as though Mr and Mrs Smeaton had

been guilty of an appalling lapse of taste, not ending their days peacefully in Dulwich.

Beth was agog. 'What happened exactly? With the boys, down at Loughborough Junction? Do you remember any more details?'

Faced with such transparent interest, Wendy retreated a little into her customary vagueness. 'Oh well, dear, such a sad story, really. So long ago...'

Beth took a deep breath, tried to count to ten, and was just about to let rip, when Katie intervened, saying in her softest, most tranquil yoga-teacher voice, 'You've got the most wonderful memory, Wendy. I've always thought that.'

'Oh, have you, dear?' Wendy preened. 'Well, I don't know much about Mark's parents. I think it was a plane crash, or maybe a train? But the incident with the boys, it's like yesterday in some ways. That poor boy, Simon Bude. Josh used to bring home his cartoons sometimes. The things he drew! Lampooning those teachers. He was unmerciful. But very funny. It was a tragedy, it really was.'

'But what happened?' Beth knew her voice was becoming shrill. She couldn't help herself. They were so near, yet so far.

'Oh, who knows really, dear? The papers all said the three of them went out there to draw on the trains – so silly, and so naughty – and, of course, only two of them came back. But they had very good legal representation. Said the stations were at fault, making access so easy. I'm not sure how they got away with it, the parents. I know the school had the boys in detention for months. But I think it was just community service, you know, collecting litter and cleaning away that stupid stuff they liked to scrawl everywhere. That must have put them off it, if nothing else would. That – and the death of their friend,' Wendy said, her voice quavering.

'Simon was the one who died?'

'Yes,' said Wendy, closing her eyes as if she couldn't bear the thought. Suddenly Beth felt as though she was there, all those years ago. The dark station, the excited boys, the cans of paint, the stink of the spray – then the whoosh of a train when they'd least expected, and the flat, deathly silence in its wake.

It was a horrible story, thought Beth. She wasn't surprised her mother was upset at reliving it. And the worst thing about it was the fact that the boys – the survivors, anyway – seemed to have got off almost scot-free.

Once they'd pecked Wendy's sweet-smelling cheek in a hurried farewell, both Beth and Katie bustled away and dashed up the road to get to the school. Suddenly, Beth grabbed Katie's coat as they passed Jane's Café, and dragged her into the doorway. Katie was about to remonstrate loudly when Beth put a finger to her mouth and pointed. On the opposite side of the road, outside Romeo Jones, was the dandified figure of Andy Kuragin, apparently stooping over to pay enormous attention to some of the pricey speciality teas in the window. With him was a man in his fifties, with a smooth pink face like a well-stuffed pork sausage, garnished with an insincere smile, and topped off with lots of white hair.

'That's your friend, isn't it? And who's that with him?' asked Beth.

'Not my friend,' Katie said quickly. 'Michael's. And that's another of his chums, he's very tight with Kuragin... I think he's in the art world, too.'

'Why is Michael so big on art at the moment? I never thought he was particularly keen before,' asked Beth.

'Oh, it's just the latest publishing fashion,' said Katie dismissively. 'You can sell art books for a fortune. All those yummy pictures.' She shrugged. 'I hate to say it, but Michael's already looking into a book on Slope.' She made a little moue of distaste. 'It looks like cashing in on a tragedy... but someone's going to do it, so why not Michael? At least he'll do it well. I bet Kuragin's here getting some colour for the book, where the artist grew up, you know, all that stuff... And that guy, I've just remembered. His name is Benson.'

'Not Baz Benson? I think he's the man who bought all Smeaton's first works all those years ago,' said Beth, peeping round the doorframe at the odd pair.

'Wait a minute, you don't think the two of them could have bumped the poor man off, to try and boost interest in his work?'

Beth looked at Katie admiringly. She was really getting into this detection business. But then she shook her head. 'Surely that's a bit too cold? Even for art dealers. Listen, we'd better get on or we'll be so late for the boys. Let's just sprint up the road, and hope Kuragin and his chum don't recognise us. We're on the other side, so we should be safe.'

Katie agreed, and the pair nipped out of the doorway and skedaddled as quickly as they could, only crossing in front of the school gates. Though a lot of the classes seemed to have gone already, Year 6 was yet to emerge from the school. Beth heaved a sigh of relief. She hated to be late for Jake.

She and Katie had a lot to mull over, what with the strange story they'd finally extracted from Wendy, and then the sighting of the two art experts. But here in the playground, it was business as usual – Belinda McKenzie was holding forth in the middle of a knot of mummies.

'I always say, it really pays to have the Discovery Channel. Gives them so much to chat about in their interviews. Now Allegra, when she was meeting Angela Douglas of the College School – there's an inspirational head for you – she had just watched the most fascinating documentary on childhood obesity in India. Really thought-provoking. They had quite an in-depth chat about it.'

Beth smiled to herself. Only Belinda could make a massive virtue out of sticking her kids in front of the telly. Then she remembered that Jake spent far too much of his own life in front of a screen, bent on killing tiny aliens. There was nothing remotely educational about that. She vowed, yet again, to winkle him away from his controller and give him a good old quiz on popular culture. It wouldn't make *her* very popular, but it was in a good cause.

Just then, Jake socked his head into her side, almost winding her. It was his preferred mode of greeting these days, now that a kiss on the cheek or even a smile was just much, much too *young* for a boy of his immense age and status at the top of the school. His first question was, 'Where's Colin?'

'Lovely to see you, too! Colin's at home, love, and we should get there straight away and see what he's been up to,' said Beth, realising she'd left the dog unattended for most of the day. Unlike Teddy, he wasn't in a cage and could therefore have run wild, if the mood had suddenly taken him.

She waved goodbye to Katie, who yelled over, 'Tomorrow?'

Before she'd thought about it, she'd nodded happily – then she remembered. She did actually have a job. Not that they'd probably recognise her at Wyatt's any more. She'd really have to go in and show her face the next day. 'Day after?' she mouthed at Katie, who thankfully understood and smiled, though she seemed a bit disappointed.

Beth chuckled to herself. Detecting certainly could be addictive. She knew that already. To her cost.

TWELVE

Beth was thinking about the price she'd paid for her interest in mysteries the next day, as she finally settled back into her chair at the archives office. Colin, the latest and perhaps most concrete by-product of her enthusiasm so far, was installed in his corner, this time with a strange rubber bone that had been in Teddy's cast-off bag. Most of the time he was completely silent, then at odd intervals he'd make bloodcurdling crunching and slobbering noises, causing Beth to break off her work in alarm until she remembered that she had company and that the company had a snack.

In some ways, Beth was amazed she'd got away with bringing Colin in again. She was sure that if Janice hadn't been on maternity leave she wouldn't have got the dog within a hundred yards of the school gates. Not that Janice didn't love dogs, but she'd consider it inappropriate to bring Colin in, unless the school's archivist had suddenly been struck blind or had a similar impairment requiring specialist canine support. But although Janice's replacement, Sam, was doing a good job, and Beth's own friend Nina was a brilliant addition to the back-room staff, no one quite had the effortless overview that Janice had always managed. With her eagle eye otherwise engaged, Beth and Colin were sitting pretty.

Still, every time there was a noise outside in the corridor, Beth braced herself to give her bête noire, the bursar Tom Seasons, a full explanation. He had always been liable to erupt into her room without so much as a by-your-leave, and Beth had the strong impression that he'd love to catch her out in some misdemeanour. Seasons' marriage had fallen apart, through no real – or maybe that should be direct – fault of Beth's. And his next relationship had come to an equally sticky end, following her last investigation. Since then, he'd really seemed to have it in for her. And frankly, he hadn't liked her much in the first place.

But, thank goodness, the bursar seemed to be keeping quite a low profile of late. If Beth hadn't been so preoccupied by Smeaton, the extraordinary haul of £30k that was currently burning a hole in her handbag (she hadn't wanted to leave it at home with Magpie), and the odd bit of work, then she would have wondered a little more why this might be. As it was, she was just very grateful indeed.

She was finally getting her head down to tackle a raft of emails that had been bobbing about in her in-box unattended for days now, when there was a single knock at the door, followed immediately by it being thrown open unceremoniously. Beth was about to have a heart attack, fearing the dreaded inspection by the bursar at last, and Colin was staggering to his feet with a wag of his stumpy tail at this sudden interruption to his frankly rather dull morning, when Nina bounced in.

With her red curls standing up around her head, Nina always reminded Beth of one of Raphael's naughtiest little painted cherubs, a wilful smile never far from her dimpled face. 'Wotcha, babe,' she trilled, then clocked Colin coming towards her with his nose inexorably focused on her crotch. Try as she might, Beth couldn't seem to break him of this unsavoury habit.

Maybe it was a Labrador thing. Or maybe Colin was just a bit of an old pervert.

'Blimey, a dog! And an, oops, very friendly one,' Nina yelped. 'Didn't know it was Bring Your Pet to Work Day.'

'Um, it's not,' said Beth, leaping up and shutting the office door quickly, before Nina had a chance to let the entire school know what was going on in here. 'It's just, well, you know. I'm on a bit of a case...'

'No! Again? Is it like Potter? Got anyone bang to rights yet?' Nina was shrill, settling herself into the visitor's chair opposite Beth's desk and clearly keen to hear every detail. 'You could have told me, babe. You know how helpful I was last time,' she said, appearing a little miffed.

That was all she needed, thought Beth. Katie dressed up in her best Burberry, like Philip Marlowe with a gold Amex, and now Nina getting in on the action, a foghorn in a puffa coat.

'Give me a chance, it's just sort of starting,' she said diplomatically.

'Great! Anything I can do?'

'Well, apart from keeping quiet about the dog...'

'Quiet as the gravy. You know me, babe,' said Nina. 'But how comes you've got a dog all of a sudden? Thought you had your hands pretty full with that cat of yours.'

Beth remembered Nina wasn't one of Magpie's biggest fans. She'd had a limited interest in being thoroughly clawed, something which Magpie definitely considered crucial in any potential human berth.

'God, it's a long story. I just sort of had to adopt him. And now I can't leave him at home all day...'

'Yeah, not with that cat,' said Nina darkly, confirming Beth's suspicions.

'...So, I've had to bring him in. But he's good as gold, aren't you, boy?' she said, patting Colin and trying to induce him to lie back down in his corner. But it was no good. Colin had defi-

nitely decided that Nina had come to play, and besides, he
seemed to have had more than enough of sitting quietly. Beth
sighed and couldn't help sympathising. She so knew how he
felt.

'Shall we cut our losses, take him to the park for a little
stroll?' said Beth, thinking guiltily that she should have done a
lot more work while she'd had the chance. That was the trouble
with her job at the moment. She had to squeeze it in around the
busy corners of her life, but she knew she couldn't do this
forever. At some point, something was going to have to give.
And since Wyatt's was paying her wages – and she definitely
couldn't hang onto the delicious £30k in her bag – it was going
to have to be her extracurricular activities.

But not today. Particularly not as it was going to be
completely impossible to contain both Nina and Colin in the
archives office. Already Nina was throwing rolled-up balls of
paper for Colin to fetch, and the Lab was doing his best impression of a sprightly young puppy, getting thoroughly overexcited.
Letting out the occasional yip, he careered forward into Beth's
latest stack of programmes from the recent Christmas concerts,
which were patiently awaiting shelving, then back into the legs
of her conference table.

With a sigh, Beth slipped on her jacket and hitched her bag
over her shoulder. She knew when she was beaten.

THIRTEEN

Harry York winced as he finally got round to listening to the messages on his phone. A case like this ate up every minute of his time, particularly in the first days. Both Beth's voicemails were in the high-pitched tone which she used when she was excited, which immediately had him on edge.

Not for the first time, he wondered how on earth they'd become involved. Yes, she'd intrigued him from the first time he'd met those grey eyes, looking up at him with such apparent guilelessness from behind a laptop screen in the office of Wyatt's School. And the fact she was small enough to put in his pocket had, somehow, tugged at his heartstrings from the off. Then, when he'd met her little son – a dark-haired miniature version of his mum, but all boy with his enthusiasms for football, on and off the computer – Harry had known he was in trouble.

He'd had girlfriends before, and he knew, without undue vanity, that his height, breadth, and even the fact he was doing pretty well in his career, made him something of an object of interest, both inside his police station and on the streets he still loved to patrol. But though he was well aware that a tiny, inquisitive, irritating little person with an ill-judged addiction to trouble was not the obvious choice of mate, somehow he'd lost that battle long ago.

He didn't know what the future held for them. Some days, like when he got messages like these, he was pretty sure it was nothing at all. Then she'd peep up at him from under that fringe and he'd feel an almighty twang somewhere in the vicinity of his heart and think it was time he marched her up the nearest aisle.

Mostly, he was veering between the two extremes – but glad they were together.

Except at times like this.

Only Beth could find yet another dead body in the Dulwich area. He shook his head as he remembered her trying to say this one somehow didn't count, as it was on Peckham Rye instead. But whatever the postcode, it was still south-east London. And the poor man had inevitably turned out to be a Dulwich resident; even she couldn't argue the toss about that. This was getting past a joke. And now, as if the situation wasn't bad enough already, it looked as though she'd stumbled on a whole heap of cash as well.

He hunched his shoulders in his navy coat, wishing the whole business would just go away. But, of course, it wouldn't. He'd have to leave Beth for later, though. For the moment, he needed to go by the book with this investigation – a book Beth wouldn't even know if he threw it at her, he thought crossly.

He turned to the DC by his side. He hoped Narinda Khan – sharp-eyed, young and ambitious – was shaping up to be the partner he'd sorely lacked since coming to work at the Met. That had been one of the reasons he'd sometimes allowed Beth such ill-judged leeway. But give that girl an inch and she'd drive a P4 bus right through the heart of Dulwich Village, he now knew that only too well.

'Go ahead then, open it,' he said to Khan, wondering what

was keeping her. She fumbled with the door keys which they'd picked up from a neighbour. People in these townhouses were the types to holiday frequently, so it had taken ages to track them down.

Dulwich was a ridiculously wealthy place at the best of times, thought York. And the people in these glamorous glass boxes seemed to have even more enviable lifestyles than most. Mark Smeaton's keyholders had been an elderly couple, but they'd turned out to be away. So, York had been faced with the choice of getting a Local Support Team to open the place up, or simply waiting. As the LST usually accomplished the job without a lot of finesse, by splintering the doorjambs and using the 'big red key' – or pneumatic ram – to crash through the lock, he'd decided to wait. But as usual, the responsibility for the decision rested on his broad shoulders alone. He only hoped he'd made the right choice.

As the door finally swung open, they were confronted with a canvas, right in front of them. It was the iconic Slope picture of ex-President Trump in Mickey Mouse ears nibbling at a piece of cheese, marked with a map of the world. The poodle signature was a tiny splodge in the right-hand corner.

'Is that...?' asked Narinda Khan faintly.

'Yep,' York was terse. They walked into the townhouse, which had the vacant quality that York had often felt in the homes of the recently deceased. He didn't know whether it was oversensitivity on his part, and he tried to shrug it off, but he definitely noticed an atmosphere, as though the place was waiting for someone. In vain.

He trod carefully, almost tiptoeing, until he realised how ridiculous that was, and followed the hallway round with DC Khan on his heels. The dark passageway opened out into a drawing room with floor-to-ceiling windows, giving a magnificent view out onto the road into Dulwich Village. The day outside was cold and wintry, the trees bare, but the wide grass verges were as green as ever, and all the light available on a grim early January day was pouring in. It illuminated the overstuffed, oversized velvet sofa and chairs, the shiny glass table between them, and the immense canvas of a defecating dog which confronted them, looming over the sofa and commanding as much attention as the view. In the air was the distinct whiff of cleaning fluids. York looked around quickly. There was no dust anywhere; the place was spotless.

'Damn, Khan, it looks like someone's been in here. Cleaned up.'

'Unless he was a tidy sort of person?' the DC ventured.

'Hmm,' said York. 'There's not a speck of dirt anywhere, though, is there? Unless he's popped back from the dead to have a quick whisk round, then no, I'd say someone else has been here.'

Khan seemed chastened. York wondered briefly if he'd been a bit harsh, but she had to learn to spot the obvious. And in truth, this spotless flat didn't fit with his vision of artists. Weren't they supposed to be above such mundane concerns as polishing their tables? Especially stratospherically successful artists like this Smeaton/Slope fellow.

York looked around, dissatisfied. As well as the canvas and the seating, there was a blocky floor-to-ceiling bookshelf next to the window. It stood out, due to the surprising lack of finesse in its design, but York could never resist books however they were displayed. He strode over, hands behind his back, and studied the shelves. As he'd have expected, most of them were great thick art tomes, any one of which would probably have caused the rickety Ikea shelves in his own much-neglected Camberwell pad to collapse instantly. Maybe he needed something sturdy and no-nonsense like this.

There were catalogues from recent exhibitions at the Tate, the Royal Academy, the National Portrait Gallery and the Saatchi Gallery; there were art history volumes; there were even back catalogues from Slope's own successful shows. Nothing there Harry wouldn't have expected. He strode out to see what else the flat had to offer.

In the master bedroom, a raspberry pink velvet throw was drawn up neatly on the king-size bed. Two bedside lights with enormous white shades dominated the tables on either side, while the matt blue-black walls had a dull but faintly erotic sheen. Flat white wardrobe doors glided back smoothly at a touch to reveal a surprisingly well-worn and frankly uninspiring collection of clothes: chinos, shirts, shoes, all stuff that York himself could have worn, if it had been in his sizes.

Smeaton seemed a bit smaller than him, but not by any means a snappy or remotely attention-seeking dresser. Was this odd? Or was it part of the disguise that had allowed him to exist in plain sight in Dulwich all this time – one of the most energetic critics of the political scene, with a trenchant, yet amusing, take on all the issues of the day? And what, anyway, was York expecting an artist to wear? Even David Hockney, who had a penchant for canary yellow jumpers and luridly striped socks, still basically wore jeans every day. For a man, there wasn't that far you could go, sartorially, to stand out – unless you wanted to attempt the full Grayson Perry. And Smeaton, it seemed, was not that way inclined.

Smeaton had been a complicated man, that much was clear, thought York. An iconoclast in many ways, yet content to merge in with the crowd in others. And the owner, he mustn't let himself forget, of that quintessentially well-heeled breed of dog, the Labrador. Harry hoped this case wasn't going to prove as multi-faceted as the man at its centre. But he didn't mind admitting he had a bad feeling about it. And with a twinge of dread that a big rufty-tufty policeman shouldn't really own up to, he realised he really ought to stop putting it off and call Beth back. Maybe whatever she thought she had found would help rather than hinder. There had to be a first time for everything.

FOURTEEN

Baz Benson sat in his office, deflated. It was a feeling that didn't come naturally to him, and in many ways it was surprising. As he had probably the best back catalogue of Slopes in the country – aside from that bastard Kuragin – he should actually be feeling cock-a-hoop right now. The death of an artist, though it necessarily meant a sudden full stop to their output, also meant an inexorable rise in the prices their existing works commanded.

A Slope sale, always an event, would now become a massive free-for-all, with bidders vying to get their hands on the dwindling pool of artworks. But, for once, Benson wasn't just counting his richly graffitied chickens. He'd actually liked Slope, or Smeaton. No need, any more, to pretend the somewhat down-at-heel middle-class man he'd often shared Soho lunches with wasn't the rebellious, hip king of the aerosols.

Poor old Mark. Benson felt a twinge of guilt – another unexpected development – at the memory that it had been he who'd persuaded his protégé to take refuge in a false name. It hadn't ever really been about the illegality of the art. It was all about that edgy image. It had been years, decades, since Smeaton had gone out armed and dangerous with a can and done what many councils considered to be wanton damage to public property. Nowadays, his works, appearing suddenly on this building or that, were rigorously coordinated beforehand, with Benson himself squaring things with the authorities, orchestrating press coverage, allowing them to sell off the art at auction. They'd used the whole costly business, involving endless backhanders and schmoozing with rapacious councillors, as a massive loss-leader for the real revenue-makers – the Slope calendars, mugs, and stationery sets that sold all over the world to youngsters who thought they were sharing Slope's rebellion. But actually, they were just helping to enrich a man who'd already been born with, if not a silver spoon in his mouth, then at least a very good chunk of Villeroy & Boch stainless steel cutlery. More often than not, Smeaton couldn't even be bothered to pretend any more. When had he last stood outside in the cold, can in hand? Hah, for the life of him, Benson couldn't recall. Nowadays Mark'd just produced his work straight onto a nice, clean canvas.

It was hard for people to understand, but just as Chanel now made so much more from its £23-a-pop lipsticks than it did from the haute couture jackets with their chain-weighted hems and even heavier price tags, so Slope's branded biros kept the money flooding into Benson's offshore accounts much more effectively than either the wall art or even the canvases. Slope's themes remained constant, though. The evils of consumerism, attacks on the capitalist system and the odd witty sideswipe at the way technology was taking over the world. Of course, it was all massively ironic when you saw the man who created it – who was every bit as pale, male and stale as the world he critiqued.

Benson sighed. He'd always liked Mark. It was hard not to. He was a decent guy and, of course, very accomplished. But there were very few who realised that his talent was basically as a copyist, not as an original artist. And the fewer who were in the know, the better.

Unfortunately, Mark had suddenly decided he wanted to be an honest man. Why, after all these years, Benson couldn't have said. And he certainly didn't know what the attraction of honesty was. He'd definitely never heard its siren song. That wasn't to say he lived on the wrong side of the law. But popping over the pathway to visit the dark side occasionally, well, that was fine. For him. And for Mark, too, for many years. But recently, the guy's conscience had seemed to be troubling him more and more.

Mark liked a drink, that had been one of his problems. And after a certain stage, he got maudlin and would be dragged back to relive certain passages of his youth. Passages which didn't reflect well on him.

Benson supposed it was an age thing, though Mark hadn't been old, by any normal reckoning. Maybe he'd had some sort of inkling that he didn't have long to live? Was that even possible? Whatever the reason, his urge to come clean had recently become a problem. And Benson had had more than enough of those to deal with.

The sound of a bell ringing in the gallery beyond broke into his gloomy thoughts. As he'd envisaged, it was yet another customer, eager to snap up a bit of history. Well. The money was at least a compensation. He rubbed his hands together, and at once was back in his comfort zone, stepping briskly out to relieve a celebrity scalp-hunter of a nice fat cheque.

FIFTEEN

Beth was at her kitchen table, grimly clutching a cup of peppermint tea in the hopes it would work its usual magic and soothe her jangled nerves. She hadn't drawn the curtains over the French doors, and in the vague mass of tangled shrubs that was the back garden, she could intermittently see the flash of twin pricks of reflected light. Magpie was keeping an eye on her and waiting until Colin had retreated to the sitting room for the night.

It looked as though their brief rapprochement was over. Perhaps that whole day home alone together yesterday had been too much of a good thing. At the moment, Colin was still stationed with his head on her feet, as a sort of pillow against the cool tiled floor. It was warm and comforting, and she felt as though he was doing his doggy best to empathise with her. Every now and then, he would sigh gustily, sounding eerily human, and summing up her feelings entirely.

She'd done her best with Harry, she really had. She'd handed over the money as soon as he'd come in, which had mercifully been after Jake's bedtime, so they hadn't had to have the whole thing out in front of wagging small-boy ears. Admittedly, the manila envelope had never looked particularly fresh, having been abandoned in the hollow of the tree. But now it was looking as dog-eared as Colin himself, as it had been lugged around in her bag all day under a thick drift of sweet wrappers, vital communications from Jake's school and her own purse – a sadly very empty affair.

Harry wasn't to know how virtuous she felt, handing over the full wad of notes to him at all. He'd probably never have felt the temptation that she'd struggled against, to peel off a note or two here and there – preferably some of those lovely crisp red ones – and convert them to something useful. He was a policeman. He'd sworn an oath to be truthful and all that. She was a little vague about what it entailed, though she had a feeling it was a bit like the Brownie Promise that she'd once longed to make. She'd been thwarted, as Wendy hadn't wanted to sew on any badges, let alone get her to the meetings, and had therefore forbidden her from joining the local troop. But Harry had actually pledged to do all the good stuff. She had not – but yet, she'd just done it anyway. Surely that deserved, if not a belated badge, then some Brownie points at least?

But Harry had remained impassive as she'd slapped the collapsing brown paper package down in front of him, merely raising an eyebrow at the state of the thing, before looking hard at her in silence. It was a tactic that never failed to make her feel very uncomfortable.

She'd found herself explaining painstakingly how she'd found it. And out of the goodness of her heart, she'd given him a run-down of her thinking on the subject, which he had been both extremely ungrateful for and very ungracious about.

That was the last time she helped him out with his enquiries, she huffed to herself, and Colin stirred in sympathy.

Honestly, how many times did she have to apologise, she wondered. It was hardly her fault that they'd come across Smeaton, accidentally acquired Colin, then stumbled – sort of –

on the money. It was the kind of thing that could happen to anyone.

Except that it didn't, but it did keep happening to her – and Beth was honest enough to admit that to herself. Not that there was really much she could do about it, unless she took a decision to board up her door and never leave the house again. Both Jake, and her job, and now Colin as well, all made that a total impossibility. Magpie wouldn't be too bothered, as long as there were regular deliveries of cat food right to her bowl.

Now Harry was upstairs, very soundly asleep, if his occasional deep snores were anything to go by. And she was down here, wishing she hadn't decided to seduce him into a better mood. It had definitely worked for him, judging by the blissful smile on his face seconds before he became unconscious. But it had most definitely not done much for her. She'd been left feeling disgruntled and resentful, and all the peppermint tea in the world wasn't likely to take those feelings away in a hurry.

By rights, she should be exhausted. It had been quite a day. She'd really hoped she'd clear a ton of work, but that had been scuppered when Nina had burst in. She'd then had to break off to take both her friend and Colin out for an airing, hoping against hope that on the way they might come across more dog walkers whose memories would be jogged by seeing the placid old Lab going through his paces. But it was not to be.

She'd had to turn down Nina's well-meant offer to badger every single person they met. It might have worked, but Beth felt they'd get further by approaching only the people who seemed to be staring at Colin or looking at his change of dog handlers in surprise. Unfortunately, a thin drizzle had started to fall before they'd completed their first circuit of the park, so they'd ended up decamping to the deserted café instead, and whiling away a rather merry afternoon until pick-up time by sipping at hot chocolates while Colin sat rather miserably outside in the rain.

Then she and Jake had come back home, with Colin now smelling like a damp doormat. Getting the dog dry and a touch less malodorous had taken most of Beth's ingenuity until Harry had arrived in a towering temper. It was all she needed, frankly.

She was just wondering if she should go upstairs, dump him, throw him out and wake him up, in no particular order, when the house phone rang. She jumped a little. Hardly anyone used landlines any more, except the poor souls condemned to pursue PPI claims. She only kept hers in case the house burnt down, though what use it would be then, she wasn't sure. With trepidation, she answered it.

'Hello?' First there was an ominous crackle. Then just as she thought a far-flung double-glazing salesman was going to start a doomed attempt to reel her in, she heard Josh's voice, as though from the bottom of a well.

'Sis? That you? Got your message, you know, about the stuff that happened way back when,' he drawled. 'You need to get out more, stop fretting about the past. Honestly, girl. That was all over *forever* ago, just get over it,' he said. Then, to her acute annoyance, he started singing 'Let It Go' from *Frozen* in a tune-less falsetto.

Beth sat up straight, all thoughts of peppermint tea and Harry banished. 'Josh. Shut up,' she said, instantly fourteen again and going from nought to incandescent as quickly as only someone with a sibling can.

Down the phone line, she heard his tinny laughter. 'Well, all right then, if you insist...'

'No, no, no, wait, don't you dare!' Beth said, realising just in time what she'd be losing if she let Josh vanish like the Cheshire Cat, leaving only his usual maddening smirk behind. 'Just tell me. *Please.* Tell me everything.'

. . .

Beth was still thinking hard about what she'd heard when she picked up Colin's lead and jangled it. He staggered to his feet, a happy smile on his wide mouth, and Beth quietly opened the door. Outside, the pavements shone, and a light drizzle made a nimbus around each street light. She turned up her collar. She was going to get wet again and so was stinky old Colin, but for once she didn't care.

Halfway down the street, she bumped into Zoe Bentinck's older sister walking their little black pug, Napoleon. For the thousandth time that day alone, Beth thanked her stars that she had Colin, not Teddy, or Napoleon might have met his Waterloo all over again. She stopped and smiled. By the time the two women parted ten minutes later, the cold rain was seeping into Beth's neck – and she wasn't smiling any more.

'Thanks, and see you soon,' she said grimly, and led Colin home.

SIXTEEN

Beth was feeling particularly virtuous as she strode past the porter at Wyatt's the next morning, bright and early. Harry had been up and gone before either she or Jake had woken, which was just as well. He'd left her a note on the kitchen table with an X marking the spot, and had taken the cash, too. He'd carefully sealed it in an evidence bag the night before, with Beth remarking this was a little bit pointless so long after the horse of fingerprint evidence had waved a fond farewell to its stable.

Jake was by now safely at school and Beth herself was striding towards her in-tray, determined to make a massive dent in it. Once her conscience was a bit lighter, her plan was to turn to the much more interesting matters which Josh had been so helpful with last night, and for which Zoe's big sister had also supplied a few surprising missing jigsaw pieces. She was busily imagining how it was all going to go, when she heard an ominous cough behind her. She faltered for a moment, then decided her best bet was to pretend sudden onset deafness and pick up her pace, but it was no good. There were two things stopping her. Colin, who didn't really do fast walking in the morning, and the bursar, who abandoned the cough tactic and just shouted her name, several times, in a successively crosser and ruder fashion.

She turned round, slowly and reluctantly, but with a hopeful smile pinned to her face. 'Good morning, Tom, how are you?' she said, inwardly full of trepidation but doing her best impression of chirpy good cheer.

As usual, the bursar looked as though he had been poured into his suit but had forgotten to say 'when'. And he was also extremely red in the face. 'Not having trouble with your blood pressure, I hope?' Beth added as a cheeky afterthought. She was pretty sure she was in for a gale force telling-off, so she decided boldly that she might as well get some retaliation in first.

'What is that?' the bursar thundered.

Beth looked around innocently, taking in the rag-tag of pupils rushing across the tarmac playground to get to registration in their form rooms, seeing the head of English dashing in the opposite direction, shedding hairpins as she went, then finally spotting Nina making her way over to the reception office in her distinctive white puffy coat, her arm raised in greeting. Beth waved in return, then let her hand drop and looked back at the bursar, her eyebrows raised as though she simply couldn't think what he meant.

Quivering now, and with his face taking on a worryingly purple hue, the bursar pointed directly at Colin, who'd plopped himself down at Beth's feet as they appeared to be taking a bit of a rest. The old dog panted up at the bursar with a wide smile, as though he'd just spotted a great friend. Beth looked down at the dog with a small but slightly sorrowful smile. Colin had probably made his most flawed judgement yet about a human.

Beth was a bit surprised later that her hearing appeared to be intact, as the bursar had reached decibel levels which he'd previously saved for the rugby pitch in his role as coach, and even then only when stuff was happening way over on the other side of the field that he needed to intervene in urgently.

Although he managed to string the whole tirade out for what seemed like hours, his point could be summed up fairly succinctly. It seemed that dogs were not allowed on the premises.

Beth had always suspected as much, though the somewhat lax regime that was in operation while Janice was at home playing with young baby Grover had allowed her to hope. But bringing in a well-behaved dog for short periods of time – the only periods that Beth worked, to be honest – did not seem, to her, to be a major crime. And besides, she was fairly sure that Janice would side with her over the bursar any day, particularly as Beth was now godmother to her beloved daughter.

Unfortunately, though, Janice was not there to rush to Beth's rescue. No one was. And if it hadn't been for poor Colin letting out a piteous howl once the first ten minutes or so of the bursar's shouting had passed, then she probably would still have been stuck in the playground now, having her ears belaboured by the horrible man's cascade of unpleasant adjectives.

Though the bursar seemed to have no respect at all for Beth – something she'd always guessed at but was now having confirmed lavishly – he did draw the line at causing suffering to animals. Here, he differed markedly from some of his recent associates, Beth was glad to note.

'Just get that creature off the premises. I'll deal with you later,' he rasped.

Beth didn't need to be asked twice. She had coped with his outburst by angling her head slightly away from the man and looking fixedly over his shoulder. While that seemed to inflame his anger, it did keep her from wanting to answer back, which might easily have cost her the job she loved. The more he shouted, the more convinced she was that the bursar couldn't have been the meaty man she'd seen racing across the Rye on the day of Mark Smeaton's death. She'd loved to have seen him in the frame, but with every jab of his forefinger and every fleck of spittle he let fly, he gave himself away. He was far too much of a philistine to have known who the artist was. She doubted he'd even heard of Slope. And this was a personal killing. No, Tom Seasons was the type of man who turned to the sports pages first, and that was that.

Once she was at home again, she put in a call to Janice, explaining the whole dog situation from her point of view, and got ticked off again – much more gently – for bringing Colin into the school. Now, with that out of the way and with Janice's assurances that of course she'd stick up for her friend and that she wouldn't get the sack, Beth breathed a heartfelt sigh of relief – and took stock.

She was at the kitchen table, in exactly the spot where she'd talked to Josh only last night. She still couldn't quite believe how useful he'd been. He was her big brother, and when he wasn't winding her up, she adored him, but she'd never seen him as an asset before, particularly not in one of her investigations. True, he did manage her mother much better than she did, and that could be very helpful at Christmas and other big family occasions. But, in return, she almost always then had to keep an eye on his girlfriends. That meant not only shielding them from her mother's sudden enthusiasm for weddings and christenings, but also deflecting any questions the girlfriend might have about Josh's non-existent interest in settling down.

But last night, Josh had surprised her. Once his teasing was over, he'd proved to have an impressive recall of those events which had taken place so long ago. She hugged the knowledge to herself. And another nugget of priceless information had fallen into her lap like a wonderful, unexpected gift. If Beth hadn't popped out to walk Colin at exactly the right moment, she'd still be blundering about in the dark with way too many suspects.

Things were now at a delicate stage. What she needed to do was flush a few things out into the open. She knew, to her cost, this could be dangerous, and she fingered the scar on her fore-head absent-mindedly. It wasn't only the bursar at Wyatt's School who seemed to have distinctly aggressive feelings towards her. In recent months, she'd discovered that people weren't exactly at their best when cornered.

She looked over at Colin, who was having a little snooze in the corner by the French windows, his paws up by his ears as though trying to block out the memory of all that shouting. He'd been through enough. Magpie, stepping gingerly through her cat flap, checked that the Labrador was properly asleep, then walked stiff-legged to her bowl and sniffed her nuggets of food with the air of a connoisseur before selecting a few to crunch into oblivion. She gave Beth a quick stare as if to say that went for her, too. Beth nodded, as if in agreement. This time around, she was going to be very, very careful.

Fishing out her phone, she sent two quick texts, then got Colin's lead off the chair next to her. 'Come on then, boy, we've got unfinished business, you and I.'

As Colin opened his eyes, Magpie disappeared through her flap in a streak of black and white, circumspect as ever in the face of a possible threat to her glossy fur and whiskers. Beth smiled her approval. She'd definitely be following Magpie's lead from now on. She quickly stuffed a few things into her bag and they were off.

It was only a short walk to the park, and Beth marvelled on the way at how safe and familiar everything looked, though for her, it was all irrevocably changed by her discoveries of the past few days. Dulwich, with its white palings, its guileless blue skies, and its seemingly endless promise of order and prosperity, was as much of a construct as any artfully created canvas.

She felt a little wistful as she walked through the park gates on Court Lane. Then she spotted someone and, try as she might, she couldn't stop a wide smile from spreading over her face.

It was Katie, with Teddy dancing this way and that at the end of a long lead. But it wasn't the puppy's boundless exuberance that had lightened her heart. It was her friend's outfit. Gone was the Sam Spade trench coat. In its place was a tweedy jacket that Beth had never seen before, a long woolly skirt that hid Katie's magnificently long and toned legs, and surely that couldn't be – but somehow was – a shapeless, saggy bag, the type that could well have a brace of knitting needles poking out of the top?

'Don't tell me. It's Miss Marple today,' said Beth, once the regulation Dulwich kisses had been exchanged.

'You guessed! I know you think it's silly, but it really helps me to get into character,' Katie said.

'You haven't actually got knitting in there, have you?' marvelled Beth.

'I would have, but I can't knit. I did find some string, though, left over from that class project on measuring,' Katie happily dug out a ball of twine. Teddy immediately jumped up at the loose end and tugged it, worrying it into the ground with a selection of impressive little growls.

Beth shook her head but contented herself with simply patting her friend's arm. 'Well, if it works for you. Maybe I should take up crosswords and start driving a Jag?'

'You don't need the props, Beth, but I do – I'm just starting out. I'll find my feet soon and then I'll be unstoppable,' said Katie, yanking at Teddy now.

'Okey-doke. Any word yet?'

'Nothing, how about you?'

Beth shook her head. She wasn't entirely surprised. But she was disappointed. While she hadn't been at all sure they'd get a reply, it would really have helped matters if they had. 'Well, come on, let's give these two a nice walk anyway, and we might as well discuss what we're going to do about the interviews.'

'Oh, don't,' said Katie. 'My heart sinks every time I think about them.'

'But Charlie is just about the best-prepared boy in Dulwich. Excepting poor old Billy McKenzie, of course.'

'I pity that boy if he doesn't get in,' said Katie, and Beth nodded. It didn't really bear thinking about. Even though it meant one fewer precious place for her Jake to snatch at, she wouldn't wish failure on any of Belinda's children; the consequences would be too awful to contemplate. Her own son would just pootle off elsewhere if he had to, but Belinda would probably commit suttee on her front lawn rather than live with the shame of a boy in a school that wasn't Wyatt's.

'Can you believe tomorrow is the big day?' Katie asked.

Beth shook her head. She was having trouble accepting it. All this stuff about Smeaton had taken her mind off the whole business, rather too successfully. She couldn't help contrasting levels of preparedness between Jake and Billy. Yes, she'd taken him for that stint at tutoring, but that had been a while ago. Jake would definitely have forgotten any topics that had been covered, and she'd made precious little effort to top up his knowledge levels since. Oh well, it was in the lap of the gods now. Though things must be bad if even unflappable Katie was dressing up as an old lady sleuth to distract herself.

Despite the looming shadow of the interviews, they had a lovely walk, wending through the rhododendron bushes at the far end of the park, out of the way of all but the most hardened dog walkers, as Katie was still apt to throw herself behind a shrub and hide if anyone with a dog smaller than a St Bernard crossed their path. 'Just in case, you understand,' she explained to Beth, while dragging a romantically inclined Teddy out of range of a pretty little chihuahua.

For once, even Jake seemed a little subdued at pick-up, and Beth guessed that Billy had been sharing his mother's favourite topic – the interviews – at breaktime. Both Jake and Charlie seemed content to go their separate ways for once, and the dogs plodded off in separate directions, too, with Katie and Beth turning round and crossing fingers at each other in a moment of solidarity as they walked away from each other. Though in theory the boys were rivals for places, their mothers were prepared to bet that neither one would enjoy their school career much without each other. It was another reason to hope against hope for the best possible outcome tomorrow.

Anticipating a somewhat sombre evening, Beth started trying to think of strategies which might lessen any gathering tension yet be wonderfully educational. Even at this last moment she was hoping for a miracle that would convert her very ordinary small boy into an intellectual powerhouse.

But after supper, just when she was about to raise the topic of global warming in a carefully off-hand manner, she was glad to hear the distinctive scrape of Harry's key in the lock.

Jake's look of joy told her he'd seen right through her, yet again, and she gave up any attempt to make the PlayStation off-limits. Soon she was washing up to the merry zing and thud of a clash between gaming Titans, and wondering if she was blowing her son's last chance.

SEVENTEEN

There was a sick feeling at the pit of Beth's stomach the next morning, and it wasn't caused by the prospect of seeing the bursar again so soon after her very public ticking-off. As she looked at Jake's pinched little face, she wondered if he was a mass of nerves, too. They were walking along the quiet streets, straight past the little Village Primary School, and on up to the daunting magnificence of the gates to Wyatt's. Interview day was here at last. It had taken such a short time to get from the exam to this point. Or it had taken every day of Jake's life so far. It all depended on how you calculated it.

Beth was sad they couldn't take Colin with them. His measured plod would have been reassuring for both of them. But the chocolate Lab was now a red rag to the powers-that-be at Wyatt's, so she'd had to shut the front door on his disappointed face and leave him to the tender mercies of Magpie.

A little while later, they were ensconced in the waiting room opposite the reception desk at Wyatt's, with two other boys and their palpably nervous parents. As usual, Beth wondered whether things would have been different if James had still been alive. She was sure they would. She wouldn't

have had to worry for two, for a start. And James would have
been quietly amused by all the hoopla around Wyatt's, and less
bothered whether Jake made the grade or not. That, Beth
thought sadly, would probably have helped a lot.

One of the mothers opposite was pecking her way through a
copy of the school prospectus, transparently not taking in a
word the glossy pages had to say; the other was simultaneously
telling her son off for gawping at his phone, while surrepti-
tiously trying to check her emails on her own. The fathers, in
both cases, seemed to have zoned out – one furrowing his brow
over the *Financial Times*, the other busy with his own thoughts.

Beth was just wondering how much longer the boy before
them was going to take, when her own phone shrilled. How
embarrassing. She was sure she'd turned it to silent. Jake caught
her eye, smiling, even as the two mothers gave her an identical
chilly stare. Oh well, it could have been worse, she thought. At
least it didn't play the *Star Wars* theme tune.

Grimacing, she fished in her bag and had a quick look at the
screen. Oh no. She didn't believe it. Finally, they'd decided to
answer her? After twenty-four hours of silence. It was maddening. But it could be her biggest – possibly only – way of solving
the Smeaton case. *Meet me on the Rye. You know where. 15
minutes.*

Beth stared at the message in despair. She couldn't. Could
she? She'd never have time to get there and back before Jake got
out... and she couldn't let him go in alone. To the biggest ordeal
he'd yet faced. Could she?

* * *

It wasn't until they were at home later that Beth realised how
near she'd come to disaster. If Jake had been green around the
gills this morning, then he'd been deathly pale when he came
out of Dr Grover's office. For once, Beth cursed her employer –

one of the most popular men in Dulwich and someone she'd always admired. She'd definitely have words with Janice, she really would. She didn't even want to imagine how upset Jake would have been if he'd come out of the head's study and found an empty seat in the waiting room where she should have been. If she hadn't been there to jolly him along, then she really would have failed her little boy as a mother. And she never wanted to reproach herself for that.

All this time, she'd been kidding herself that Jake didn't realise how serious the interviews were, and just what a difference those twenty minutes could make to his future. But she hadn't reckoned with how fast he was growing up. He was no longer a little boy, oblivious to the world around him. And kids talked at school, of course they did – especially Billy McKenzie. Beth had been naïve.

He'd known all along what an ordeal was facing him, and he'd gone in uncomplaining and done his best. The fact that it took him half the walk home to regain his usual colour probably told her all she needed to know about how well it had gone. She decided she wouldn't press him for details. He'd tell her about it in his own good time – and knowing her lovely boy, that might well be never. For now, she was just so glad that she'd failed to heed that blasted text message and had realised where her priorities lay. She was shocked, in fact, that she'd dithered for even one minute. Jake came first, before everything – especially before a mystery that was none of her business in the first place.

Beth was so over the whole thing that later that night she let down her guard and confided in Harry that she'd had a brief wobble about what course of action to take. She was only telling him in order to reinforce, to him as well as to herself, the knowledge that she'd made the right decision in not going to the rendezvous. But to her surprise, he didn't tell her how well she'd done, but just fulminated, yet again, about the way she got involved in stuff that was none of her concern. She was seriously worrying he was going to wind himself up to bursar-style volumes, and wake up Jake as well, when her phone pinged.

She couldn't believe her eyes. She'd thought all chance of resolution had been thrown away, but now she was being offered a second bite at the cherry. It was too good an offer to refuse – especially as she already had a babysitter in the house. She took a long, steady look at Harry, sitting there like a fixture on the other half of the sofa, his blond hair ruffled this way and that, his shoulders broad in a big cuddly jumper, his long legs splayed in front of him. A pair of reading glasses was perched halfway down his nose. Though he insisted he hardly needed them, she'd noticed him reaching for them more and more recently. He was deep in *The Franchise Affair* by Josephine Tey. Feeling her scrutiny, he looked up, his eyes crinkling into a loving smile. Then he saw her face and sat up straighter.

'No need to look so serious.' Beth smiled and dropped a kiss on the top of his head. 'I'm just popping out with Colin for his last airing. See you in a bit.'

* * *

It was very cold on the Rye at this time of night, even with every button done up and a huge scarf swathed around her neck. The sky was inky velvet, with darker blotches representing the copse of trees up ahead which had become such a familiar, and grisly, sight even in the daytime. It was a whole lot worse in the dark. There were street lights, yes, but they were all positioned round the outer perimeter. There was nothing here, near the deserted middle, where it was so sorely needed.

It was so typical – all the emphasis was on stopping wealthy mothers clipping the bumpers of their BMWs. There was no thought for those who had to be out at this hour. What about clandestine walkers? What about insomniacs? What about people with incontinent dogs that had to be taken out last thing? What about reckless private eyes risking everything on a hunch? Didn't anyone ever think about them? If she got out of this alive, she was definitely going to email the council and complain, Beth thought. People sneaking about in the middle of the night paid their council tax too, she fumed. Or, at least, she did.

There was a moon, but like a shy child it hid its face behind the scudding clouds. The wind was biting and there was a suspicion of rain in each gust that blew. If Beth could have had her pick of weather for a midnight showdown with a potential murderer, this would have been the last combination she would have chosen.

She looked around the windswept Rye and thought for the thousandth time what an absolutely terrible idea this was. Just when she had resolved never to put herself in danger again, here she was, standing in the middle of a common which might look deserted but was probably bristling with rapists, muggers and worse behind every bush. Plus, of course, the person who'd lured her here with that damned text. At least she wasn't risking Colin's life. She'd left her alibi for leaving the house firmly locked in the car, much to his disappointment.

Anyway, it was too late now to do much more than curse her insatiable curiosity, stamp her freezing feet in her little boots, and hope that she wasn't going to die of cold before someone even had the chance to kill her.

The minutes ticked past, each one lasting at least a year, and her ears caught the buzz of traffic, sounding like a far-off box of bees being shaken up by an unseen hand. It was some slight comfort to think that there were still motorists ringing the Rye and, if anything bad happened, all she needed to do was shout loudly enough.

But just then, a gloved hand was clamped over her mouth.

EIGHTEEN

Instantly, Beth jumped in terror. Somehow, through the force of sheer blind panic, her leap turned out to be much higher than anyone could have reasonably expected for someone of her stature. Like an Olympic dressage pony pulling off a gold-medal-winning performance, she even managed to whip round in mid-air – wrenching free of her assailant in the process. She landed, somewhat heavily it was true, but still upright, unscathed and out of the attacker's grasp. Every vein in her body was now pumping what felt like pure adrenaline. She was facing the dark figure head-on.

It wasn't much fun, she thought, her breath coming fast and shallow from shock, knowing she was now confronting the person who'd left Mark Smeaton as a crumpled heap, breathing his last on the Rye. But at least she was still all in one piece.

Just as she had the thought, the moon peeped out from behind the clouds and glanced off something being waved in front of her. It was the wickedly sharp blade of what looked like a Stanley knife. Only an inch or so long, admittedly, but surely quite enough to do substantial damage? Immediately, one part of her brain detached itself from the scene playing out in front of her, and she wondered whether you could actually stab someone deeply enough to cause death with something like that.

Harry, blast him, hadn't thought to share any of the post-mortem details with her. She'd seen Smeaton's wounds for herself, and the fact he was extremely dead suggested that the knife had been up to the job, but this still didn't look nearly as fearsome as half the knives in her kitchen. Despite herself, despite every inner voice warning she needed to tread carefully, she couldn't help relaxing a little.

'You wanted to talk?' she said, and although her voice came out as a bit of a squeak, she let herself off. Being capable of any kind of speech wasn't bad going in this sort of situation, she reckoned.

'Well, I said that. But now we're here, it's pretty chilly. I'm wondering whether I shouldn't just finish you off and have done with it,' said John Grey, before lunging towards her with the blade.

Beth's brief moment of relaxation was definitely over. She staggered backwards for a few very quick steps, feeling wildly behind her to make sure she didn't come up against a tree in the dark. 'It's not just me, though, is it? What about the police? What about, erm, your mum? I'm sure I'm not the only one who's onto you,' she said wildly.

'Mum might have her suspicions, but she's never going to turn me in,' said Grey, proving to Beth she'd struck lucky with her guess that Rebecca Grey was more than ambivalent about her boy. 'And the police, well, they'll be happy enough to let the whole thing drop. Just another unsolved case. There are enough of those in London.'

Privately, Beth knew Grey wasn't far off the cold reality of crime in the capital. Harry wouldn't bat an eyelid, and nor would any of his colleagues. They'd seen it all before so many times. Even a murder, and a high-profile one like this, could be dropped and left to gather dust without anything more than a bit of hand-wringing from the press. But this was definitely not the moment to admit that.

'I have a partner, someone I've been investigating with, and she knows everything, too,' Beth faltered, then realised with horror what she was saying. The last thing she wanted to do was make poor Katie a target as well.

She decided to widen the net. If Grey thought that loads of people, not just her and Katie but everyone else in Dulwich, was in the know, then surely he'd decide killing them all was too much like hard work?

'Um, it's not just my friend, it's, you know, *everybody*. The people at Wyatt's... And my mother... The Bridge club...' This was getting worse and worse, Beth thought. She was now pointing a killer towards her entire community.

But she needn't have worried. Grey reacted with amused contempt.

'Well, I'm terrified now. If a whole bunch of Dulwich mums and Bridge players know, then that's it, I might as well give up. Perhaps you'd like to make a citizen's arrest?'

From the way Grey was advancing towards her with the knife extended, Beth rather thought that this was his idea of a joke. She was pretty sure, under the circumstances, that she could be excused for not joining in with a merry laugh.

'Look, Mark Smeaton was famous. I hear what you're saying about the police, yes, sometimes they just let things drop, but he wasn't just another random person, was he? He was a celebrity.'

'Don't remind me,' said Grey through gritted teeth, the knife waving at her again as he advanced. 'That bastard.'

'Why did you hate him so much? I thought you were supposed to be such great friends,' Beth said, her curiosity outweighing even her terror. She'd finally hit on the right thing to say. Grey halted, and snorted bitterly.

'Friends! That's hilarious. Smeaton didn't know what real friendship was. He was a thief, had been for years.'

'A thief? I don't understand what you mean.'

'All his inspiration, even his signature... the very idea of doing graffiti in the first place. It was all stolen. Every single bit of it.'

'Where from? How can you steal graffiti?'

'You don't have a clue, do you? Who Smeaton really was. *What* he was.'

'Tell me. Make me understand. It's true, I don't know anything...' Beth said, falling over the words a little.

'Ha, you're just playing for time, aren't you? Hoping someone will come and rescue you? Well, take a look around. There's no one here. No one but us. We're alone. Or I soon will be. You – you'll be gone,' said John Grey, his teeth flashing briefly in the moonlight as he smiled with every appearance of cheerful anticipation.

Beth shivered and looked about wildly. Even if she'd been able to see properly in the gathering gloom, he was right. There was nothing else stirring on the Rye except the bitter wind, which whipped up the edges of her scarf and ran its impatient fingers through her fringe. What if she made a dash for it? Could she get as far as the road, the safety of the traffic? But it was so far away and flowing more slowly now. Even in London, people stopped driving and went home to bed eventually. And she didn't have to think about sprinting off for longer than a second before she'd dismissed it as hopeless. With his long legs, John Grey could outrun her and stab her in a moment. She'd do better just standing her ground and, as he put it, playing for time.

Unfortunately, Grey had other ideas. 'Come on, we're too visible here. Even if no one's coming to save you, we'd be better off hidden. Let's make for where I stabbed Mark. It's nice and secluded there. Plenty of atmosphere.'

Again, there was that flash from his teeth as he bared them in a smile, but Beth wasn't enjoying his sense of humour at all. She braced her little legs in the grass, but he waved the knife in her face again and she thought better of her token opposition. *Keep him sweet, go along with everything. And, most important of all, keep him talking.* Didn't they say that was the way to survive a hostage situation? She hardly dared hope that this would last long enough to merit that description, but she owed it to Jake, Magpie and even Colin to try and drag things out, create some sort of rapport with Grey. Though she was seriously beginning to doubt whether that was possible. He seemed quite definitely unhinged.

Grey grabbed her by the arm and they started to walk. He was taking great strides, hurrying them under cover. Beth was trotting along to keep up, the knife waved in front of her nose if she stumbled or slowed down. She was out of breath by the time they reached the first of the trees that marked the copse where Mark Smeaton had died.

'Look, can I just take a breath?' Beth said, putting an arm out to steady herself on a tree. Instantly, the blade flashed out and she felt a sting. She whipped her arm back, and saw a slash in her jacket, the shiny lining beginning to puff out. Under it, her arm started to throb. She wasn't sure if she'd been cut or just scraped by the blade. And now, perhaps, was not the moment to find out.

Grey laughed, the sound bouncing off the trees. Almost immediately, it started to rain. Oh great, thought Beth. I'm going to get killed, but of course I'm going to get drenched first. And I washed my hair this morning as well. Just my luck.

'What did you mean, about Smeaton being a thief?' she asked desperately, wiping her damp hair out of her face with her free hand, trying to re-establish some conversation. Being led to her doom was no fun at all; she had to slow things down if she could. To her immense relief, Grey stopped walking and turned his face up to the heavens, seeming to enjoy the patter of drops on his face.

'Mark would have loved this. He was out here, rain or shine. With that mutt of his. Yes, he was a thief. But why should I tell you about all that?'

'I think you want to tell me how clever you've been. That's why you agreed to meet me, isn't it? I've heard some of it. From my brother, Josh. He knew you at school. But only you know the real story.'

'Josh? Oh yes, that short-arse. I remember.'

Beth, fuming, nearly remonstrated with Grey. Josh wasn't short. He towered above her. This man was definitely deranged! Then she remembered who was holding the knife. She bit down her anger and carried on.

'It was the three of you...'

'Me, Mark and Simon. Yes. The three little pigs. But Mark turned out to be the big bad wolf. He blew Simon's house down.'

'You mean, he killed him somehow?'

'No, you silly little thing. He was as shocked as I was about what happened that night at Loughborough Junction. Well, he was as shocked as I pretended to be. He didn't see me. I only meant to trip Simon, teach him a lesson. I didn't realise how fast the train was coming. Mark was a bit behind us. He was always a dreamer. By the time he caught up, it was all over. Splat. Poor old Simon. Boo-hoo.'

Beth was suddenly chilled. She hadn't expected this. After speaking to Josh, she'd known Grey had to be responsible for Mark's death. And after that chance encounter on the street just afterwards, while walking Colin, she also knew that neither Kuragin nor Benson, shifty and untrustworthy though they were, had been anywhere near the Rye at the time of his death. The bursar, who she could have sworn she'd caught sight of that day, had no motive and knew nothing about either art or

Smeaton. But she'd never guessed that Grey had another death on his conscience as well.

Grey was still talking, his voice taking on a sing-song quality, as though he was reciting a familiar tale. 'But that didn't stop him from pinching Simon's ideas, did it? Simon was the leader, the graffiti fan, the one who was always pushing us to tag. He was the creative mind. Mark just copied stuff, and I, well, I was much better with my hands, the practical stuff, than either of them. Mum always said so.'

'You mean...'

'Yes. Mark just stole all Simon's ideas, once he was safely in the ground. Mark made a fortune on the back of it. Sure, he tried his own work, and it had a bit of success – his first show was a sell-out. But he never seemed able to repeat it, and then he chickened out, just fell back on the graffiti – and that went global.'

'But all the satire, the images, the dog... that was his own work, surely? Simon couldn't have created everything before he died at what, fifteen?'

'The dog was Simon's, yes, but Mark embellished it, took the ideas, embroidered them. He improved it, made it all sharper. But the whole operation, everything he did, was based on the original, stolen concept. He wasn't creative like Simon was. He was just good – very good, if you like – at copying. He didn't have a truly original thought in his head, and he knew it. That's why he dried up after one show. Then he just nicked Simon's work. Oh, he felt guilty about it, I'll give him that. Every day, he tried to atone. Living alone, working like a madman. But he was a bastard, too. Using the poodle signature, that was a dig at me.'

'Why would he want to do that?'

'Oh, he resented having to pay.'

'Pay?'

'Well, of course he had to make amends. I was the one who

knew where he'd got his ideas from. I'd always known. So, when the money started flooding in, it was only right that he shared it.'

'Shared it? You mean, paid you off?'

Grey, who'd been in a reverie, stared hard at her again, then smiled with that flash of teeth. 'Call it what you like. It was a tax on his success, I suppose. The price he paid for being a fraud.'

The final piece of the puzzle fell into place in Beth's mind. She just hoped she'd survive long enough to tell someone else how clever she'd been.

'So, he'd leave the money in the tree? Why there?'

'It was somewhere we had in common. I always had to walk Mother's blasted poodles. He was always out with Colin. And it meant we didn't have to see each other or talk. He'd leave the money; I'd pick it up. Simple. Though the last payment went missing,' he spat. 'I didn't have time to get it, could hear people moving around in the copse, I had to leg it. By the time I came back, it was gone. If he ever even put it there in the first place. I wouldn't put it past him to try and cheat me, the bastard.'

Beth didn't feel it was the moment to correct Grey. It was hardly cheating if the blackmail victim finally decided not to play ball. Though, in fact, Mark had carried out his side of the bargain, as usual. It was Grey who'd wrecked things by going crazy and killing his golden goose.

He'd zoned out while he'd been reminiscing. Now he narrowed his eyes at Beth again. 'You've been snooping around, I know. I've been watching you. Did you see it? Did you take it?'

'No! No, think about it. I'm a shortarse too, aren't I? Like my brother. I could never have reached it,' Beth said quickly. Grey seemed satisfied with that, and fortunately didn't ask himself how Beth knew so much about the money. She rushed on to keep him distracted. 'But I don't understand what made you do it? Why did you stab him?'

Through the drizzle, she could see Grey staring at her. 'He was waiting for me. It was an ambush. He wanted to talk.

Wanted to stop. He'd had enough, he said. Didn't want to atone any more. He wanted to come clean. But he didn't understand. He could never stop. He had to keep going, forever.'

Again, Beth felt Grey's logic twist away from her. Smeaton might have wanted to stop, but it was Grey himself who'd drawn a red line under the whole business. In blood.

'Why did you take the dog's lead away with you?'

Again, John gave that strange smirk. 'Mark loved his stupid dog. It was asleep when I stabbed him. Pathetic. Not like our poodles. They're so intelligent. I thought about killing the dog too, but then I thought I'd just take his lead, then he'd wander off, get run over. Serve him right.'

Beth felt her anger mount, trying its best to displace the terror running through her veins. How could he have been so mean to poor old Colin? Instantly, she vowed that if she got out of here alive, she'd take the dog on. Mark had no friends or relatives who'd stepped up anyway – and the decision made her all the more determined to survive.

She didn't say a word, but maybe John Grey felt her resolve as he fell silent, then started coming towards her, lethal determination in every stride.

Then, crashing out of the bushes on the right-hand side, another figure burst into the clearing. Salvation! Beth's heart leapt. 'Thank God you're here. Please help me, John is...'

Rebecca Grey moved out of the shadows and stood in front of her son, wiping hair and rain from her face, her sensible dog-walking coat slick with wet – and a wicked blade in her hand. Beth felt her heart plummet into her boots as she struggled to understand what she was seeing. First John, now Rebecca Grey?

'Oh, don't tell me what my son is,' Rebecca Grey hissed out of the corner of her mouth, her sensible, pleasant features distorting with rain and raging emotions. 'Don't you think I know by now? Stupid boy, always leaving me to tidy up his mess. Thank goodness I was on the Rye that day, just to finish Mark off. I always carry this penknife. A habit from picnics with the boys, when they were young,' she said. It was eerily mumsy – though the knife in her hand was anything but.

'Poor Mark. But I couldn't have him telling everyone what John had done. And John, you fool, just look at the blade on that Stanley knife. You can't kill someone with that, you blithering...' But words failed her, and she just shook her head, advancing purposefully on Beth instead. 'Time to finish this off neatly, then we can all just get on with our lives. Well, most of us.' She bared her teeth in a horrible smile, and Beth realised John Grey didn't only share his madness with his mother. Rebecca, too, had a deeply non-infectious sense of humour.

Right. She'd given the talking thing a good old go, thought Beth frantically, but now it was definitely time to try a different tactic. She turned on her tiny heel and started to run down the track. The rain lashed in her face, the bushes seemed to reach out to grab at her, her bad arm throbbed, and the darkness, away from the open spaces of the Rye, seemed to close in on her in a ridiculously unhelpful way. After a few seconds of flight, during which she virtually felt the killers' breath on the back of her neck, Beth realised this wasn't going to work, and broke the habit of a lifetime for the second time in recent days, plunging right off the path.

Fighting her way through the tangle of shrubs, Beth blessed the government cuts which had allowed all this undergrowth to sprout so magnificently. It was like trying to insert herself between the twin brushes of a car wash. She was soaked and scratched but, so far, she was alive. Grey, so much taller and bulkier, was having to crouch down and was being hit in the face, satisfyingly hard, by all the branches she bent back during her headlong flight. His mother was staggering this way and that, trying to find a way between the shrubs.

All Beth could hear was her own laboured breath in her

ears, and the jolting thump of her heart banging away frantically in her chest. So intent was she on getting away that she
kept battling forwards for some time, even after helpful arms
had grabbed her and pulled her out of the soaking bushes – and
she'd emerged into a ring of pulsating blue lights.

NINETEEN

A tall figure cut short a terse call on his phone and strode forward to fold Beth into a familiar navy peacoat, warming her instantly. Then he crushed her small body in a mighty hug until her ribs hurt and her arm throbbed.

'Thank God you have absolutely no poker face. You looked so shifty taking Colin off 'for a quick walk' that I mobilised all units. I was just about to go in and get you out,' said Harry into her ear.

'About time, too! I thought I'd had it.'

'Don't tell me this has finally put you off all this amateur sleuth nonsense?' said Harry, scanning her face optimistically.

'Well, it's definitely put me off something,' said Beth, wrinkling her brow under her wet fringe.

'What's that?' Harry asked, bending to place a series of delectable small kisses along her jawline, while the other officers were distracted with cuffing and cautioning John Grey. He'd been dragged from the trees, sopping wet and swearing, along with his mother, whose middle-class, middle-aged features had morphed into an uncanny representation of Edvard Munch's *The Scream*.

'Who'd have thought that Wyatt's would turn out a murderer-cum-blackmailer? And send his mother completely mad into the bargain? Are you sure we're doing the right thing, trying to get Jake in there?'

Harry York smiled, and bent to kiss Beth again.

TWENTY

Beth and Katie stared at each other over their cappuccinos. It was all quiet in Jane's at the magical hour of 11.15 a.m., the moment when the toddlers, mummies and au pairs of SE21 were otherwise engaged.

'But I don't understand, why didn't you ring me and let me in on it all?' Katie's eyes were wide with betrayal.

'Are you crazy? You're not telling me you'd actually have enjoyed being out on the Rye in the middle of the night, with not one but two homicidal murderers trying to stab you? Plus, it was raining really hard. Look at my hair, it's a disaster.'

'But it's the principle of the thing,' said Katie doggedly, eyeing Beth's ponytail. 'Anyway, thank God Harry was on the case. I'm so glad he was there in case things turned nasty.'

'Believe me, it *did* turn *very* nasty. And Harry was only just in the nick of time. But yes, thank goodness for his suspicious mind. Colin didn't miss me at all, he was having a lovely sleep in the car. He might have started barking eventually if I hadn't come back, but I'd be in small bits on the Rye right now if I'd been relying on him,' said Beth.

Katie patted Beth's arm, and Beth winced and put it down

by her side. She'd been lucky, she knew that, but it looked as though she was going to have another battle scar to remember this business by.

'It could have been a lot worse, though,' said Beth, with a reminiscent shiver. 'I was lucky to get away. You know, John Grey even said he was hoping Colin would get run over, on the day he killed Mark Smeaton. Imagine that.'

'The man was evil.' Katie tutted, glancing towards the doors. Teddy was tied up outside in an experiment both women suspected was not going to last that long, but the old Labrador was placidly waiting for Beth, the new centre of his world, at home. 'What's going to happen with Colin?'

Beth sighed. 'Well, there isn't anyone to take him. Mark Smeaton's parents are long gone, and none of his friends have begged to have him. I guess there's nothing for it.' The words sounded resigned, even resentful, but Beth's smile said it all. She couldn't bear to part with Colin now.

'What about work?' Katie asked.

'I've spoken to Janice, and we've come to an arrangement. Colin will be allowed in, but only for half days.'

'But you only ever work half days anyway – if that,' Katie said.

'Shh! Anyway, all that's going to change. I'm going to really get down to it this term,' said Beth.

'Right,' said Katie, smiling. 'Is that OK with that awful bloke, the bursar?'

'Seems to be. Well, what can he do? Dr Grover's word is law – and Janice has very kindly told him what to say.'

'What I don't understand is how you knew it was John Grey, in the end? Even though it was actually his mum, if you see what I mean.' Katie wrinkled her brow.

'It was partly what Josh told me about the three boys. John was always the whiny one, hanging onto the other two, but also getting them into trouble accidentally-on-purpose. He seemed to be bitterly jealous. And imagine how much worse that must have got when Mark made such a success of things, and John was still living at home, making crappy furniture.'

'But still,' said Katie. 'It's a long way from thinking he might be a bit dodgy, to being sure that he was a killer.'

'Well, meeting Zoe's sister Magenta while I was out walking Colin was a breakthrough. Because I didn't know it, but she'd worked for both Kuragin and his awful friend, Benson, as an unpaid intern.'

'Poor girl,' said Katie.

'Yes, it's put her off the art world for life; she's becoming a lawyer now. But it turned out, while we were talking, that she'd seen both Kuragin and Benson on the day Mark Smeaton died. Neither of them would have had time to kill him and get back to their central London galleries in order to see her and give her a hard time about this and that. So, you see, I was able to make the leap to John Grey. It was either him – or some psychopathic stranger.'

'Or an insane mother.'

'Yes,' said Beth, and both women fell silent. Beth had certainly felt the odd murderous rage boiling up when her own son was upset by other kids at school. How far would she go to assuage the wrongs done him? Not as far as Rebecca Grey, obviously. Well, she certainly hoped not.

'Does it make you think twice about Wyatt's?' Beth asked her friend.

'No, of course not. Why?'

'Well, it just got me wondering. I mean, Josh has turned out the way he has... then there's John Grey. And his mother was probably sane when he was in Year 7.'

'Josh is a really successful war photographer, Beth. Mark Smeaton was a global phenomenon, though it was under a false name. And John Grey, well, he might have turned out even worse at another school,' said Katie, with her usual sunny smile.

Nevertheless, Beth was thoughtful as she made her way home. She turned her key in the lock to find not only Magpie lying down in the hall for tummy tickles, but also Colin, sitting bolt upright, with something pale and unfamiliar in his mouth. For a second, she wondered if it was his first mouse. Magpie was definitely leading him astray. He'd be demanding top-notch dog food next.

But wait a minute, that wasn't a sorry little woodland creature at all. It was even worse than that. She dashed forward and dragged something out of his jaws. There, slightly splattered with doggy drool, was a battered envelope with a rather smeared Wyatt's postmark in the left-hand corner. The fateful letter, at last.

Her heart was beating almost as fast as it had that night on the Rye, as she shut the door to her little house.

A LETTER FROM ALICE

Thank you so much for choosing to read my book. I love writing about Beth Haldane and I hope you've enjoyed finding out what she got up to this time. If you'd like to know what happens to Beth next, please sign up at the email link below. Your email address will never be shared and you can unsubscribe at any time.

www.bookouture.com/alice-castle

If you enjoyed the story, I would be very grateful if you could write a review. I'd love to hear what you think. I always read reviews and I take careful account of what people say. My aim is always to make the books a better read! Leaving a review also helps new readers to discover my books for the first time.

I'm also on Twitter, Facebook and Goodreads, often sharing pictures of cats that look like Magpie. Do get in touch if that's your sort of thing. Thanks so much again, and I really hope to see you soon for Beth's next adventure. Happy reading!

Alice Castle

Alicecastleauthor.com

Printed in Great Britain
by Amazon